Copyright ©2007
Gin Phillips

Library of Congress
Cataloging-in-Publication Data

Hawthorne Books
& Literary Arts

Phillips, Gin.
The well and the mine: a novel/
Gin Phillips.
–1st ed.
p. cm.
ISBN 978-0-9766311-7-0

1.   Cities and towns—Alabama—
     Fiction.
2.   Depressions—Fiction.
3.   Coal mines and mining—
     Fiction.
4.   Alabama—Fiction.

I. Title.

[PS3616.H4556W45 2007]
813.6–DC22
2006100637

9   1221 SW 10th Avenue
8   Suite 408
7   Portland, OR 97205
6   hawthornebooks.com
5   *Form*:
4   Pinch, Portland, OR

Printed in Canada
through Print Vision

Set in Paperback

First Edition
Fourth Printing

To Virginia Kirby,
Clara Trimm,
Roy Webb, and
Carson Webb

You are
better than fiction.
I love you.

Acknowledgements

MANY SOURCES—including my family—helped me firm up the details of 1930s Alabama, particularly in terms of mining. I drew from *The Challenge of Interracial Unionism: Alabama Coal Miners 1878–1921* by Daniel Letwin; *Race, Class, and Power in the Alabama Coalfields, 1908–1921* by Brian Kelly; *The WPA Guide to 1930s Alabama*; *Blocton: The History of an Alabama Coal Mining Town* by Charles Edward Adams; *Outside the Magic Circle* by Virginia Foster Durr; *Poor But Proud* by Wayne Flynt; *Black Days, Black Dust: The Memories of an African American Coal Miner* by Robert Armstead; and *Coal Mining in Alabama*. I'm grateful to the Carbon Hill Library and the Alabama Mining Museum, as well as to Fred Leith and Shelby Harbin.

Thanks to Kate Sage for generally being spectacular and for specifically leaving every page of this stronger than she found it. Thanks to Tillman and Anne Sprouse for always being there for fact-checking and storytelling, to Barry Flowers for the legal advice, to Brad Daly for mining museum treks, and to Brittney Knox for research help. Mom, Dad, and Lisa—no one could have asked for more support in work and in life. I appreciate you more than you could know. Diann Frucci and Karen Etheridge, you're the best. Thanks to those who read this early on and put up with unwieldy stacks of paper—to Jamie and Beth for being thorough and thoughtful, to Brooke for always being so sure. And to Fred for reading a whole lot of drafts of a whole lot of stories and making me a whole lot better.

The Well and the Mine

A Novel

Gin Phillips

 HAWTHORNE BOOKS & LITERARY ARTS
Portland, Oregon | MMVII

Introduction

I FIRST MET GIN PHILLIPS IN BIRMINGHAM, ALABAMA,
in 1997 while serving as co-chair of the Birmingham-Southern
College GALA weekend Women of Distinction awards. She was
the student assigned as my escort for the weekend, and while
walking from function to function, she mentioned briefly that she
wanted to become a writer. Having heard that from students so
many times in the past, I wished her well and honestly forgot all
about it. When I received a letter from Hawthorne Books asking
if I would be willing to read a book by a young Alabama writer,
I was surprised and delighted to find out it was Gin Phillips and
that instead of just talking about it and thinking about it,
she actually sat down and wrote a book—not only a book, but a
wonderful book!

I know Alabama well, and *The Well and the Mine* takes me
back there. But this story doesn't so much re-create a place as it
does a life—lives, really—a town and a family full of hopes and
oddities and hidden fears. Life is boiled down to its fundamentals
for the Moores—hard work, family, the taste and smells of land
and home. Their whole world consists entirely of Carbon Hill,
population three thousand. No Fireside Chats yet, no money to get
a newspaper, and only the occasional *Grand Ole Opry* on the
radio. Alabama in 1931 assumes a texture in these pages, palpable
and alive. It's a texture made up of the details of domesticity,
from the way a mother washes her floors to the way lights crackle
in an electrical storm. It's a texture thick with the mechanics and

fatigue of coal mining. And it's a texture dotted with young girls' imaginings and plottings.

There could be a tendency to idealize this past, to give into nostalgia and turn this story into *The Waltons*. And, admittedly, it is an alluring past, with unlocked doors and a close-knit family and dinners spent talking and laughing around the table without a television in sight. But it isn't a one-dimensional ideal. This is a past that's ripe with complications, be they racial barriers or a baby down a well. Right next to the sweet tea and long porch nights, tragedy is always lurking, so close and so possible. For a miner, the thought that you might not make it home from work that day is as much a part of your morning as a cup of coffee. The Moores have no safety net, no protection against the worst other than Albert Moore's good health and paycheck.

This is a book that opens with a baby thrown down a well. It's also a book that's funny. So, speaking of texture, it's not exactly a predictable pattern.

When you watch Tess and Virgie scouting Carbon Hill for the Well Woman, when you follow Albert down into the mines or Leta on the way to a Birmingham hospital, you step into their lives. When you close the book, you'll miss these characters. But *The Well and the Mine* doesn't just give you characters who stay with you—it gives you a whole world.

FANNIE FLAGG
Author of *Fried Green Tomatoes at the Whistle Stop Cafe*

THE WELL AND THE MINE

1 Water Calling

Tess AFTER SHE THREW THE BABY IN, NOBODY BELIEVED me for the longest time. But I kept hearing that splash.

The back porch comes right off our kitchen, with wide gray-brown boards you can lose a penny between if you're not careful. The boards were warm with heat from the August air, but breathing was less trouble than it was during daytime. Everybody else was on the front porch after supper, so I could sit by myself, nothing but night and trees around me, a thin moon punched out of the sky. The garden smelled stronger than the leftover fried cornbread and field peas with onions. And the breeze tiptoed across the porch, carrying those smells of meals done and still to come, along with a whiff of Papa's cigarette and snatches of talk from out front. It was the best time of the day to sit with the well, its wooden box taking up one corner of the porch and me taking up another.

I loved the well then.

I leaned against the kitchen door and looked through the wood posts of the railing, even though I couldn't see anything but black. There weren't clouds covering that slice of moon or the blinking stars, but they still didn't throw enough light. The light from the kitchen door let me see to the edge of the porch. But the woman she didn't see me, I guess. Sometimes the Hudsons down below got their drinking water here—they didn't have their own well—and I thought it was Mrs. Hudson at first. But she was like a bird, and this was a big, solid woman, with shoulders like a man. She climbed the stairs two at a time. Then she hefted that heavy cover off the well, like a man would, with no trouble.

I couldn't see the baby at first 'cause it was underneath her coat. But she took it out, a still, little, bean-shaped bundle wrapped up like it was January.

I could have reached her in five or six steps. If I'd moved.

She held the bundle like a baby for a minute, tucked under her chin like she was patting it to sleep, whispering. The blanket fell back from its head, and I saw a flash of skin. Then she tossed it in. Just like that. Not long after the splash—just a quiet, small sound—she lifted the square cover again and fit it back into its cutout space, settling it in with careful little touches. Even with all that weight, the porch boards didn't creak when she left.

The splash wasn't so much the sound of the baby hitting the water as it was the yelp my well made; it sounded shocked and upset knowing something inside it was awful. Wanting my help.

I felt my teeth dig into my bottom lip, maybe drawing blood, but I was quiet as a mouse and stiller than one. Mice scatter like marbles.

After I don't know how long, Virgie pushed at the door. I knew the sound of her feet on the floorboards. I scooted up, and she poked her head out.

Virgie wore cicada shells, pinned like brooches at her collar. We used to wear them all the time, rows of them like buttons down our shirts during summer, but since she'd be going to the high school next year, she wouldn't wear them to school no more. She'd gotten too old.

"We're all out front—why're you hidin' back here?" She looked down at me, then up at the well. "I swear, you'd marry that well if it'd give you a ring."

Beyond it was pitch. The kind of black you think you'd smash into like a wall if you were to run into it. The woman was gone.

"Some lady threw a baby down it," I said.

Virgie looked at me some more. "Down the well?"

I nodded.

She laughed, and I knew without looking at her she was rolling her eyes. "Hush up and go inside."

"She did!" My mouth was still the only part of me I could make work—it felt like I'd taken root in the floorboards.

"Nobody's been near our well. Quit tellin' stories."

She knew I didn't tell stories. I swallowed hard, and it loosened my feet. I pushed myself up and took a step toward the well. "She was, too! A big woman with a baby in her arms. And she threw her baby in without sayin' a thing."

"Why would she do it with you watchin' her?" She said it like she was grown-up, not just 14 and only five years older than me.

"She didn't see me." My voice was high, and my chest ached with wanting her to believe. At the well, I tried to slide the cover back, but it was too heavy. "Look in here."

"You don't have a lick of sense."

"Virgie…" I was begging.

She looked a little bit sorry, and came over to stroke my hair like Mama did when I got upset. "Were you daydreamin'? Maybe you saw somebody walk by the porch and you imagined it."

"No. We have to look in the well."

"How do you know it was a baby?"

"It was."

"Was it cryin'?"

"No."

Finally she looked worried, looking out at the night instead of looking at me. "Somebody mighta thrown some garbage or somethin' in there outta spite. But who'd do it?"

"It wasn't garbage. It was a baby. And I'm gone tell Papa."

I turned and marched off toward the front porch, going back through the house with Virgie right behind me. That last week in August, the nighttime wind was enough to cool your face but not enough to carry off a day's worth of sunshine. The sun was twice its normal size at the tail end of summer. We'd all stay outside until it was about time to go to bed. Papa and Mama were in their rockers, with Mama shelling peas and Papa smoking a cigarette. They were lit from the lights in the den—Papa was still smudged, even though he'd washed and washed his face and hands. He was bluish instead of black.

Virgie announced it before I could. "Tess says she saw somebody throw somethin' in the well."

Papa caught my arm and pulled me over to him. He curled one arm around my waist and set me on his lap. I reached down and felt the leather of his hand, snuggled closer to him.

"What did you see, Tessie?"

"It was a woman, Papa. And she had a baby in her arms, wrapped up, and she threw it in the well." I spoke slowly and carefully.

Papa used his knuckle to nudge my chin up. "It's awful dark out back. Maybe you just saw some shadows."

I shook my head until a curl popped loose from my ribbon. They were always coming loose. (Virgie had gotten her blond angel hair bobbed to her shoulders and she curled it like in magazines at the newsstand.)

"I saw her. I did. I was sittin' by the door, and I was gettin' too chilled so I was gone come in, but then I saw her walkin' up the back road. I didn't know her, but she was comin' right straight here, so I sat and waited and nearly said hello to her when she got to the steps, but then she didn't walk towards the door at all. She stopped at the well. She looked around, moved the cover, and tossed a baby in. And then she left."

"I think maybe somebody tossed an old sack of trash or maybe a dead squirrel or somethin' in there just for meanness," Virgie said.

I looked straight at Papa. "I swear, it was a baby."

"Don't ever swear, Tess," he said with a little shake of his head, looking back toward the dark. Two lightning bugs went off at the same time.

Mama looked puzzled, the lines in her forehead deeper than usual. "Why would she throw it in our well?"

Virgie looked mad at me. "Now you've upset Mama."

Albert I DIDN'T BELIEVE her when she told me. Even though her face was white as chalk and her eyes big as silver dollars. They've all got Leta's eyes, wet-earth eyes. Rich like good soil.

She was always a dreamer, but the girl never made up tales. Didn't look for attention. Some girls her age did that, though. And it didn't make no sense what she was saying. Land's sake, no woman'd toss her baby in a well.

But Tessie kept on about it, nagging me. Not like her one bit. There was a sweetness about Tess. She liked to please, didn't like to upset nobody. Not to say she lacked spirit. She'd bend, but that girl wouldn't ever break.

The night she was so wrought up, I lifted the cover off and looked down in there, but she just said, no, I couldn't see proper without any light. I ain't never home during good daylight when I'm on the day shift, so I told her the next night I'd shine a lamp down there and we'd have a good look.

If there's one thing I'm good at, it's shining a light in the dark. I know the dark. I'm stained with it. It's caked permanent in the creases of my elbows, in the lines on my hands, under my fingernails. I can taste it deep down my throat and I cough it up in the middle of the night. Up in the daylight, men sort and clean the coal we bring up, picking out slate while they squint in the sun and crisp their skin, and I am no part of them. I wasn't that much older than Tess when I started tending to the mules, getting used to hours without the sun, headed down and down and down, my boots clomping along next to the hooves. I got used to the heft of an axe and the smell of burned powder and the burn of dirt falling in my eyes and every bit of it was in pitch black with the fuzzy weak lamps on our heads and on the walls making just the slightest dent in that pitch. So you would think this one thing my baby girl asked of me, this one time she wanted me to shine my light in the dark for her, I could have done it as easy as breathing. Wouldn't have cost me nothing but a little time. But I didn't have it for her. Thought there wasn't nothing to it, no reason to give up those few precious minutes of sitting in my chair and letting the day roll off me.

'Course then the next day afore I got home, Leta felt the bucket hit something when she was getting water to boil the corn. Pulled up the bucket, and it had a blanket in it.

Leta   I THOUGHT SURE we'd get sick. Can't even think about it—the poor little thing. But in the drinking water.

I waited 'til Albert came home from work. When I pulled up the blanket with the morning water, I knew Tess had been telling the truth, and we'd all ought to have known that. She's a good girl. I didn't let the bucket down again, just sat the blanket on the side of the well. I hurried to the store and bought a new tin bucket, too, thinking I wouldn't want to be using that one again if the night passed like I thought it would. When the girls and Jack came home from school, I told 'em we'd be having cornbread and milk for lunch. Couldn't do much else with no water, and I wasn't touching what I'd already drawn.

"You found it didn't you, Mama?" Tess asked. Her voice was hoarse, and she was chewing on her braid. I didn't get on to her for it.

"Found a blanket. We'll get it all straightened out when your Papa comes home."

"You believe me now, don't you?" She seemed concerned, like I might actually still say she was making things up. I knelt down, took the braid from her mouth, and kissed her forehead—dirty already from who knows what.

"I believe you, Tessie. Get washed up for dinner."

I poured fresh milk over dewberries for dessert. None of them complained.

With the last touches of sun in the sky, backs sore from peering in and eyes tired from squinting, we thought we'd have to find some netting. Then, when we'd lost count of how many times we'd tried, Albert pulled it up with a tiny, pale arm hanging over that tall tin bucket. It was naked, and it was a boy.

My mama died when I was four, and I remember her laying there with the blood soaking the sheets and the sweat not even dried off her face. I saw the baby she'd had die two days later, its face blue and its body shrunk like a dried peach. I've seen men carried home from the mines with eyes torn out and arms just about ripped clean off still hanging by pieces of skin. None of it stuck in my head like that little swollen thing that used to be a baby hanging over the side of our water bucket.

Virgie I THOUGHT SHE made it up at first. To feel important. Tess was the hatefulest thing when she was little. Mama would leave me watching her, and she'd wander off and I'd have to drag her back just a'screaming. The white fence around the yard had to be built to keep her in. Then she just learned to unlatch the gate. She wouldn't mind worth a flip. And after Jack came, she didn't ever get tired of tattling on him. But she never told lies.

She couldn't sleep that first night, and I didn't even say a word to her. I thought she was being silly. I lay there mad at her, listening to the sleep sounds coming from the rest of the house. Papa's snores. Mama's restless shifting—even in her sleep, she couldn't be still. Jack murmuring as he rolled over. The train whistle outside. Wind against the glass panes. But no sounds from Tess. She was lying there awake just like I was, and I didn't even say good night.

The next night, the night the baby had laid on top of our well covered in its still-damp blanket and the sheriff had come and carried it off in a basket, Tess didn't say a word to me. I watched her for a while, tucked into a little S with her back to me in bed, and I inched over to her, even though the pins for my curls stuck into my head when I moved.

"Tessie," I whispered. It tickled her ear, and she hitched her shoulder up.

"What?"

"Y'alright?"

She didn't answer me. I poked her with my big toe, aiming for the sole of her foot.

"Stop."

I jabbed at her calf next.

"Stop it, Virgie," she hissed. "You'll draw blood with that toe."

"Roll over."

She did, looking sleepy and put-upon. Her pretty black curls were spread over the pillow, falling into her face, too, so that she kept swatting at it. She kicked at my feet. "Keep your feet on your side."

I slid my hand over, just touching her arm.

"Keep your hand on your side," she whispered.

I flopped over on my back, looked at the ceiling for a while, then met her wide-open eyes. "I'm sorry I didn't believe you."

"I know," she answered, and that was that.

I woke up hours later to her thrashing around, moonlight streaming through the window. She'd pulled the sheet off me and twisted our top quilt, the one with the bluebirds on it, around her like a cocoon. Her legs were flailing, and she was talking nonsense. I couldn't make it out.

I said her name softly. "Tess, Tess, wake up." I touched her shoulder, shook her lightly. "Tess, it's alright. Wake up." A little louder. Still mumbling and tossing. I felt her forehead for fever.

"Shh. You're having a nightmare."

She rolled to the left suddenly and, thump, she was on the floor. I lurched toward her, peering over the bed. Soon a head popped up.

"I fell out of bed," she announced. She shifted and the moon hit her so that I saw the tears streaked down her face. I didn't say anything.

She looked around, looked at me, looked at her empty pillow, and repeated—for no good reason— "I fell out of bed."

My mouth started twitching then, and so did hers, and soon we were sniggering so hard we had tears rolling down our cheeks. She climbed back in bed, and we both struggled for breath.

Finally we settled down, tugging the covers back over us, burrowing down in the feathers, and I felt sleep pulling me down. "I dreamed I was in the well with him," she whispered, but before I could answer, we were asleep.

Albert THE THING WAS, you'd have to work to take the cover off the well. That cover was a square of wood no bigger across than from my elbow to my fingertips—just big enough to let the bucket go down—but it was wedged tight into its slot. I'd sawed it out of the center of the wooden piece that made the well top, before I nailed the top onto the wooden sides, so the cover always fit snug. Rain blowing on it over the years had warped it, making it mighty hard to pry out, especially on muggy days. Plus it was heavy, thick pine, unwieldy enough to make Leta gasp when she moved it, strong as she is for a woman. You had to grab it just right, wedge your fingers underneath, and lift in one great pull. And I worried that only somebody who'd seen us do it, who knew how it worked would be able to get it off in one tug. Wouldn't be no spur of the moment thing.

Tess I MISSED MY WELL. There wasn't much space in the house for five people, even when one of them was as small as Jack. At the front of the house was the sitting room on one side, with a door leading out to the porch; the bedroom where Virgie and I slept was on the other side, with another door to the porch. Our bedroom connected to Mama and Papa's bedroom through a big, open space with no door—from our pillows we could see just their heads, small and still against the big curli-cued headboard at night—and off from their bedroom was the dining room connected to the kitchen. Five rooms for five people. The two fireplaces, one in each bedroom, shared a chimney, and we closed the doors during the winter so only the bedrooms stayed warm. No use wastin' heat, Mama would say as she went around tugging doors shut, them scraping against the frames before they clicked, shiiii-shunk. Jack got his own bed because he was the boy, but it was just a pallet near the fireplace. Ours was a feather bed like Mama and Papa's. Not from our chickens—Grandpa Tobin made it for Mama when she got married. I felt sorry for those hens, naked and cold and wanting to curl up with us in their stolen clothes.

But, still and all, Jack had his own place. Mama had her rosebushes. Virgie took off for long walks in the woods. Papa had the mines ... even though he wasn't really alone there and sometimes walls fell in and killed bushels of men. He still had a place that was separate. And I had my well.

The well was really only a planked-in holeful of creek—a part you could keep and watch and have, like a June bug on a string. Underground, a little stream trickled into the well, stayed awhile, and went on its way, but you could pull up a bucket of that stream anytime you wanted. After sunset, the back porch was quiet and closed in by trees; the sounds of frogs and crickets reminded me of when I stayed too late swimming and had to run back for supper. Of course, I couldn't swim in the well water, but sometimes I could draw up a bucket and take a swallow straight from it, even though Mama told me it wasn't right to drink from something that hung where bugs could land and crawl on it. (I saw flies land on the tea pitcher sometimes when we'd forget to lay the cloth back over it, but Mama'd just wipe it off and still pour from it. But that was inside and different somehow.) She always poured the water from the tall, narrow well bucket to the inside bucket, shorter and squatter, and only from there would it splash into our washbowls and pitchers and cooking pots. But I'd take long, cool mouthfuls at night, then dump the rest back into the well's black mouth.

I was the only girl who would swim in the swimming hole, and first all the boys went off for a while, telling me they'd never come back if I was gone be mucking around, but they did. Papa didn't like me swimmin' with them, but I started taking Jack with me, and that made him feel better. Jack'd play with the boys if they were around his age, and I'd stay separate, seeing how deep I could dive, pushing my arms back and forth through the water to make butterfly wings, letting my hair swirl around me and pretending I was a sea witch with seaweed hair.

But you couldn't go to the creek just anytime. The well was always there, waiting. I could smell the water in it, and I knew that at the bottom it was cool with slippery moss like on creek rocks. I used to stare down it and imagine that we might scoop up mermaids or talking fish with the bathwater.

Don't throw the baby out with the bathwater.

After the dead baby, I didn't like to stare down there anymore. I didn't think about talking fish. I thought about the nightmares. They started with me diving down underwater with my eyes open, and then I'd see a baby reaching for me. I was running out of breath, but I couldn't swim up because the baby's hands were in my hair, and I couldn't move him. I couldn't see his face at first, but when he lifted his head, I could see he had black holes where his eyes should be. It was the first nightmare I could ever remember when I woke up. And I'd remember it all day long until I fell asleep the next night.

Virgie PAPA SAID IT was an abomination what that woman did. That God would judge her. But I wondered did that woman think she couldn't scare up enough food for another lunch, and with the others barefoot and winter coming, this would be the better way. Or did he just cry and cry until she thought her head would burst? Was it that she couldn't handle it anymore, that this was the fifth or the sixth or the tenth little one underfoot and it was more than she could stand?

I wondered did Mama ever stand by the well and think how her life could be easier.

Tess   NOBODY TALKED MUCH at supper that night. Mainly the forks and knifes went *clank, clank*. Then there'd be chewing, tea-swallowing sounds, a little smacking from Jack. Then Mama'd say, "Don't smack your food, Jack." Then *clank, clank*. Good yellow squash and sugar snap peas and some fried ham and biscuits. We hadn't had ham for months and we didn't even have to kill a pig, Mama said. She told us to tell the Hudsons thank you when we saw them.

Finally, Papa wiped his mouth. He was always the first one finished. "Enjoyed it, Leta."

We all echoed him, telling Mama how good it was. She smiled and said "thank you" as fast and soft as she could. Then she looked at my plate and frowned. "You're not eatin' much, Tessie."

"You still upset?" asked Papa.

I didn't know how to answer that. "Just not too hungry."

"You're leavin' your ham on your plate?" asked Jack, sounding like it was the same as taking my head off and leaving it there.

"'Course not," I said. I started to nibble on the ham again. You didn't leave anything on your plate.

"Don't know why a baby in the well's got anything to do with eatin' ham," he muttered.

"You shouldn't talk about the poor thing like that, Jack," said Mama. "It was a child, same as you or Virgie or Tess."

Papa put his hand on mine, the one that wasn't holding my fork. "Tessie, you got every right to be upset. Must've been a shock to you. Still is. It don't matter about the ham."

"I'll eat it," said Jack.

I kicked at him under the table. "Not if I eat it myself, you little pig."

But that kick didn't have much feeling behind it; I only

managed it out of habit. I couldn't get worked up over Jack being a bottomless pit. I knew Papa was feeling guilty. Mama, too. Wasn't no reason to—I knew they didn't have space in their heads to be thinking on babies being in the well.

"I'm gettin' better 'bout it," I told Papa.

"I heard you tossin' in your sleep," Mama said. "You were whimperin' like a baby."

I put my fork down. "Just bad dreams," I said.

"Aren't y'all thinking about it?" Virgie asked, looking back and forth from Mama to Papa. "'Bout who did it? Why she'd do it?"

Mama and Papa looked at each other but didn't really answer. I couldn't bring myself to pick up my fork again, even if Jack did get to eat my ham. Mama noticed that I'd wiped my mouth and given up.

"Sure you don't want her ham, Albert?" asked Mama. Papa shook his head and flicked his hand toward Jack. "Go on then, Jack," she said.

"I can't imagine," Virgie said, as Jack forked my ham.

"But eat your squash," Mama said to me.

2 Daylight

Jack WE COULD HEAR THE TRAIN FROM OUR HOUSE, even though we couldn't smell the coal burning. Our place was just before you got to the painted "Welcome to Carbon Hill" sign, down a rutted road that made your head nearly hit the car roof on the drive to church.

My first memory of town is the train whistle blaring. The wind from the wheels or the cars themselves or maybe everything together blowing hot on my face. The train seemed terrifying and alive and it blocked out the sun and the whole town, and I couldn't look away. That was a knee-high child's version of the Frisco Railroad, where we'd see our Grandma Moore when she came back from visiting Pop's oldest brother in Tupelo. The train would head on through Jasper into Birmingham and on to parts foreign and strange to us. Later it'd take me to St. Louis for an accounting course—which I hated— and then to Washington, D.C.—which I loved—to work in J. Edgar Hoover's office as a typesetter in the months before Pearl Harbor.

But in those days, the days when Virgie and Tess and Mama and Pop made up the known corners of my world, all the Frisco line did was bring Grandma back to us.

The whole town ran down the hill it was named for, with churches and houses a little farther up the hill, then all the shops lining Front Street. The railroad ran beside Front Street straight through town, with all the offshoot tracks or truck routes leading to the mines like so many legs and arms off a backbone.

Galloway was the biggest company, and its commissary was on the corner of Front Street and Galloway Road, across from the Brasher Hotel. You'd head left up the Galloway Road for a couple of miles and hit the main mine. Or if you kept going a little farther down Front Street and turned right at the tracks, you'd curve around and find the No. 11 mine where Pop worked most of the time.

Galloway was the pair of thick-muscled legs that moved the whole town, then there were the spindly little arms, local mines that didn't have the staying power of Galloway. Howard Mine was up Fish Hatchery Road, and there was Brookside and Hope and Chickasaw, all with truck after truck packed with coal that ran down to the main depot, where the chute would empty the coal straight to the railcars. By 1931 those small ones were suffering, mostly shut down. Galloway struggled on with fewer men and fewer tons.

My memories of that summer aren't too clear. I remember a red-headed boy at school whose father had died the year before, that a beam had broken him nearly in half when it collapsed. I worried about that.

The Warrior Coal Field, north and west of Birmingham, covering all of Walker County, was rich with coal deposits. A gift for a state that otherwise was mostly prying vegetables and cotton out of the land. But it was a gift with strings attached. Its coal seams tended to be thin and broken up, so it was harder to mine. Too much slate and shale meant cleaning the coal took more time. So more men picking and loading and more men washing and sorting. All that came together to mean that ten men in Alabama produced the same amount of coal that three and a half men could produce in Indiana.

I read that when I went away to college. I assumed they didn't want to publicize that in Alabama. Sort of demoralizing.

I worried off and on as a boy, afraid of things that were really just shadows in my head, not full-out ideas or images. But I knew we were on the edge of something. That Pop was between us and falling. Just falling and falling until we smashed into some terrible bottom that people only whispered about.

Accidents happened all the time. I remembered when Pop broke his jaw, and we all knew he could barely see out of his right eye anymore. Plus he'd broken both arms and a leg and both his ankles and torn something in his back. That was all before I was born. I wouldn't have known about any of that if it weren't for Mama asking him about the aches sometimes. He just kept quiet about it and pretended he was in one piece.

But I knew it was likely he wouldn't come back through the door at night after he left in the morning. And then I'd be the man. Some boys my age were already in the mines. Pop wouldn't let me. He said I should go to school.

I couldn't figure out how I'd get the money to support the family if something happened to Pop. Needed to be twelve, maybe eleven, to get a paper route. I could've gotten paid to stack shelves at the commissary, maybe to deliver orders. I could do a man's work at the mines at twelve if I lied a little. But that wouldn't have been good enough. Not if Pop was killed before then. I thought Virgie could get a teaching job somewhere way out in the country, even without teacher's college maybe. Tess was too little to do anything. Nobody would hire a little girl.

We had the farm and the milk and the chickens. That would feed us. Might have to let go of the electricity. Could always sell the car.

Nothing ever did happen to him, nothing dramatic or sudden or tragic. But I never felt like I was away from the edge of that cliff until long after I was earning a man's paycheck.

Leta I USUALLY WOKE up a minute or two before the rooster crowed. I hated that rooster, and many a morning I thought of twisting his neck and turning him into soup. That little bit of meanness shoved at me and got me out of bed. My braid was long enough to twist into a bun and I could sleep on it without it coming loose, but I'd usually sleep with my hair completely down. Albert had a foolish liking of how it covered my pillow. I obliged him, even though I'd wake in the middle of the night and have to yank at my hair and push at my husband to get free of his weight. Before my feet hit the floor, I was plaiting it again, twisting it into a bun, and grabbing a pin from the nightstand to hold it in place.

My green housedress hung in the wardrobe, and I slipped it on without a sound louder than cotton sliding against skin. Albert stirred at the splash of water from the pitcher hitting the porcelain basin. Spring and summer, he'd sleep past me, not needing to build the fire to warm the room before the children woke. I washed my face, patted it dry with the towel, fingering a hole that needed to be patched. I hated using the pot on the porch unless I couldn't wait—instead, I stopped at the outhouse on my way to feed the animals.

Opening the door softly, I walked the eight steps to the kitchen without needing a light. The stove fire was my doing. I stoked it, then drew a bucket of water to fill the girls' pitcher so they'd have fresh water for their faces. But instead of taking it to their dressing table, I poured it into the stove reservoir. Albert would lay there another ten minutes, and the children would sleep until the rooster crowed, probably another thirty minutes, about 5:30. I didn't ask the girls to help me with breakfast—it gave Albert and me a few minutes, a little silence before even the sun joined us. His coffee—tasted like poison to me—would be ready by the time he dragged himself over to his chair by the stove. I preferred to work by firelight in the kitchen instead of turning on the overhead bulb. Electricity's too harsh for early morning. Even the sun knows to start gentle. After I got the fire built in the belly of the stove, I measured out the grounds and set the coffee on to boil.

Albert walked in while I was kneading the biscuit dough, flour up to my elbows, fingers grasping and pressing. Flip, punch, mash mash. Flip, punch, mash mash.

"Never understand how you do that in the dark," he said from just behind me. He tucked a stray hair behind my ear.

"Same way you know your way round No. 11." I nodded toward the fire. "And it ain't dark."

I knew without looking that he'd picked up the girls' pitcher where I'd left it on the table planning on filling their wash-bowl himself, and I caught his arm when he stepped toward the porch. "Take it from the reservoir," I said, pointing him toward the stove.

He looked puzzled, then nodded and walked over to the side compartment of the stove where the water heated. It couldn't have been too hot yet, but I felt better for making the effort.

"Ain't no need to heat the water," he said. "It ain't gone bad." But I only handed him a dipper, and he went on. By the time he came back from the bedroom, the coffee on the stove was boiling. I pulled his coffee cup from the cabinet and poured over the sink, with the heat from the cup warming my fingers as the brew rose to the top. Just a ground or two floating. Black as night, so hard looking it didn't seem right that a spoon could move through it.

"Must taste like coal," I said under my breath, stopping up the pot's spout with a bit of cloth and setting it back on the stove to keep warm.

"Coffee?" He took a sip, smiled, and closed his eyes as he leaned back. "No, ma'am. Tastes like daylight."

Since I was twelve, I could make biscuits in five minutes flat. My oldest sister taught me, and it took me awhile to get the feel of it. You feel a good dough in the tips of your fingers—when you need to add more milk, when to throw in more flour. It's gotta be soft like a child's cheek, but not so dry it'll crack. I never even looked as I poured in flour and milk at the same time, tossed in a pinch of baking soda, salt, cut in the lard.

I threw the biscuit circles in the iron skillet and set 'em in the door of the stove. Ten minutes. Lay a couple of slices of ham in another skillet—the Hudsons had brought us a part of their pig. Not much left, but enough for everybody to have some to go with their biscuits. A jar of pear preserves on the table, slab of fresh-made butter. The children didn't smear it on their bread like they used to before they started churning it, so it lasted longer. From the back of the cupboard, I took a jar of honey. Albert saw it, and his eyes, blue like robins' eggs, lit up.

"Thought we were out."

"Just told them that." Honey was too precious to have it dripping on them from head to toe after one piece of toast. Albert loved it.

We sat there, not touching, as he sipped his coffee. "I heard Henry Harken's boy is sweet on Virgie."

"Ain't they all?" he answered me. "You'd swear that girl was walkin' an inch off the ground. Pretty as a picture."

We didn't ever mention Virgie being beautiful, partly because we didn't want Tess to feel like she was any less beautiful, and partly because we didn't want Virgie getting a swelled head. Sometimes it was hard to ignore, though, especially since she was getting older. I'd often look over to tell her to fetch something for me, and she'd just take my breath away, like fireworks or fresh snow. She never fit in a town where everything was covered in a layer of black dust.

"You're gone have to beat the boys off with a stick soon," I said.

"Likely."

I looked at Albert, with his lovely eyes, his lined face pale from lack of sunlight, his jaw still crooked where it had been shattered. I looked at my own hands, always cracked and dry from doing dishes, and thought of my tired face, leathery from too much sun.

"How'd we make her?" I asked, half to myself.

"Looks just like you did," he answered immediately, talking around his cup. "Ain't no surprise."

I pointed at his right eye, gone weak from a stray rock in a cave-in. It looked normal, but he saw less and less out of it each year. "You done lost your memory, well as your sight." I looked to check for the girls, then kissed him quickly on the forehead. He smiled.

I took out the biscuits, forking two on his plate. He smashed the butter into a pool of honey as it streamed down on his dish. He scooped a forkful of the golden stuff on top of a biscuit half as I put out plates for the children and slid the biscuits onto a plate in the middle of the table. I covered them with a towel to keep them warm.

"Not gone eat with me?" he asked.

"I'll eat with them," I said.

The rooster crowed, and Albert gobbled down his second biscuit, using the sorghum syrup on it instead of the honey. He wanted to stretch that honey out for another few weeks. I took his plate from him, waited for him to drain his coffee, and set the dishes in the basin. He pecked my cheek, looking out the window behind me at the sky. "Not gone have time to do the milkin' today, Leta-ree. Promise I'll make it out in time tomorrow."

"I don't mind," I said. "Lord knows I'm down there with the rest of the animals anyway." He did the milking most mornings, knowing that I didn't enjoy it. Not many men did the milking before they headed to the mines.

I could hear the girls stirring, and they'd wake Jack so I wouldn't have to. That boy could sleep through a cyclone, even if he was swirling around in it. I could do the milking and feeding and get the eggs before the children left for school.

Before I got out the door, Virgie called to me, sitting on the floor and pulling on her shoes with the curling rags still sticking out of her head. "Want me to get the eggs, Mama?"

"You eat your breakfast and get your brother ready. We'll see about them eggs after that's all done." I knew I'd have time to gather them before they finished up.

She looked at me sideways. "You eat yours with Papa?"

"I had all I wanted."

I headed out to the cow. She'd be suffering if I didn't get to her before proper sunrise. The sky was already touched with pink, but I stopped at the chickens to throw them a handful of feed. Moses whipped her head around to greet me, rumbling deep in her throat. That signaled a bad mood, and I gave a wide berth as I grabbed the stool and approached her from the side. After a little cooing and stroking, she seemed calmer. I rocked forward on the stool, unevenly balanced on its three legs so you could flip backward if the cow was more ornery than you thought. She stayed still, and I pulled the pail under her udders. She was heavy with milk, and I welcomed the chore, the peace and routine of it. There's a rhythm to good milking, like stitching at the Singer. Your fingers settle in to do the work, and your mind purely floats away.

When Virgie was seven and Tess just a toddler, I'd been run to death trying to take care of the two of them, plus I was getting rounder and rounder every day with Jack. Tess had the croup, and I had to go feed the animals. So I had Virgie sit in the rocking chair pulled right up close to the fire, and I told her to hold Tess and not to move. I said, "She can't get cold, now. She's got to stay warm, so you don't move from this fire. Don't you move a bit."

By the time I came back, she'd baked them both good. Faces red as a sunburn. Tears in Virgie's eyes, and when I started to fuss at her, she said, "You told me not to let her get cold, Mama. You told me not to move."

It's funny—you'd think with that porcelain doll face, she'd be a selfish one. But Virgie'd lay down on a fire-ant hill if it'd help us, especially the younger ones. Ever since Tess was born, she's been like that. Like one look at those mewling little faces woke something in her that tied her to them for good.

Albert I CRANKED UP the Model T, slid onto that almost-leather seat, threw my coveralls and boots and cap on the floor. Every morning I made the drive to work I was glad for it. I watched my parents scratch and claw in the dirt in a little shack on land the Tennessee Company owned and promised myself and God it'd never be me, with my family and my home at the mercy of the same grabbing hands that decided my paycheck. To be a man, you need your own home, not company-owned land. Need your own land for crops and a few animals so strike or no, you've got some sureness of food. Built the house with my own hands, and pulled in every favor I was owed from brothers and friends. Always wanted to add a second story, but never seemed to be any extra.

I didn't bother closing the window flaps unless it was raining—I liked the feel of the sunrise to hit me on my face. I just barely got to see a bit of pink in the sky before I headed down No. 11. Those drives to work, with the bounces from the ruts in the road, cool smell of the wet grass, and the taste of sorghum still on my tongue, was the best time I had to myself. And usually I'd give somebody a lift, so it wasn't really to myself. Then again, I wasn't friends with many big talkers. Wished it took me half an hour to get to the mine instead of fifteen minutes. I'd drive the back way, keeping out of town and its waking-up sounds, just rolling through the almost-dark, trees on either side. I didn't care much for town at all, to be honest, not like my girls, who were always wanting to go for penny candy or get a soda for a treat. Too much all crowded together for my taste.

Jonah was walking by the side of the road not a quarter mile from the site, so I stomped the brake and pulled over.

"Ride on in with me," I yelled as he turned around.

"'Preciate it." He climbed in, cap in his hand, already wearing his coveralls. The colored part of town was fairly near the mines, maybe a half-hour walk. "Doin' alright?" he asked.

"Fair."

"Heard about that baby there in y'all's well. Family takin' it hard?"

"Alright, I s'pose."

Jonah's father worked the mines and was still going down below when I started with Galloway Coal. Might say the father got pushed into the line of work—learned it in prison. Convict lease. Six years for vagrancy, and he spent that six years treated worse than a pit mule. Jonah's papa served his time and made it out alright, but mining paid better than farm work, which was the only other work about any colored man could get. So he left off the prison uniform and headed back down. Union man. Jonah growed up in Dora, in what folks there started calling Uniontown. Negro strikers all of 'em, who got pitched off company housing during the strike of 1920 and cobbled together shacks out of trash, boards, rotten timber, whatever they could find. Said they'd never again live in a house they could get throwed out of. And even after the strike was over and they headed back to the mines, they never did go back to company housing. Jonah said they'd stuff paper in the cracks when it rained, watch the stars out of the holes in the roof when it was clear.

Me and him rode on in, hearing the mine—smelling it, too—before we saw it spring up around a curve in the road. The gob pile, just a wide, long hill of the trash sorted out of the coal, gave off a heavy sulfur smell that hung low in the air. The clang of the cars bumping into each other, the clatter of the conveyor belts, yells from men hollering to one another. All the above-ground workings were clear as a bell, bared to the sunshine and anyone who happened to walk by. The tipple stood above it all, part wood, part machine, the wood supports of it seeming too tricky—like a spiderweb from a distance—to be so solid. The sorters and washers worked on the coal when it went past them on the rumbling belts, the good coal rising higher to the top of the tipple, where it got dumped into storage. Finally it'd be loaded into the coal cars to make its way down to the depot. Nothing but dust and smoke and wood and metal, nothing green or growing anywhere in sight. Nothing alive but men. And them just another part of the big machine of it all.

All the day shift was filing in, with just a few of the men looking at me funny on account of Jonah being in my car. I reckoned it didn't make no difference if I offered a man a ride to work as I was passing him on the road. It would have been different if I'd gone by his house and picked him up. I'd only been to Jonah's house once, when his first child died one night in his crib. Only time I'd ever been through those Negro houses, just boards slapped together. It was a shame Jonah had to live like that—he was a good man, a hard worker, good to his family. Had my kids call him Mr. Benton, not by his first name like some boy who ain't never shaved a beard.

Jonah and me didn't say a word climbing out of the car. He nodded and went on, and I hung my legs out the door while I pulled on my coveralls. Cracked my back as I stood up, trying to loosen up my spine.

I pulled my cap off the seat and unhooked the lamp. Spit in the top chamber a few times, unhooked the bottle of carbide from my belt and poured a bit in the bottom. The oil and spit would come together and make the gas that reflected off the face. The old kerosene lamps wobbled this way and that like a drunkard. A carbide flame was a steady thing.

Bosses'd have you believe you were part of something special, toting the world on your shoulders at Galloway Mine No. 11, with four hundred men going into its belly every day and prying out Galloway Lump. One of the biggest coal basins in the world here in Carbon Hill, they said. Always heard tell that long after Pennsylvania and Virginia mines had been picked clean, Alabama would supply the world. Was hard to conjure the future by the light coming off my cap.

Tess   COAL WAS SCATTERED around the ground like beetles, all shiny black shells. My hair was that color, not corn-silk yellow like Virgie's or silver like Papa's or dirt-road-colored like Mama's. Coal colored.

But there was no coal rock in our yard, only down past the chickens. They were the start of the animals, who were all in a line down the hill—chickens then Moses then Horse then smelly pigs. Then outhouse. And then creek. Our part of outside was as neat and tidy as inside the house: The yard was swept hard and smooth, a brown, still lake with rosebush islands. It wasn't hardly ever dusty because Mama swept it every day. It shined like peanut butter when it rained.

We'd got home from school, and Virgie'd gone straight to see if Mama needed anything. I hugged Mama then headed right to the warmer over the stove, cracking open its door to see what Mama left for us. Biscuits, still soft and warm. Mama'd always make a few too many at breakfast or lunch; they made for the best eating after school, once you ripped one apart and spread pear preserves inside. I was licking my fingers by the time I headed to the outhouse, walking a wide path around Moses, who was always sharpening her hooves to stomp me or gritting her teeth into points to snap at me. Mama nor Papa neither one would listen to me, but that cow was full of hate and vinegar. Virgie and me both knew it. Once maybe she was a good cow, pure white like her milk, but then some evil spirit came on her, eating her up inside and turning her soul black as sin. That's when the black splotches started spreading over her hide. That cow always looked like she'd like to tear me to bits, even though without me, she wouldn't have had a name.

I didn't like the outhouse. You had to hold your breath, and it was dark and my bottom was bony and might could've fit through the hole, I thought. (It was a two-seater, but both the holes were adult size.) Before I pulled the door open, I took a deep breath, then jumped in and hiked down my bloomers just as fast as I could, counting the whole time. I could only hold my breath up to sixty-three.

Usually by forty, I'd finished my business, pulled out the bit of Sears Roebuck catalog I'd carried down in my pocket, and got out with a good ten seconds to go. If I could, I held my breath till I was back up by the horse instead of gulping air by the pigs.

I was done by thirty—Aunt Celia was coming, and I didn't want to miss seeing her spit—and I leaned down for my bloomers. But right on the seat next to me was a fat spider—not a daddy long legs or a little grass spider, but something foreign. It wasn't like nothing I'd ever seen before, all legs and squirming body the size of a finger. I jumped up and thumped it hard, and down it went, disappearing down the hole. It made me scream, and once I started, I couldn't seem to stop. I hollered and hollered, took a gulp of air, and hollered again.

Virgie MR. DOBSON SHOWED up at the door, sack of pears in one hand, his straw hat in the other. He nodded at me, just a blink with his whole head.

"Thought I'd bring your ma some pears."

"I'll get her, sir."

Mr. Dobson stood still, like he wasn't even breathing, except for his right foot tapping. He'd do that until Mama got to the door. He brought pears about once a week, and I always paid attention to that foot. He looked somewhere over my head, at some spot on the wall that wasn't at all interesting, and I didn't feel it was right to look him in the eyes when he was doing such a good job of avoiding mine. So he watched the wall and I watched his foot and it was a few seconds before I remembered I needed to run get Mama.

She hated for us to holler for each other in the house like we were calling dogs.

The Dobsons didn't have much besides their three pear trees. Mama would give him a basketful of vegetables and prob-ably some cornmeal to take back with him. She always acted too happy about those pears, her smile wide and bright, and I knew she hoped the cheery, cheery pleasure in her voice—which made her sound like someone who wasn't my mama at all—could distract Mr. Dobson from thinking about how he got a basket a lot fuller than the one he brought.

Mama was on her hands and knees in front of a bucket of sudsy water, and she said she'd just rinse off her hands and be right out. I passed that along to Mr. Dobson, whose foot was still beating a rhythm on the porch. He thanked me, then jerked his head toward the creek.

"Might be somethin' wrong with Tess—I hear her yellin'."

By the time Mama came through the doorway, I was headed down the hill, wondering what had happened to Tess. She always hated the outhouse. When she was little, she used to sneak and go in the bushes instead until Mama told her it wasn't ladylike.

I walked toward Moses, who jerked her head at me as soon as she saw me. Tess wanted to name her Jesus at first. You can't name cows after the Son of God, but she was only five. So she got to name her Moses. After the confusion about Jesus, nobody had the heart to bring up that Moses was a boy name for a girl cow.

She was the meanest cow we ever had. Mama tried to teach me to milk so she and Papa wouldn't have to do it every morning, but I couldn't. Their teats looked soft and pliable, like they'd be no rougher on you than squeezing a sack of water, but there was a knack to how you pulled them. Trying to learn the feel of it, your wrists swelled up and your fingers felt like they'd been skint on gravel.

I called for Tess, hoping she'd answer me before I had to pass Moses. The cow was just outside the barn, grazing, and I wished Mama had left her in the stall. She started shaking her black-and-white head. I wanted to turn around, but I could tell she wanted to run at me, and Papa always told me to walk on by her and don't let her know I was afraid. But she knew.

I stood like a statue, and Tess came from behind the barn. She wore her favorite dress, lavender-checked with pockets shaped like chickens, embroidered with black trim around the bottom and the chickens. Our Aunt Merilyn had sewed it.

"She's gone run at you," she whispered.

"Shhh." I kept staring at Moses, who was still shaking her head, eyes rolling. She looked at Tess and seemed to hate her about as much as she hated me. Tess took two steps back.

"Papa says don't show her you're afraid, and she'll go right on grazing," she said, not sounding too convinced. But she lifted her pointy little chin up higher.

"I know." I stepped back, too, and it made me mad that this wobbly thing with her awkward swinging udders and too-big tongue made me afraid. Chickens and pigs and Horse—they all knew their place. Even the rat dog Papa kept around the barn. But this cow thought she had some hold over us. Like she knew we needed the milk and that gave her some kind of confidence not at all proper for an animal to have. That cow was overfull of pride.

I looked back at her, looked her straight in the eyes. I almost took a step toward her, but she moved enough, just a twitch, to scare me. I looked away then, and so did Tess. We both ran all the way back up to the road, dresses flapping up around us. As always, I tried to hold mine down.

"Were you yellin' at somethin'?" I asked, smoothing my hair.

"A spider." She looked up at the porch and grinned, then took off like a shot toward the steps.

Papa's sister Celia was standing on the porch, leaning over the railing to spit. She had Papa's blue eyes, and curly, dark hair that fought her braid every step of the way. She spiraled it like a snail shell at the back of her neck, and it was bigger than an orange. Her face was all angles, and she was tall as Papa. He always smiled whenever she showed up.

Aunt Celia was also the spittiest woman I ever saw. She spit Copenhagen way out, over the porch rail, over the rosebushes, and sometimes almost clean to the road. She thought it was disgusting for women to smoke cigarettes.

Tess ran up to her and hugged her neck. "Did ya hear, Aunt Celia? About the baby in the well?"

Aunt Celia situated herself in a rocker, then made a V with her fingers and spit through the V—*ha-ick puh*, over the railing. The O of her lips hung there between her fingers for a second, then she went back to her normal mouth.

"That's why I'm here, Tessie Lou."

Tess's middle name isn't Lou, but Aunt Celia liked to call her that.

While she was talking, I hugged her neck, too, not squeezing as hard as Tess had. Then I backed off, settled against the railing, the shadow of the roof falling on me. Tess crowded against Aunt Celia, just touching the edge of her sleeve. If Tess could've sewn herself onto Aunt Celia's dress like a big curly-headed button and stayed with her ever and always, she would've.

I liked Mama's sisters best of all, especially my Aunt Merilyn, who moved like she was dancing. She could fill up a whole house with laughing and talking and fluttering around—there was nothing delicate or fluttery about Aunt Celia. Her mind and her mouth were as sharp as her cheekbones, and Tess would sit and stare at her like she was a picture show. She made me antsy. She made me want to stay out of range. Once when I was little, I hid under the bed when she came over.

Papa was leaning against the wall of the house, one foot propped on the porch railing.

"Sheriff came," he said. "Looked at it and took it to Jasper for Dr. Grissom to look at. To guess how old he was and see if they could figure out anything."

When Papa worked days at the mines, he didn't get home until near or after dark—"on at seven off at six," Mama'd tell us over and over when we were little and couldn't remember when we'd see him again. When he did finally get home, if there was still daylight, he'd go straight to either the garden or down the road to the farm until the last of the light was gone. But the mines had cut back everybody's days, laying some men off completely. He no longer worked there six days like he used to, and sometimes for two or three days in a row he'd be farming when we came home from school. He'd wave to us as we walked by, but he had stopped altogether for Aunt Celia.

His soft gray shirt was wet from working in the garden, and his nose and cheeks had turned pink. Like Aunt Celia, he was all angles; his arms, neck, even hands were corded, not soft at all.

Sometimes I thought if the mines fell down around him, Papa would still be standing, harder than the black diamond. In his wide-brimmed straw hat—not his mining cap—he was a railroad spike.

"Couldn't you tell how old he was from looking at him?" Aunt Celia asked. She snorted before he could answer her. "'Course you couldn't, but couldn't Leta? Think a woman would know by the looks of him."

Papa looked at Tess and me and frowned. "Couldn't say. Not quite normal after the water and all. Thought he might be undersized, too, if he'd gone hungry. No tellin' what a mother like that might've done to him."

Tess sat on Aunt Celia's lap, even though she was too big, and kept her arms around Aunt Celia's neck. "I dream about him, Aunt Celia."

"What do you dream?" Aunt Celia's mouth stopped moving as she peered down at Tess.

"I see his little fingers and toes and sometimes I think he's in bed with me."

"You ain't said nothin' about that in a few days, girl," Papa said, eyebrows sloping down toward his nose. "You still havin' trouble sleepin'?"

"I sleep. I just keep havin' nightmares. I never even see his face good." She snuggled into the crook of Aunt Celia's arm, looking a little silly with her legs hanging all over the place. She looked at Aunt Celia, not at Papa or me, and asked almost in a whisper, "Do you think he's hauntin' me?"

Aunt Celia didn't pause for one second. "Nah," she scoffed. She turned her head to the side. *Ha-ick puh.* "Why would he haunt you? He ought to haunt that poor excuse for a woman who threw him away like a corn husk."

"You believe in ghosts?" I asked her.

"Not the kind that torment you, Virgie May." My middle name is Elaine.

"I'm right there in the bed with you, Tess," I said. "I'd snatch a ghost baldheaded if one tried to get near you."

She didn't look at ease. "But what if he's a good ghost?"

Papa walked over and put a hand on her head. He always comforted you different than Mama did. She stroked and petted with the tips of her fingers; he didn't move his hand at all. He'd lay it on your head or shoulder or back and keep it there, steady, letting you feel the weight of it. "If he's a good ghost, he'll understand he needs to leave you be. And if he won't, send him on over to my bed."

She smiled. "Yessir."

Aunt Celia glanced at Papa. "Y'all's water safe?"

"Oughtta be." Papa shrugged. "Baby was only there for a day, and bein' stream fed, there'd be a steady flow of water down there. Leta's been boilin' all the water anyway."

Mama swung open the screen door, carrying two cups in her hands. Aunt Celia liked coffee in the middle of the day, so Mama had put some on to perk. Papa had decided he'd have some, too, I guess, which I couldn't understand with him already sweating. Children weren't allowed to have coffee.

"Albert's already been after me to stop the boilin'," Mama said, handing them each a cup. "Which I guess I will. Don't have the time for it anyway, but it made things seem a little cleaner."

After the morning coffee boiled, Mama always put a little piece of cloth in the spout of the pot so that no bugs would fly into it. I could see how a dead baby in our water would trouble her.

"Ah, you'll be fine. Come join us," said Aunt Celia, waving to a rocking chair.

"Floors won't keep with the soap on 'em," said Mama. I saw her hands were red from the hot water and the scrubbing. "But come see me before you leave, Celia. Makin' some fried peach pies." She looked at Tess sprawling over Aunt Celia's lap. "And after you've squashed your aunt flat as a fritter, you girls can come in and help me with the floors."

"Yes, ma'am," we both said. Mama's skirt swished when she went through the door.

"Don't know if it's hot enough," Papa said, holding the cup up to his face.

Aunt Celia, quick as a flash, reached over and stuck her finger in his coffee. "Reckon it is," she said, finger still in there.

Papa smiled big enough that we saw the hole where his side tooth used to be.

"You hear President Hoover gave up control of that power plant in Muscle Shoals?" she asked. Papa never talked politics with Mama, who said not one politician was worth a flip. But he and Aunt Celia would talk about the president and the governor and people losing their jobs. I don't know if she liked politics, but she did like to argue.

"You gone beat that dead horse?" Papa asked after he took a sip of coffee. "If it was federal, we'd get jobs and power from it. Ain't a bad deal."

"You damn Bolshevik."

"Celia..." Papa said, looking at us.

"Ah, they've heard a helluva lot worse from school kids. And you are a damn Bolshevik."

"I don't think you even know what a Bolshevik is," Papa said, just ignoring her language that time. "Main thing is that President Hoover don't think the government should get involved. Thinks folks should just up and volunteer to help."

"And what's wrong with that, Albert? You got a short memory. Everybody pitchin' in got us through the war."

Papa shifted his shoulders up and down, then rolled his neck a little, taking his time about answering. "You know better than that, Celia. You got sense enough to see the difference. For every man with a job here—shoot, from here clear to Birmingham—there's two men without one. They's a lot more to be volunteered on than to do the volunteerin'. Just look around...," he stopped, and I knew he was on the edge of getting in a real stew. I could see the vein just over his ear bulging. But he waited awhile and just smiled.

"Heard the governor of New York might run against him next year," he said finally.

"New York." *Ha-ick puh.*

Tess had slid to Aunt Celia's feet and was looking at our aunt's mouth, her eyes narrowed and nose squinched up. "Aunt Celia, will a man kiss you tasting like snuff?" she asked.

"Tess," I scolded, but Papa nearly spewed his coffee laughing, and Aunt Celia just cocked her head.

"Ain't had no trouble yet in that department," she said. She looked like she wished she could spit for emphasis, but she took a sip of coffee instead. "Had your first kiss yet, Virgie?" she said, turning to me.

I couldn't even look at Papa, couldn't even open my mouth to say something back. I just shook my head, and at the same time Papa said, so natural and comfortable, "She's only fourteen, Celia. Don't be rushin' her."

"Nearly fifteen," she said, winking at me. "You married Leta when she was sixteen."

"Ain't the same now."

"'Cause her daddy didn't skin you alive the way you plan to the first boy that comes callin'?"

"Ummm." He nodded. He was looking back toward the garden, though, and draining the last bit from his cup, tipped his head back in one quick motion. "Only an hour or so of daylight left," he said, squeezing Aunt Celia's shoulder. "Best be finishin' up. Don't forget to take Leta up on her pies, and tell Mama I said hello."

I was glad they'd left me out of the whole conversation.

Papa clunked down the steps, and I boosted myself up onto the porch rail, with my legs over the side toward the house, where nobody from the street could see up my dress. "Hope the sheriff catches whatever lunatic did this at any rate," Aunt Celia said.

"Do you think she was crazy?" I asked.

"Have to be off-kilter in some way."

"Who do you think did it?" asked Tess.

"I don't know, but it's the baby, not the mother, that's your concern, Tessie Lou."

"What do you mean?"

"It's him you're seein', you say. If that's so, if you feel like he's calling to you, you've got a responsibility to him." *Ha-ick puh.*

"To do what?" Tess looked confused.

"To do right by him."

"How?" I asked, puzzled.

"You girls know about my baby?" she asked, just as casual as if she was asking if we knew about the new hat she'd bought.

We didn't answer her for a long while. It seemed like half an afternoon we sat there, her rocking, us still as stones. Finally I said, "You had a baby?"

"Yep," she said. She'd been married a long time ago—I knew that. He'd been a miner like every other man around, and he died before I was born. Something bad wrong inside him. "Only ever carried the one, and she was born early," Aunt Celia went on. "Lived three days, then I buried her up at Pisgah. Buried Marcus next to her the followin' year."

"Who's Marcus?" asked Tess.

"My husband."

"Your husband?" Tess looked at me expectantly, as if I'd jump in and argue that, no, Aunt Celia couldn't have had both a husband and a baby that disappeared into thin air, that it was nothing more than a story.

"My husband," she repeated. "But what I wanted to tell you was that after my baby girl died, she'd come to me in my dreams. Crawling, though, not like she was in real life at all. Older, with chubby cheeks and healthy color. Cooing and happy and grinning. Sometimes she'd come to me when I was awake; not in a vision, like, but I'd feel her heavy in my lap. Feel the heat of that little, squirming body. That went on for a year, and for a while I thought

I was plumb crazy. But then Marcus fell over dead in the yard, quick as a wink, and I started looking forward to that weight in my lap like I'd never yearned for anything before. I'd sit in my chair for hours at night just waiting for her to come. Never saw her there, just felt her... held her. Rocked and sang to her.

"About a year after Marcus died, I didn't feel her anymore. Didn't dream of her. Like she'd moved on. I think she stayed with me out of kindness, 'cause she knew I'd need comfortin'. Maybe she figured I'd have to deal with losin' him, so she stayed until I didn't feel such an ache no more."

I tried to picture Aunt Celia sitting there, a baby in her hands instead of a snuff tin. Making silly, pleased-with-herself mother sounds to the top of a fuzzy head instead of spitting and sticking her finger in cups of coffee.

"I sure don't feel like he's doin' this out of kindness," Tess said. "He don't comfort me. He makes me feel sad. Nothing but sad."

"I'm sayin' he's got an attachment to you and you to him," insisted Aunt Celia, shaking a finger at Tess. "For whatever reason. Sounds like it's him that needs the comfortin'."

"So what should I do?" asked Tess.

"Well," she said, "s'pose you could figure out who he was. Find who threw him in and give him some peace."

Albert HALF MY LIFE was spent taking things out of the ground, the other half spent laying them in. Trying to dig my way into the dirt from up here, then praying I could get to the surface from down there. The tenants—Talberts their names were that year—farmed the sixty-acre piece of land up the road for me. They got a share of it. But the patch by the home place we did ourselves. The five of us setting out potato slips, tomatoes, and pepper plants. Blistered noses and hands black with dirt.

The sun was strong, and I was calmed by the heat, the sweat. Amazing the difference between the smell of the earth, warm and moist, full of cucumbers and tomatoes, watermelon and corn, compared to barren dirt, ripe with only black rock. I loved sucking up great breaths of that growth and green — full-sized lungfuls of peas and squash and soil instead of careful, shallow sips always testing for a pocket of after damp or black damp, one of the stranglers.

Picking beans still bent the back, but I could stand whenever I pleased. That small freedom numbed the ache. Leta wanted to can a mess of squash and beans on Saturday.

"This one ripe, Pop?" Jack poked his head around the tomato vines behind me, hair sticking up in front like a peckerwood. I turned, and he rolled a watermelon twice as big as his head around the edge of the row.

"I see you went ahead and picked it," I pointed out.

"Had to show you to ask you."

"Didn't think to bring me to the melon?"

"Didn't want to trouble you." His eyes got big and innocent. "You're workin'."

Smart boy—promised myself I'd never let him see the inside of a mine. He'd go to business college, maybe lawyer school. Have clean fingernails every day of the week.

"Reckon you'd like watermelon for dessert," I said.

"Yessir."

It looked ripe, and I stepped over and thumped it good, lifted it to smell where the vine had been. Could smell the sweetness.

"It's good. Run give it to your mama." I watched him out of the corner of my eye: That melon weighed twenty pounds if it weighed an ounce. But he wedged his arms under it up to the forearms, little paws latching on the other side. Before he started to heft it up, I stopped him.

"Bend your knees 'stead of your back."

"Nothin' the matter with my back, sir," he said, still hunched at the waist. His feet were bare with garden between the toes.

"Son, it's like me liftin' a watermelon the size of a car."

He bent his knees a smidge, still taking the weight on his

back. I let him. Couldn't tell my kids nothing once their minds got set—mules, every one of 'em. The melon got a couple of inches off the ground, then thudded back. He didn't raise his face, just stood there panting, not saying a word.

"Don't kick that melon, Jack."

He met my eyes then, all squirrel cheeks and hard little line of a mouth. Mad as all get out.

"Grab this basket and start on that row of beans," I said. "I'll bring in the melon later."

"I can get it."

"Be more help to me with the beans."

He backed away slowly. "Yessir."

"Hold on, Jack." I stooped back to the tomatoes, but I couldn't help think of Tess's nightmares. Jack was even younger than she was—no telling what he'd got in his head. "You upset 'bout that baby?"

When I looked at him, he was already swinging the basket as he trudged off.

"No, sir."

He seemed pretty sure about it, and I didn't waste any more time worrying. The tomatoes had turned out better than I expected. Blight had been going around, but they looked red and juicy. My mouth watered at the look of them, insides about to burst through the skin. I plucked one and bit into it like an apple, juice running down my chin.

"Come 'ere, Jack."

I pulled another one off and handed it to him, still tasting summer in my mouth, seeds stuck in my shadow of a beard.

"Virgie and Tess don't get none," he said, looking pleased.

"Girls," I called. "Get down here."

They were there in a flurry of flying skirts and legs and wide smiles.

"In the middle of the afternoon?" asked Virgie, as Tess reached to grab one.

"Any one you want," I said. "Pick the biggest, sweetest one

you see." I smiled at them all, chattering and slurping, teeth and tongues and hands and arms covered in tomato innards.

"They're happy vegetables, aren't they, Papa?" asked Tess, chomping great chunks out of hers. "Cheerful and excited. Like lemons are pouty and peaches are flirts."

Virgie took tiny bites, bending over to hold the tomato away from her dress. But her's was the best, fuller and redder than the others. "Tess thinks they all have a personality," she said.

"If she can eat it after she makes friends with it, ain't nothin' wrong with it," I said.

We all picked beans until supper time, sticky and sweating, licking our fingers and hands and tasting tomatoes and dirt. When I swung Jack and Tess up the steps on the way in, our hands didn't want to come apart.

Virgie MAMA DIDN'T EAT MUCH. She gave everybody else a helping before she helped herself, and sometimes she'd leave herself out altogether. Especially with meat. She'd usually take a spoon of everything when she fixed her plate, but she'd never get seconds. Sometimes she'd skip a meal if she thought no one would notice.

We had fried pies for dessert, and Mama flicked them out of the skillet with a fork, one on everybody's plate except hers.

"You ain't havin' one, Leta-ree?" Papa asked.

"Full up," she said, sitting down.

"You love peach pies," I said.

There were two left, and I knew she was thinking she'd let us have them after dinner the next day or pack them in Papa's lunch tin. I sat there looking at my pie, smelling the cinnamon and butter, and didn't touch it. Tess and Jack stuffed their cheeks with pie, not saying a word. Mama smiled at them.

"Eat up, Virgie," she said.

I pushed it around my plate, a puffy half circle with forked-down edges. Then I sliced it in half, brownish orange filling smoking as it oozed out. "I just want half."

"I'll have it," said Jack, already reaching.

I ignored him, blocking him with my elbow. "Take half, Mama."

"Jack can have it," she said.

"How'll you know if it's good if you won't have any?" I asked.

"Take it." I plopped it on her plate before she had a chance to answer.

She looked like she'd argue, but then she just stared at me, eyes squinted a little, like she was trying to figure out her next move in checkers. "Alright, alright," she said.

She bit in, and I started on mine. It was sweet and delicious, like always.

3   Cicada Shells

Jack   AUNT CELIA CAME AROUND ABOUT ROOSEVELT eventually, long before his train pulled into Carbon Hill. Tess was in high school, I had one more year of grammar school, and Virgie'd come home from Livingston for the weekend by the time Franklin and Eleanor's train swung through town—it turned out that some old-time city commission wrote into their contract with the Frisco line that any train tour on the line had to include a stop at Carbon Hill. So Jasper got passed up and we got a look at Mrs. Roosevelt. Pop and Aunt Celia and the girls and I walked to the train station to see them, along with most of the town. Only Mrs. Roosevelt came out of the car.

People had their Sunday clothes on for that split-second wave from Mrs. Roosevelt, who I thought was homely, Tess thought was splendid, and Virgie thought was uppity. Aunt Celia yelled louder than anybody—she hadn't called anyone a Bolshevik in years—and when some of the men tossed their hats, she got carried away and tossed her bonnet. She never did find it. But she apparently thought of it as her own sacrifice to the altar of the Roosevelts and told the story with plenty of theatrics for the next few decades.

You never saw such New Dealers as the whole town was then. Whatever seedlings we might have been before the Depression, we'd all grown into fine Democrats, warmed by TVA and fed by Works Progress. By the early '30s, the mines had nearly halted altogether, and the town was 75 percent dependent on those mines, according to a pleased-with-ourselves letter the city commission sent to the federal government. Property values were down by 60 percent. Then the president's safety net fluttered around us, with over $180,000 from the government matched by over $100,000 from local citizens. Roosevelt's public works program spit and shined Carbon Hill into something unrecognizable, giving us curbs and sidewalks and more paved road—for the longest time we only had five paved blocks—a swimming pool, a gymnasium. We got a new high school—the one Virgie and Tess went to had twenty rooms for eight hundred kids. Before Roosevelt, we didn't have hardly any indoor toilets in town, and those that were there would drain into ditches that ran right along the streets and the stench nearly knocked you over in the summertime. The new sewer system took care of those ditches.

You could smell the difference the New Deal made every time you walked through town.

Even before Roosevelt, though, the town was solid enough. Physically. Little pigs could have survived a wolf just fine under any roof—I can't remember more than three wooden buildings left in downtown. Nothing but brick. There'd been fires that did some damage, but then a cyclone cut a swath through the middle of town in 1917. It destroyed the churches and the high school and a slew of other buildings. A few years later a bigger fire took out most of the town, from the Pearce Hotel to Sweat's Restaurant. Then came the rows and rows and block after block of brick.

It had always been a town shaped by forces of nature. Wind and fire and earth that demanded a few lives every now and then in exchange for the coal we kept prying out. And one man in a wheelchair was as big a force as any of it.

Albert THE SUN HAD turned grapefruit-colored when Cecil Bannon—Ban we called him—and Oscar Jones stopped by. Leta'd finished putting the dishes up, and she'd just eased into her rocker and picked up her needle when we heard them holler from the road. By the time they came up the steps, it wasn't hard to figure what they'd been doing. I could smell the home brew on Ban's breath, but he knew better than to pull out his flask on my porch. My kids thought of liquor as some far off thing from stories, and I didn't intend to let them get a closer look.

Still and all, they wasn't men to let a few drinks rattle them. Walking steady, they'd taken the steps several at a time, nodded their heads politely at Leta. Long as she didn't get within breathing distance, she wouldn't guess a thing ... or at least she wouldn't be forced to admit she'd noticed. She said hello, then stood up from her chair, waving off Ban and Oscar's don't-trouble-yourselfs, and walked over to the girls. Which I thought meant she'd caught a whiff but was in a forgiving mood. She slid to the top step smooth as a leaf falling, pulling Tess toward her to smooth her hair. I'd lost track of what Oscar was saying.

"... say Pete's never gone see again. Blind as a mole."

"Thought we'd take up whatever we could for him," Ban said.

Pete had gone to work for DeBardeleben in Birmingham after Galloway let him go, and he'd lost his eyesight in an explosion a month or so back. There'd been some thought he might get better, and he'd had them bandaged since it happened, hoping they'd be good as new when he got unwrapped. That was the way I'd heard it anyway.

"DeBardeleben send anybody over?"

"Gave him and his wife nothing more than pocket change," Oscar said. He was a block of a man, short, with arms so thick you could hardly see the elbows. His wife was bigger than three of Leta and probably couldn't have squeezed into the rocker. I couldn't shake the thought that he must roll into the center of the mattress every time she got into bed. Now her, she could've gotten the cover off the well lickety-split.

"Yep, we ought to take up a little something for him," I said.

"They're comin' back to town next week," Oscar said, propping his feet on the rail. "Wife's got family here to help out.

Thought we'd let you collect the money if you don't mind. Fellas'll
feel better about you holdin' on to it."

I nodded. Now I knew Oscar's wife hadn't had a baby anytime recent, but I couldn't help but think that nobody'd have
noticed if she was carrying a child. She didn't strike me as a cruel
one, though. She packed a good lunch for Oscar, sometimes
slipped in ginger cookies.

Wasn't a normal thing for me to be thinking on women.
Leta was Leta, of course, and it didn't seem right to lump her in
with all the rest. The rest were made up of dresses and small
hands and hair twisted into complicated knots. Ban's wife was
just his wife. Oscar's wife—though I puzzled over the size of
her—wasn't no more than his wife. I had no notion of what went
on underneath those complicated hair knots.

"So that's alright with you?" Oscar leaned back with his eyes
closed, not even looking at me.

I left off thinking about wives. "Yeah. Sure, I'll take up the
money."

We'd done it plenty of times before. None of the operators
wanted to do a thing for you. Living in their big houses with
maids and gardeners, cream in their coffee and roast chicken
whenever they wanted, they could empty out the change in
their pockets and pay a crippled man a year's wages. But they
didn't. Could be money was a sickness that spread through their
veins, but they couldn't ever have enough. They'd let a man die
from bad mine construction, with his wife and children looking
forward to starving as soon as the funeral was over, and they'd
no more than toss a bill or two on the coffin. Hearts choked off,
no feeling at all. Like a woman who could kill her own child.
We couldn't do nothing about them. But we might could do something about her.

The sky turned a darker and darker pink-red that night,
with trees blowing toward the burning pink like they were trying
to warm themselves.

"Carried the nigger fellow to work yesterday, did you?" Ban asked.

Crickets were just beginning to chirp. Only half-hearted sounds, like they were caught up with the sunset, too.

"Yep."

"Good buddies with him," Oscar piped in. He wasn't a mean man, and his words didn't have much bite. More like he felt he needed to get his two cents in.

"You've known him for years, both of you," I said. "He's got a name. And ain't nothin' in the world wrong with Jonah."

It came out more tired than bad-tempered. But it floated up with the smoke and hung out there awhile, nobody arguing with it. I took my time wrapping my next cigarette, smoothing the paper on my thigh and pulling a pinch from the tobacco tin.

"Niggers just don't work as hard as we do," Ban said finally, after I'd taken my first puff.

Made it through half a cigarette after that comment, rockers creaking. Nice thing to sit and rock and smoke. You can tell a man by his rocking—slow and steady, antsy and skittish, lazy as a slug. Ban's rocker creaked timidly, like he thought the porch might rear back and bite if he came down on it too hard.

A word or giggle drifted over now and then from the children. Now those kids, they no more knew what it was like to look eye to eye with a Negro child than I knew how to dig a shaft to China. Leta neither, other than when their paths crossed during some trouble at the mines. Some coloreds did drink up their wages, and some of 'em were shiftless. Wouldn't show up to work unless there wasn't no money in the house. Don't know as that had all that much to do with them being Negroes.

But you work shoulder to shoulder with a man, push his cars with him, he pushes yours, that changes how you look at things. A few years back, five men were burned to cinders in a gas explosion, and when the bodies got brought out, they was all black as coal. There'd be a Negro woman and a white woman star-ing at the same body. When your wives stand next to each other trying to sort out if one of those charred logs is their husband, that means something.

"Shouldn't have let them in the union," Oscar said.

Now he and Ban were only tossing things out, not mad about anything, not really caring that I gave Jonah a ride to work. Just talking the same old words. Like kids and nursery rhymes. I kept rocking. They'd seen the same things I had, and Oscar was grasping at an old straw to bring up the union. Wasn't even a union anymore. But even with all the hue and cry over coloreds and whites pulling chairs up to the same table, the union had mixed smooth enough. Weren't no choice, for one thing, because the UMW stood firm on it. For another, any thinking man understood how all the gears locked and turned together in the big machine of it all.

Bible says, "Inasmuch as ye have done it unto one of the last of these my bretheren, ye have done it unto me." Real truth is what you do to the least of these, you do to yourself. Long as the Negroe's wages were in the dirt, ours were bound to be. Long as the bosses rid them hard, couldn't force them to do better by us. All go up together or all stay down together.

The state finally killed off convict lease in '28, not because it was wrong putting fellas to work in the mines instead of jail, but on account of the big operators not liking the advantage the convict mines had. Didn't have to pay 'em and nine out of ten of 'em was colored, so they didn't have to treat 'em human. Whipped 'em like animals. Worked 'em from six in the morning to ten at night, kept 'em in line with the whipping and the sweat boxes and no food. Kept us white men's pay down, a'course, because why pay somebody when you got slaves, and that's what they still was, just called 'em by a different title. You hold a slave up to a man expecting fairness and wages and you tell him he can take his leather grips to Kentucky so far as you're concerned, because you don't need to pay nobody for what you got a body to do for free. You come to the bosses complaining about short-weighing and needing more safety inspections and they just wave that slave in your face.

Those men mostly done nothing more wrong than steal a sack of meal, maybe get too drunk and make noise walking home. And they got thrown underground with a whip to their back. Wasn't much different from us, but at least no white man got a whip.

I didn't say none of that. I noticed we had a dirt dauber's nest under the eave of the shed. Might have been an old one.

"Awful good sunset," Oscar said. "Makes you hate to see night."

"Sure does," I said.

"They's just not the same as we are is all I'm sayin'," Ban said, like he was hoping I'd agree as much as I agreed about the sunset.

"Seem to recall Ben Barrett sayin' somethin' like that," I said instead.

Eleven years ago, during that same 1920 strike, a Negro union man threatened other Negroes about turning scab. The sheriff, had words with him at the commissary about those threats. Then Hill—a white fellow and another union man— went after the sheriff and shot and killed him and his deputy. For the sheriff's words to the colored fellow. 'Cause at that moment I guarantee Hill thought of him as a union fellow. I knew Hill, and he was a spittin' snake of a man, all the time howling at the moon about something. Sometimes he was howling about the coloreds. Then he went and died for one.

The sun was down so that all we could make out of one another without straining was the glow of our cigarettes. Still we rocked. Tess was in Leta's lap getting her hair plaited. Virgie was playing bucking bronco with Jack in her lap, holding on to his hands while she swung her knees back and forth, making him whoop.

"Mine were crazy about that one," said Ban, waving the glow of his embers toward the kids and their horse game.

"Only got to hit the ground once before they change their minds," said Oscar. "My youngest one's slippery as a crappe."

Ban and me didn't even try to keep from laughing at him. "Only happened the once," said Oscar.

We got ourselves together finally. "Best be headin' home," Ban said, pulling out change from his shirt pocket. "Here's my fifty cents for Pete."

Ban's wife, she seemed to have a good head on her shoulders. But he had a daughter that was a little wild, had turned down three proposals. That didn't mean nothing, really. I couldn't get around that all I knew about any of the women was what they put in a lunch pail. Couldn't think how a ham and biscuit would tell me anything about slaughtering a baby.

Tess   IT WASN'T UNTIL a couple of days after we saw Aunt Celia that we talked about what she'd said. And it wasn't so much us talking as that Virgie up and announced her plan.

We lived on the porch more than in the house through summer and fall. The steps had big concrete sides to them instead of rails, wide enough to sit on. While Mama and Papa rocked, Virgie and me sat on the concrete, me on the top one and Virgie on the bottom. She liked to lean against the L-shape where her slab met mine, and I liked to be taller than she was. It worked out good.

Mainly we'd watch the lightning bugs, sometimes count their flashes, sometimes catch them in our hands. Papa would smoke, and as long as there was a smidgen of daylight, Mama would do the hand stitching that she couldn't use the machine for. She'd finally quit working when she couldn't see no more. People were always passing and saying hello, maybe coming up on the porch to chat; sometimes Virgie and I would walk down the street and say hello ourselves to the shadows on the other porches. She didn't care for that as much as I did.

But sitting there on the cold concrete that night, Virgie surprised me.

"We should make a list," she said, clear out of the blue.

"What?"

"Like Aunt Celia said. We should figure out who did it."

"Make a list of babies?"

"Well, I s'pose of women who's had babies. If we know who's had babies in the last six months or so, we ought to be able to go 'round and see who's missing one."

"How do we know he was six months?"

"Prob'bly less than that, but we'll be safe thinking it's six." She'd crossed her ankles, and her legs were stretched straight in front of her. Her dress came to a little above her ankles, but the way she was sitting, I could see the tops of her stockings rolled down. I didn't wear stockings, of course. I didn't even have on my shoes—I'd tossed them by the back door as soon as I got in from school. I didn't care for them, even though Mama said I should be grateful to have shoes. She said plenty of kids didn't, like those little Talbert kids whose parents worked Papa's land. She said worms could crawl up into the bottoms of your feet and make a home there.

I could see those little worms setting up house in my heels or big toes, carving out little living rooms in my feet, building nice warm fires and bringing in tiny mattresses and kitchen tables no bigger than freckles.

Mama said that was not how they did it at all.

But she always kicked off her shoes, too—was sitting there sewing with her bare feet tap-tapping on the porch—so she couldn't get too worked up about me.

"What're you girls plottin'?" called Papa, jarring me.

"Nothin', Papa," we answered at the same time.

He looked at Mama and flicked the ashes from his cigarette. "That's trouble if I ever heard it," he said. But he didn't ask again—just went back to flicking and rocking.

Virgie went and got her school tablet and a couple of pencils. She always kept her shoes on, not caring at all about how trapped and sweaty her toes got. "So let's start with the people nearest to us ..."

"Virgie?"

"Lola Lowe had one a few months back, I know."

"Virgie?"

"What?"

"Why're you doin' this?"

"What?"

"I know you don't believe in ghosts. And you're not havin' nightmares. What's your hurry?" It wasn't like Virgie to leap into something with both feet. She liked to stick a toe in.

She kept staring out at the animals, didn't even look at me. "I don't want you to have nightmares, fussbudget. And it's only right. To give the poor baby a name."

That didn't explain how excited she'd got at Aunt Celia's idea. She'd been quiet ever since then, and I knew she'd been thinking. She never could talk and think at the same time. But after all that thinking—whatever it was—she wanted to get started right away, come up with steps like you'd do to solve a math problem.

"I'm not sure I want to," I told her. "I want to put it out of my head."

That got her to look at me. "Don't want to know who did it?"

I looked away and swallowed, trying to make my mouth less dry. I'd thought about what Aunt Celia said, too, and it had weighed on me. I was more selfish than what she'd talked about, though, about owing that baby something. I wanted my well and my creek and my dreams back. Some nights, sitting out there on the porch by the well, I'd thought that view was the most beautiful, perfect thing in the world. And the more I thought about the baby, the uglier everything got. I wanted to stop thinking about it altogether.

"Don't you want to know why she'd do it?" Virgie kept on.

"Why don't we just leave it be, Virgie? Just try to forget about it."

"You can't just forget about it," she said. "That kind of thing doesn't up and disappear."

"It might. You don't know, Virgie."

"Think about that baby, Tess. Think about what Aunt Celia said about the baby wanting you to help him."

I was not happy with that baby for turning me inside out, and I wasn't really inclined to help him out none. It seemed like he might be nicer to me—maybe give me dreams of soda crackers and peanut butter and lemonade—if he wanted me to comfort him. But then again, maybe if we gave him a name and a mama and a house and a life, maybe he would let go of our well. And then it'd be mine again.

"You think if I helped him out he'd go on to heaven and leave me be?"

I could tell Virgie wanted to argue that he was already in heaven because there wasn't such a thing as ghosts, but she also wanted to get me to go along with her without much more fussing. After chewing her lip a minute, she settled for answering, "Everybody'd be better off if he had a name and a proper burial."

As it was, he'd have to be buried in the section for pitiful people who didn't have nothing, not even a headstone. I felt bad about that, but I felt like she'd gotten me off track.

"And he'd leave me be?" I repeated.

"Well, Lord, I don't have a rule book on it," she huffed. "Look, right now you're tryin' to ignore it away. And you still have the nightmares. So that's not workin'." She looked out toward the woods again, then reached around and tapped my ankle, which I guess was the easiest part of me for her to reach.

"And you shouldn't be mad at the baby, you know. It's the mother who caused all this."

That was true. And she hadn't gotten in the least bit of trouble, which wasn't fair at all. Instead I was tossing and turning and waking up gasping while she probably slept like a big ole log. I could just imagine her, mad-eyed and covered in pockmarks, chuckling to herself in the pitch black as she went to sleep in a narrow, hard bed. Without me wanting to, I saw her start to move. As she drifted off, one strong hand would reach out and pat the space beside her, claws tapping the place where a baby had been. And every time she felt the empty space, she'd laugh all the harder. I saw her clearer than I ever saw mermaids.

"You goin' to do the talkin'?" I asked. "Go in first if we stop by anywhere?"

"Yes," said Virgie, even though I was the talker.

"And if I don't want to go somewhere, you won't make me?"

"'Course not."

"Okay. I'll help you," I said, wishing I could toss the Well Woman out of my head as easy as she tossed away her baby.

Jack walked up to us, curls falling over his forehead.

"You playin' tic-tac-toe?" he asked. That boy loved to doodle and draw, always wanted a pencil in his hand. Mama said he always was a marker. (Back when he could barely crawl he got hold of a pencil and drew all over the sitting room wall. I was too little to remember it myself and Mama wouldn't tell what happened after, but I sure would've loved to known what his punishment was. It must've been a doozy.)

"No, Jack," I said.

"Can I play?"

I started to tell him to go catch lightning bugs, but Virgie scooped him up and settled him in next to her. She drew a tic-tac-toe board on a sheet of paper, then ripped another one off and handed me a pencil. She handed the other pencil to Jack, telling him, "You go first. You can be Xs."

To me she said, "So let's go on and get started. I already been thinkin' about who's had babies: there's Lola Lowe, Pride Stanton…" and she kept going with a whole string of names. I scribbled them down as she and Jack scratched out Xs and Os. She let him win twice, then won twice herself. By the time we finished, the sun was down, and the last of the names were slanted down the side of the page. But we had fourteen women we knew who'd had babies since March.

"Wouldn't you think we'd know?" I asked.

"Know what?" Virgie said, craning her neck around to look at what I'd written.

"If we came across who did it. She couldn't just blend in."

"Why?"

"Because she's crazy. Or evil."

"That's just what she's doing. Blending in." Virgie let her hand dangle by the concrete, the pencil in one curled finger. "We could be lookin' her in the face every day."

"But you can tell crazy," I said.

"If it's so plain, why doesn't she stick out? Crazy or evil must look different than we thought."

"Who's crazy?" asked Jack.

"We're just talkin'," said Virgie. "Don't pay us any mind."

"Who's crazy?" he said again.

"The woman who threw that baby in the well," I said too sharp.

"Oh," he said, frowning. "I was only askin'."

"Well, don't be such a Nosy Parker." He was always trying to get in on everything.

"I think you're just as crazy as anybody," he muttered.

"What?" That boy wasn't right in the head.

"You still believe there's mermaids and fairies and such."

"So?"

"There's no such thing. Don't know about mermaids in the ocean, but you say fairies live in the woods. And they do not."

"Sure they do."

"Then why don't we ever see them?"

"Oh, quit it," huffed Virgie. "You're like two puppies yapping back and forth. Don't pay her no mind, Jack. She's just grumpy."

With a glare at me, he went back to waiting for Virgie to draw a new board. She did, smiling at him and cutting her eyes at me. It wasn't fair that the littlest and cutest one always got to be right.

"Still want to argue that you can tell crazy from not-crazy?" she asked, talking softly and hardly moving her lips. "Oh, that's the whole thing, Tess." She caught her lip with her teeth for a second. "We can't tell crazy. We can't tell anything. It's not like she's got big googly eyes that turn around in circles. We have to be smart to track her down."

"I didn't say she has googly eyes." That was stupid.

"And if you're not going to be serious about it, I'll do it myself."

"I'm serious," I insisted. Virgie didn't say anything. "I am. I'm very, very serious. Serious as a funeral."

She looked mad.

"I didn't mean it like that," I said.

I didn't. Sometimes you make a bad joke when you really don't mean it, and my mouth could be too fast for my brain. "I'm very serious about it."

"That's fine then. As long as we can be grown up about it."

"Yes," I nodded quickly. "Just like we're sheriffs."

She twisted around and took the list off my lap. "Oh, I didn't think," she said after she read over them. "These three had girls." She crossed them off.

"Why y'all namin' names?" asked Jack, drawing curlicues around the edge of the paper while he waited for Virgie to make her move.

"Oh, just 'cause," Virgie said. "No one special." She blocked his row of Xs and he forgot about it.

"Virgie, how many people are in Carbon Hill?" I asked.

She looked up, chewed her lip a minute. "Papa," she called, "how many people in Carbon Hill?"

"'Bout three thousand," he called back.

That worried me. "We don't know all them three thousand."

She thought about that. "Well, she put him in our well. She must live around here, probably knows us." She looked down at the list. "I think we ought to go check the babies."

"We gone knock on their doors and ask 'em to hand 'em out?"

She scanned over the list. "Well, we ought to see some of 'em at church on Sunday. Then we'll start on the others."

"And you're doin' this so the baby will be at peace?" I still wasn't quite clear.

She answered right away. "I just want to know if too much motherin' and tendin' and cleanin' ends up pushin' you to this."

Virgie IN OUR PRIMERS, "outside" was listed as a preposition.

"Put the ball outside the box." But here "Outside" was a thing you could touch. A noun.

The woods started at the edge of the creek, and the sound of moving water blocked out the sound of birds until I got deep into the trees. Then the ground was speckled with shadows and leaves and sometimes sunshine, and my shoes made loud sounds that made me feel like I didn't belong. But if I was still, I could be completely quiet, and I could sink into the woods, maybe lean against a tree or sit down on a flat rock with no moss or bugs. I could hear pecans or hickory nuts hit the ground. No one else there. No one watching, no one listening. I liked the woods best when I could be alone.

Ella and Lois were with me this time, but I knew them so well it was almost like being alone.

The trees were mostly green, just tinged with fire as we walked, with a little spark of yellow or orange drifting down around our heads every now and then. Ella had a sackful of chinquapins, and Lois collected all the hickory nuts. I had the wild blueberries. We all sampled from our sacks and snitched from the others, and even with our bellies swollen and ready to pop, we'd still have enough to take home for roasted hickory nuts and berry pies and cobblers.

Back behind Highway 78, up along the mountain, was a dinner table always set.

"So if he is sweet on you, are you gone let him call on you?"

Ella asked. She crunched a chinquapin, tossing away the shell with its mouth still gaping from losing its nut.

I frowned. Henry Harken was the son of a big mining inspector in town, well-to-do. He made me nervous. His family had plenty of money, and his clothes must have cost more than mine, Tess's, and Jack's put together and doubled.

"I don't know."

"You better get t' thinkin'!"

I didn't like how he never introduced himself as Henry—he always said Henry Harken, Jr. I thought that was right snooty. I watched Ella and Lois in front of me, walking so close their arms touched, like paper dolls still attached at the elbow. I hadn't known any other twins, so I didn't know if they all acted like mirror images—their movements, gestures, the way they walked. It was like God had given lessons with just those two in the class. When Mama and Tess and I walked and the sun lay our shadows down in front of us, we looked like that, like triplets. But we were stick-figure women, all legs and arms and skinny middles, and Ella and Lois had enough curves to wear girdles on Sundays. I didn't weigh a hundred pounds soaking wet.

Ella and Lois loved talking about boys, but I didn't have any fondness for it. I didn't like how they looked at me, how a group of them would holler when you walked by. Like suddenly you were on a stage but you didn't know any lines to say. Aunt Celia lived with Grandma Moore, and I wondered if that wasn't the better way to go about it. It seemed simpler.

Grandma Moore had separated from Grandpa Moore before I was born, leaving him in Fayette and moving here to a house Papa bought her. That was the first house she ever lived in that was her very own. And Grandpa Moore's mother had divorced her husband and changed her name and all the kids' names back to her maiden name. That's why we were Moores. He must've done something awful to make her want to go out and not just erase him out of her life, but erase his name, too. Whatever he did, if he hadn't have done it, we'd all be named Adams.

Nobody ever talked about what those men did, but that was two generations of women who'd picked up and moved along.

"Know whose baby that was yet?" asked Lois, her hair catching the sun where the trees thinned out.

"Uh-uh," I said as I stepped over a log. "We haven't heard anything. Have you?"

"Mama says must have been a no-account."

I wondered if it was another woman who wanted to pick up and move along and that baby was only a weight holding her back. I didn't have dreams like Tess—the pictures in my head of the woman and her baby came during the daylight. She liked these same woods. And liked how cool and damp the air was. And felt like it was the only place that was really hers.

"What's the matter with Henry?" Lois asked.

"He's nice-looking. Sweet on you for sure. Good manners," added Ella.

"He makes me nervous," I said, knowing that'd just make them hound me more.

"Shoot, everybody makes you nervous. You'd think lookin' like Mary Pickford, you'd have sense enough to know you're good as anybody."

"I don't look anything like Mary Pickford." I popped a chinquapin in my mouth and took my time chewing. I looked like Papa's other sister, who lived in Memphis and visited by train every spring. We had the same hair, same chin, and same Moore nose with a hump in the middle of it.

"Virgie Moore," declared Ella, "you better learn to take a compliment. Somebody tells you that you look like you could be in a picture show, best just to say 'thank you.' Quit blushing and standing there like a stump."

I looked to Lois for support; she shrugged.

I didn't blush. But I didn't like to feel like I was on display with everyone looking at me. With boys and most grown-ups, you ended up feeling like they were holding up some yardstick to you. I didn't like being measured was all.

"I'm only sayin' it because I have this..."

Ella interrupted me. "You do not have a hump in the middle of your nose, so don't get started on that. We don't want to hear about it anymore."

Arguing with Ella was a waste of energy. So I stopped talking. Scanning the trees as we passed, I jerked to a stop. Tucked into the pulled-back bark of a pine tree, the cicada shell was almost invisible. Brown and crisp, slit down its back. I crunched through the weeds and leaves over to the tree, hiking up my navy skirt to avoid the brambles.

"Wait a second," I said to Ella and Lois, barely loud enough for them to hear. They were a good twenty feet ahead of me then. But they stopped and backtracked, not looking at all surprised.

"Found you one?" asked Lois.

"Mmm-hmm." I pried it off gently, not breaking the little leg husks. It stuck to my collar like it'd been waiting to get a nicer home than that dirty bark. I'd add it to the box under our bed at home. I liked to keep enough to wear them sometimes in winter. They kept real well if you were gentle with them. And I didn't wear them out in public, of course. Just at home.

Ella looked disgusted. "I can't believe you throw a fit if your hair musses, but you'll wear a bug like it's made of diamonds."

"It's not a bug. The bug's gone. It makes its own sculpture of itself and leaves it behind." I didn't usually do my shell collecting with an audience. It seemed more serious—and a lot quieter—when I was alone.

"It's skin," said Ella, wrinkling her nose.

"I know," I said. "But look how perfect it is." It was my first memory of something that was not Mama or Papa or warm fire or dinner table. I'd been wandering around in the backyard, while Mama was hanging clothes on the line, and I came across a cicada shell, which, of course, looked just like the one I'd just found ten years later or so. They weren't creative creatures. I stared at it until Mama pulled me away, and when she did, I pulled it off the tree. Crushed it in my hand with a grip not used to being gentle. I was horrified that I'd killed it, and Mama kept telling me it wasn't alive to kill. But the next time I found one, I picked it up as gentle as if I were holding a butterfly by the wings.

Ella had plopped herself down on a stump, hands on her hips, just like her mama did when Ella sassed her. "If you're not partial to Henry Harken, what about Tom Olsen?"

Tom lived next to Ella and Lois, and he served as our personal messenger service. When they had a message for me, he'd ride his bike over to our house, give me the note, then wait until I'd responded and carry it on back to the twins. He had pretty gray eyes with long lashes like a woman's. I'd mostly noticed his eyes—I'd had time to look because he never looked straight at me, mainly looked over my shoulder or kicked his bicycle tires. But he was always smiling, showing his barely crooked teeth to the space over my shoulder. His eyes and crooked teeth seemed nicer to me than Henry Harken's expensive clothes.

"What about Tom Olsen?" I said. I fingered the cicada lightly, checking if it was stuck good.

"Don't you think he's absolutely divine?"

"Ella…" She thought most boys were absolutely divine.

"Well, the first basketball game's at the end of the month, and I'll go with Hanson, 'course." He'd been calling on her for six months—her parents weren't as strict as Mama and Papa, so boys had been walking her home ever since she turned fourteen. "I want his cousin to take Lois, and Tom could take you. We could the six of us go together."

"With the boys?"

"Yes," she said patiently, hands still on her hips. "That's what makes it six. With no boys, it'd be three."

"Likely that's the highest math she can do," said Lois.

"I don't think Papa would let me."

"You could ask him," pointed out Lois. "It'd just be as friends. And all six of us would be together the whole time."

"Hanson'll drive us. He's got loan of a car while his brother's working in Kentucky."

I'd never ridden in a car with anybody but Papa. He got the first car in Carbon Hill, and the five years since then, he'd been carting everybody around. Relatives needing to go to the doctor, men riding to work with him, shopping trips to Birmingham. Sometimes he'd get woken up in the middle of the night to go get the doctor if somebody was having a baby. I think Mama'd ridden in the car twice other than going to church on Sundays— every time she was about to get to go somewhere, somebody squeezed in and took her place. And she'd stay there at home, smiling at us and waving from the porch as we left.

Leta   I WISHED THEY hadn't've come on canning day. I know word about the baby must've spread all over town before the sheriff even carried him off, but somehow the women all waited a week to drop by. And then all at once, like locusts.

Midway through the morning, with two pots boiling on the stove and the fire going strong, even with the windows open, my face was red with the heat. No matter how often I swiped at my forehead, I could feel the salty drops running down my cheeks and upper lip. My dress was wet under the arms. I was pouring more sugar into the pickles when I heard a shout at the front door.

"You home, Leta?"

"Come back to the kitchen!" I recognized the voice—Charlene Burch from down the hill. Small woman, big eyes, voice like train brakes squealing. She stepped into the kitchen, nose lifted.

"How many jars of pickles you done?"

"Six quarts so far. Second batch has another day to go. Just got sugar left." I moved to the first bowl, the smell of vinegar sharp and strong, and carried it with both hands out to the back porch. I poured the vinegar off, then came back in and started to carry the second bowl out to do the same.

Charlene had set down at the table and was biting into a sliced pear from a bowl. It'd been soaking in sugar over night, and she took tiny, mousy bites like it was a piece of chocolate.

"Didn't grow cucumbers this year," she said. "Kids ain't too fond of 'em."

"The boys doin' good?" I asked, calling over my shoulder as I stepped on the porch. "Jolie gettin' on well at the high school?" Jolie was their oldest, a year ahead of Virgie.

"They're all just fine. Our youngest is startin' a paper route next week—bring in a little extra. Yours gettin' on?"

"All right as rain." I poured the sugar on the cucumbers, covered 'em with a towel. Water in the reservoir was hot enough to start on the preserves.

"Not upset by the poor baby?"

I filled up the pot halfway, ladling water slowly. "Not so's you'd notice. Tess was real shook up at first."

"She saw the woman—that's what I heard at the post office."

"Just shadows."

"Who do you think would do it?"

"Can't say." I leaned over and pulled the sugared pears away from her.

"Think it might have been Lola? Lord knows she's got plenty young'uns around."

I sighed. "She's a sweet woman. She's got a good heart."

"There's somethin' about her, though. Can't ever tell what that one's thinkin'. Or Eleanor Lucid—she's never been quite right. Living like she does with no man or children around. Wouldn't know what she might do."

I stirred while she talked. Charlene never expected much talking back. She kept right on, and I never did understand where she thought Eleanor Lucid could've got her hands on a baby, touched in the head or not.

Anna Laurie Tyler came in when all the pear preserve jars were lined up on the back porch, lids off, cooling. I was starting the figs.

She looked near tears when she came through the door— she'd come up the back way like she did a few times a week. She was just a'staring at the well when I looked over.

She felt my eyes on her and looked up. "Up for company?"

"Come on in and set a spell," I called back.

"So this is where he was. It's a horror—just makes your blood run cold."

She seemed to think it must've been a girl, Virgie's age or so, not married. She named a few women's daughters she thought were the most likely. I put her to work stirring figs while I started scalding more quart jars.

The Bingham sisters—married, though, so they weren't really Binghams anymore—came after lunch. Didn't even sit. They wanted to know if the baby had marks on him, if it looked like he'd been beat. Seemed they thought they'd heard a baby screaming too loudly at the neighbor's place the week before.

"Not normal baby hollerin'—sounded different. I told Johnny it made shivers run down my spine," one of them whispered. "Haven't seen that baby in days and days."

The next one had heard it was two babies. And the one after that thought his head had been missing. Those two helped me lay the paraffin over the preserves.

Celia stuck her head through the door before the girls and Jack were due home. "Got a porch full of preserves out here," she called. "And looks like you've done gone and pickled yourself along with the cucumbers."

I smiled to see her. My apron was splattered with vinegar and fruit juice, my hands flecked with wax. My head felt hot enough that I swore I could feel my brain swelling with the heat. I did feel unsteady, light-headed. "Get yourself in here, Celia."

"You get yourself out here. Get some cool air on you."

"I ain't even started supper."

"Won't be startin' nothin' if you keel over into the stove."

I took off my apron and followed her. The back porch wasn't as social as the front— it looked out over the trees instead of the road. "Like some tea?" I asked, pausing at the door.

"Sure would," she said, but grabbed hold of my arm and steered me outside. "Stay there." She disappeared, then popped back with two glasses, walking over to the silver pitcher near the well. She pulled back the cloth covering it and poured the tea quickly, without spilling a drop.

"Need to drink you three or four of these," she ordered. "Done sweat out all your fluids." Her dark hair was sleek as ever, curls smooth and tidy tucked into a twist. I'd never seen Celia sweat, even though she could crank the Model T with one hand or snatch up a bale of hay like it was a toddler.

The tea tasted good. Sweet enough to cut through the layers of fumes and hot air stuck in my throat.

"Saw all the cluckin' hens come through here," she said. "Showin' Christian concern?"

I smiled again, nearly chuckled. We were standing right by the well, and all I could think was how much I'd like to pour a bucket of water on my head. Or have a run down to the creek like one of the girls. "Mainly they was namin' names. So horrified by it they just can't quit talkin' about it."

Celia finished her tea and pulled out her snuff. It was an awful habit, but she'd done it for the eighteen years I'd known her. Got to where it seemed like another woman pulling out her sewing. She pulled her fingers back from her mouth and narrowed her eyes at me. "But you ain't talkin'?"

"About it?" I breathed out, ran my fingers over my hair. "Don't see no reason for it. It's done. That baby's in a better place."

"What about his mama?"

I'd thought about that, but I'd ladled it into a jar and sealed it up tight. "Ain't my concern. That's for the sheriff."

I'd got the preserves done—pear and fig—and pickles'd be done the next day. Enough to last through next spring, plus a jar or two for Albert's brothers who were bound to come by looking for whatever they could get. Just had the beans left to do.

Tess   WE COULD GO over the list only in our heads during church—no pencils and paper—because you had to sit straight and pay attention the whole time or you'd get a pinch on your arm from Mama. If I was caught writing, Papa'd probably whip me when we got home. Virgie was too old for being whipped.

It was awful hard to sit still, because even though there was a breeze outside, all the bodies heated up the one room like so many person-sized fireplaces. We all sweated except for Papa; most everybody'd picked up a fan from the stack by the door on the way in. Square with little folded pleats, they advertised Garrett as "sweet, mild snuff," which made it sound like taffy or mints. During prayer, all you could hear was those paper fans whuh-whuhing through the air, and the old men hacking up phlegm. (I asked Papa about that one time and he said it was the mines that did it, made your spit hard and solid where it caught in your throat. Then Mama came in and he had to stop explaining because she didn't care for us to discuss spit and the like.)

The Baptist church had a stained-glass window, but we had no color in ours. The steeple had been reattached with metal bolts after it got blown off once, but other than that little reminder of some sort of excitement awhile back, it was a dull building. Just two columns of pews, small windows, plain wood floors. Nothing to look at but the people.

There were lots of hats and nice dresses and shiny shoes with ankle straps. Virgie wore a two-piece green dress that Mama said was starting to fit too tight. It was hard for anything to fit her too tight—she didn't stick out anywhere. Mama's corset, which Virgie helped cinch, made her seem softer and rounder under her navy blue dress and jacket. Papa just looked uncomfortable in his tie and white shirt that Mama ironed early in the morning along with the tablecloth. Mostly the other men looked as itchy as Papa in their suits, but the women looked scrubbed and pleased in their getups. We'd had plenty of time to look at everybody since most of the church had come up asking about the baby and wondering how we were doing, especially me. But most of them hardly looked at me when they asked how I was holding up, and nobody let me get more than a word out before they asked what it looked like and how we got it out and who we thought did it. Papa sat there not saying a word, and Mama answered mostly with shrugs and tight smiles and "Couldn't say."

The preacher was friendly looking with white hair puffed up like a cloud and a young face. He led singing, too, better than most of them, his big, deep voice settling in my belly like a swallow of hot soup. He'd come in town for a contracted meeting, so we'd be back at church most nights, probably. Maybe he'd be up at Winfield or Eldridge some of those nights, and we might stay home, depending.

The first song we sang was the bleeding sheep song.

Tho your sins be as scarlet, they shall be as white as snow
Tho they be red like crimson, they shall be as wool...

We sang about washing a lot. Water and blood.

Lola Lowe wasn't there. Other women were, with their babies in plain sight, and I checked them off the list in my head. We still had Pride Stanton and Mrs. Taylor—I thought LeAnne was her first name—to check for sure, along with Lola Lowe. Those three lived fairly close and we knew them a little bit, so it made sense to see about them first before we got to tracking down anybody else. I made a note in my head to say that to Virgie.

Ms. Genie had to pop her two-year-old on the hand during the prayer because he was making a fuss. It shocked him long enough that he was quiet a few seconds, then he started howling. But the man saying the prayer (he had a steady, bee-buzzing voice that made you nod off during his prayers) was saying "Amen" anyway, so she shoved the little boy's face into her chest, her hand wrapped around the back of his head, and carted him outside, where she probably wore him out. Then came the Lord's Supper, which Virgie took and me and Jack didn't. She'd been baptized in the creek two summers ago, and ever since then, she got to have the sip of grape juice and bit of bread that looked so good as it passed by late in the morning with dinner still an hour or so away.

A better song came next, with a sweet soprano part that poured over you.

When peace like a river attendeth my way/When sorrows like sea billows roll/Whatever my lot thou hast taught me to say/It is well, it is well with my soul.

I fidgeted, wishing the pews weren't so hard, and Papa looked at me so quick I almost missed it. I settled down and just twitched my toes as a compromise.

The sermon wasn't shouted, not even an occasional word, and the warm-soup voice made my eyelids heavy. I looked over at Maddie Reynolds, an apple-shaped woman with lots of yellow hair. She was holding her baby, who'd been asleep the whole service. She swayed side to side just a fraction, eyes flickering down at him every few seconds.

And we thought she might have killed him.

Finally we were out, Papa and Mama getting caught up talking, and me headed to the door, wanting some cool air. And, I swannee, that slick-haired boy Henry Harken was waiting for Virgie outside, asking if he could walk her home.

Virgie OH, I JUST about died when I saw Henry Harken standing there in his Sunday suit. But I was already at the top of the stairs before I noticed him, and he'd seen me for sure. So I walked on down the steps, sure everybody was watching and thinking how I'd never before had some boy waiting for me. He didn't even go to church with us—he was a Methodist. His church was only a few blocks away, but I knew it couldn't have gotten out at the same time we did. I wondered how long he'd waited.

I watched my feet going down the steps, proud that I'd shined my lace-up shoes and that I'd gone to the trouble of putting on garters. My green two-piece dress, belted at the waist, was the nicest I had and my favorite length, tea-length, halfway down my calf. It's the most flattering to your legs. I smoothed my white gloves as I stepped, trying to make it look natural. Soon enough, though, I was at the bottom step, and Henry's black shoes and gray pants were in front of me.

"Hi, Henry," I said. "Nice to see you."

"Hello, Virgie." He smiled and nodded like a grown man. "I thought I might walk you home if you wouldn't mind."

I'd never been walked home, and I was sure Papa wouldn't allow it. But Henry was marching up the steps toward Papa before I said another word. I guess I'd looked like I wouldn't mind. Papa was halfway down the steps himself, with his hat tipped back to get a better look at Henry. Tess was nearly stepping on his heels.

"Mr. Moore, sir, good afternoon. My name's Henry Harken, Jr., and I'd like to walk Virgie home if you'd allow me."

Papa didn't answer right away, standing there in the middle of the steps with the whole church filing out around him. "I know your father," he said, people streaming around him like this conversation wasn't even happening, sometimes slapping his shoulder. "You gone walk through town, bring her straight home? Don't want to be holdin' dinner for her."

"Yessir."

Then Mama was there, her hand light on Papa's arm, watching Henry with her dark, warm eyes.

"Afternoon, ma'am. Pleasure to meet you..." he started, but Papa cut him off.

"Henry Harken's boy," he said. "Wantin' to walk Virgie home."

Mama smiled at that and nodded. "Nice to meet you, Henry."

Papa tipped his hat back down to where it shaded his eyes. "You'll have her back shortly? We'll be drivin' home, so we'll beat you by a good bit."

"Yessir. We'll go straight to the house." He turned toward me, then looked over his shoulder. "You have a good afternoon, sir. Ma'am."

He almost got a smile from Papa, but it turned into a nod. Mama and Papa both looked straight at me when Henry's back was turned to them, Mama looking like she'd love to tell me something, and Papa looking—well, I couldn't guess then, but it was probably uncertain. I didn't recognize the expression on him.

So we started toward Front Street, and I knew my shoes would lose their shine. Only Front Street had sidewalks and paving; everywhere else was covered in red rock—some sort of leftover dust from the mines. It didn't muddy easily, but it settled from nose to toes. Even with all the red rock, I liked the walk down the hill. Carbon Hill proper was ugly, all brick, standing as plain as a set of blocks lined up. But no churches were on the main street—you had to turn left and head up the hill to get to our church, and just a few blocks over was First Methodist and a few blocks over from that was First Baptist. The shiny white marble and the stained-glass windows of the Methodist church seemed like they suited Henry Harken to a T. And really I liked it myself—not as much as Tess did, though. The Holy Spirit really called to her from those stained-glass windows. Myself, I liked best of all to walk past the neat rows of houses, yards swept clean and little fences sometimes separating neighbors.

But at the bottom of the hill, the happy houses stopped and stores started. All the same brick, no trees, no grass, no color. Just that red dust everywhere. You could taste it on your tongue.

Home was just a mile or so from town, but the house shone white, repainted by Papa and his men every few years. The front yard had great dollops of red and pink from the roses, and out the kitchen window you saw nothing but oaks and pines, dogwoods, and two massive sweet gum trees. We had soil, not dust. Downtown made me thirsty.

"You're quiet," said Henry, which made every word I knew fly out of my head.

"I was thinking," I finally said. We crossed one of the small wooden bridges over a ditch at an intersection, our last block until Front Street. All the ditches were filled with weeds and water, and I could hear the hum of mosquitoes and flies and whole clouds of winged things.

"You mind me walking you home?"

"No," I said quickly, knowing how rude he must think I was being. He wasn't bad looking, and he was awfully clean. Even his fingernails were clean. His shirt looked stiff and smooth, not like cloth at all. His skin was blotchy, though, like all the boys, and that made me feel a little better.

The sidewalk was crowded with after-church traffic, and we had to dodge people. And nod "hello" as we were weaving. And I was trying not to look embarrassed, wanting to seem like, no, Henry Harken was not walking me home and really we'd just bumped into each other accidentally and happened to be moving along the same patch of sidewalk.

But I tried to make it easier for him. "It was real nice of you. Real nice."

I ran out of words again just as a car rolled by, hiccupping over a rut. Henry, walking next to the street, put a hand on my arm and nudged me a little closer to the storefronts.

"Wouldn't want you to get mud on your Sunday dress," he said, even though the street was dry. Still, it was thoughtful.

We passed the Elite Store, with its fancy hats straight from New York, all the latest fashions, and I barely glanced in the window. I didn't know a soul who could actually afford one of those hats. I moved toward the storefront when a little boy in checked short pants barreled between Henry and me. His mother, not much older than me, followed close behind him, snatching at his waistband to slow him down.

"I am so sorry," she said to us. "He's like tryin' to hold hands with a tornado. Theodore, say you're sorry for nearly running into this lady and gentleman."

As she clamped her hand around his wrist—not even bothering with his wiggling fingers—and he forced out a "sorry," I got a better look at her face. She'd been a few years ahead of me in school. Christy something. She had a run in her stocking and her shoes were scuffed at the toes.

"Say 'Sorry, ma'am' and 'Sorry, sir,'" she corrected the tornado.

Still hunched over the boy, she smiled up at us. I tried to look behind her eyes. What was there besides politeness? Was she miserable or something worse? She had dark circles under her eyes and not much color. Definitely tired, but would she rather get rid of this boy altogether than deal with him for another day? Had there been another little one at home that she had decided to get rid of?

She was gone then, and when I looked over my shoulder, I saw her smile at Theodore even as she dragged him so that his feet left the ground every few steps.

"Handful," Henry said, looking back at them. He was only making conversation, but it irritated me that he thought he could sum them up in one word. I tried to shake the feeling.

"So what time did y'all get out of church?" I asked.

"We usually get out about a quarter 'til twelve."

We did, too, but with the visiting preacher, we'd run late. Papa's pocket watch had said 12:30. "Thank you for waiting." I thought of another question pretty quick, even though I knew the answer. "You don't live in town, do you?"

He shook his head. "Our place is east of town, opposite end of yours."

Across the street I saw Annie Laurie Tyler, who always looked like she was on the verge of some nervous collapse. Mama always seemed tired after Annie Laurie came to visit. The woman had too much emotion. She didn't see me, and I angled myself so Henry was between me and her. Now, Annie Laurie—that was the kind of woman I thought might up and lose her mind completely and drown her baby. But her youngest was around Jack's age.

We covered a couple more blocks, coming up to Dr. Strickland's Drug Store. Henry stopped suddenly, looking pleased with himself. "Would you like some candy?"

I didn't have any money, and I didn't feel it was right that he should buy me anything. "Oh, we'll be eating dinner soon as I get home." I started down the street again.

"I'll buy you a piece of whatever you want," he said. "Just to eat on the way."

There was a wheedling in his voice that irked me. "No, thank you."

"I can get free candies from the commissary anytime," he said. The Galloway commissary had big barrels of penny candies—caramels, licorices, gum drops. Sometimes Papa gave us each two pennies and we'd spend an hour deciding. I didn't think it would taste as good if it was free.

"Don't you get sick of it?" I asked.

"Nah. Too many kinds."

In the corner house, Maxine Horner stood in her doorway with a broom and dustpan, wearing a stylish jacket the color of buttercups. She and her husband, Bob, ran the Pastime theater, which was two streets up. She hadn't had a baby recently.

I'd only been in the Pastime once, for a Saturday afternoon Western.

"Afternoon, Virgie," she said. Her eyebrows arched a little, and she smiled when Henry turned toward her enough for her to get a good look at his face. "And afternoon to you, Henry."

We both smiled and waved, and I knew everybody'd know he'd walked me home by tomorrow morning.

"Did you see *Frankenstein*?" he asked after a bit.

"No, I haven't been to the theater in awhile."

"*Dracula*'s coming next week. With Bela Lugosi. Do you like vampires?"

"Don't know as I'd say I'm fond of them." I was afraid he'd ask me to go with him, but he didn't. Just went on about vampires for a while. Awful—whoever heard of liking such things.

The Brasher Hotel seemed busy enough, and men were standing in line to get into the restaurant on the top floor. I looked up and had a clear view of a man's behind perched on the railing. From my angle, it didn't look like a behind at all, all

misshapen and smooshed, and I craned my neck a little as I kept
walking. I didn't crane it for too long.

The sidewalk and the paved street stopped there, so we
were back on red rock. I watched my skirt switch against my legs,
and I tried to make my feet stir up as little dust as I could
manage. If I put down my toes before my heels, I barely made a
puff. I could see Henry's feet moving alongside mine. He kicked
up great storms of dust, but I kept concentrating on toe-heel,
toe-heel.

We walked past Nigger Town, the little group of shotgun
houses that ran up the hill. No coloreds were out that I could see,
but the path didn't take us too close. The high school had a
Kiwanis minstrels group that would make your sides hurt from
laughing. They'd paint their faces black and dance around stage,
mispronouncing things and falling all over one other. One year
we had a group of real Negroes come and perform for the grammar school near Christmastime, and they weren't nearly so
funny. They didn't seem to know at all how colored folks were
supposed to act.

Tess SUNDAY DINNERS WERE the best dinners. We almost
always had mashed potatoes, piles of them, so much you
could take seconds or even thirds. And Mama also made gravy.
Usually I liked white gravy the best, but I loved brown gravy
on potatoes. And also you could put scoops of English peas in the
middle of your potatoes and make a bird's nest. And that didn't
count as playing with food.

That Sunday Virgie walked home with Henry Harken I had
fun with it. Jack, too. Soon as Virgie got in, Mama called us
to dinner. Papa asked Jack to say the blessing—"Dear Heavenly
Father thank you for this food this day and all your many
blessings in Jesus' name, Amen." Girls could only say the blessing if no men were at the table.

Jack shoveled in some potatoes and said, "You gone marry
him, Virgie?" Then we watched her turn red.

"Hush," she said.

"Did he kiss you?" I asked. "I hope you didn't let him kiss you."

"You two don't be talkin' foolish," Mama said, even though she was trying not to smile.

"No," said Virgie, trying to look all proper.

I saw how the boys looked at Virgie, how they'd get flustered and punch each other in the arm when she walked by. Sometimes they couldn't look her in the eye, which worked fine because she never looked at them either. It was an interesting thing to watch, and I felt sure no boys would ever act quite so ridiculous around me. They only act all stupid when you're beautiful.

"Did you want him to kiss you?" Jack asked.

"That's enough," said Papa.

I just couldn't help it. "If he does kiss you, I bet you smell pomade."

Papa looked at me until I started shoveling potatoes in myself.

But Jack added one more before Papa gave him the that's-really-enough look. "You could name your babies Henrietta and Henry and maybe another Henry. Those Harkens are big on Henrys."

4 No Pay for Slate

Jack OF COURSE WE DIDN'T KNOW WHAT IT WAS TO BE
hungry. Not really hungry. With Papa having land, food
was never hard to come by. At least not for us kids—we just ate
whatever Mama sat in front of us, after she and Papa had
sweated and labored to get it out of the ground and clean it and
can it and cook it. No meat, but with Mama's cooking you never
noticed what wasn't on the table.

The men with no land, the ones living in mining camps or
renting property, didn't have that cushion. When the mines
started closing, there was nothing to go on the table. No other
jobs, either. And there was nowhere for those men or their
families to go. Maybe a handout from a church or free meals from
a relative, but that didn't last. Day in and day out, as weeks
stretched into months, what hungry people mainly did was starve.

We didn't see any of that. Not for a while. All Papa's
brothers farmed at least little patches of land, and Mama's sisters
had married men with clean white shirts who always had pens
in their pockets.

Lola Lowe's boy Mark was my age, and he had a tough time
of it in school. A lot of the really poor boys had the advantage
of being tough and hard and mean as snakes. No one would mess
with them. But Mark was always small, and he never seemed
healthy. He just seemed poor and pitiful and uncomfortable, the
kid who everybody's mother told you to be nice to. And frankly

nobody was too mean to him—there would've been no sport
in it—but nobody sat with him or asked him to play ball, either.

In third grade, he turned orange, like he'd been colored
with a crayon. And he had a potbelly on him. That thin body, nothing but bones, but an inflated belly you couldn't help but
notice. He stopped coming to school, from embarrassment more
than sickness, I think.

It turned out all they had growing in the garden was carrots,
and that was all he'd eaten for months. And then they had the
doctor bills from all the tests run to figure out what had turned
him orange. A few of Lola's other children turned splotchy
with rickets. By the time I graduated, she'd lost her four youngest.
Different names to what killed them, but poor nutrition at the
root of it. Mrs. Lowe handled losing the husbands a lot easier than
she did the children. I barely remember her from childhood,
but when I was in college, Mama started having me take Thanks-
giving dinner over to her.

To me Lola Lowe was the stooped, thin woman who never
said anything but "Fine head of hair on you, Jack. Thank you. And
tell your mama thank you."

She was two sentences to me.

Albert BIRDS KNOW FIRST when there's a storm coming up,
and I could hear them hollering. I'd heard the cawing
from the kitchen, and when I stepped out on the porch, I could
feel the storm in the air myself, the wind whipping around
the porch, smelling of electricity. The jays and crows and martins
sounded their warnings to one another while I stayed out there,
standing, waiting for the rain to hit. Nothing like the minutes
before an electrical storm, all the force of it making the hairs on
your arms stand on end, the trees nervous and shaking. I crossed
my arms and waited until the sheet of rain slammed into the
yard. The first line of lightning cracked. The birds went quiet,
hiding.

At shift change at 6 pm, the men coming on told us both

banks in town never opened that morning. Word got around quick that they'd closed without a word of warning to anyone. Doors locked, shades down, everybody inside just gone. Supposedly weren't going to open again period. None of us at the site had any money in 'em anyway, but the town was chock-full of fellows banging on the doors trying to get their money. A few went over to Jesse Bridgeman's house to bang on it for a while. Figured since he ran the bank, he was to blame. They banged for most of the afternoon, though, because he went home and killed himself early that morning. Wife died a couple of years before and kids were at school, so nobody noticed until finally one of the fellows walked around and peeped in the back window. Jesse was laying in a heap on the ground, hadn't even sat down to pull the trigger.

'Course in '29, banks wobbled and shook, businesses shut down all along Main Street. Went broke. Must've been a quarter of those storefronts boarded up. Didn't make much difference to me. Mines stayed open—with a few less men put to work in 'em—and life went on. No better, no worse.

I knew Jesse—not so as we'd do more than nod to each other in passing, but I'd thought he was a solid man. Didn't understand it. He had two boys and a girl, the youngest one of them about Virgie's age. I didn't know how you shrugged that off. Thought maybe it was different when there was money. Maybe the wife had rich parents who'd take care of the children.

I'd been in a few accidents, but the only one that I thought I might not get out of was in No. 5, down at Chickasaw.

I was loading then, shot the coal myself and then filled car after car. Like most things, your body fell into it after a while, scooping up the chunks of coal—slate, too, that'd be sorted out up on top. Didn't get paid for slate. Hefting it all into the car, I didn't hear a single voice, only coughing from time to time. Or the frustrated sound of a shovel hitting a slab of slate that wasn't jarred loose. No clock, no such thing as time or minutes, only a shovelful and the next and the next. And you settled into the

bosses' system alright—how long didn't matter, only how much.
One ton per car. We filled them regular and smooth, me and
Jonah, knowing to ignore the aches and soon enough they'd give
up and quiet down.

The prop under one of the blasts wasn't set right, and the
whole side of the tunnel caved. Floor and ceiling seemed like
they met each other in the middle, and I was blinking the dirt and
dust out of my eyes, spitting it out of my mouth, blowing it from
my nose. When I reached up to wipe it off, I couldn't move my
hands. Buried in it to my chest. It didn't take me half a second to
figure out that was the first problem needed to be solved. First
I worked on wiggling my fingers, getting them loose enough
that I could start to twist my hands. Then I hollowed out a bigger
space by circling my wrists. That freed up my arms below the
elbows some, and bit by bit I could feel the earth breaking up
below my shoulders. I kept moving and shifting, pulling loose the
same way the cat ate the grindstone—a little at a time. Once I
had my arms out, it got easier. Then I could use both hands like a
dog digging up a bone to push the dirt away from my body. I
carved out a space around me until I got to below my hip bones,
then I heaved myself out.

I had to take a few deep breaths before I could call for anyone. I'd heard grunts and shouts down the tunnel a ways while
I was digging. I'd ripped a few fingernails off and had to tear off a
piece of shirt to bandage my fingers up. They kept on bleeding,
and a few times I tried to clear my eyes of the dust and got an eye-
ful of blood instead. Digging in a cave-in ain't nothing like in
a garden. The dirt was full of splinters and chunks of wood, coal
and rock, a few bits of metal. Once I got to wrapping up my
fingers, I saw my hands were bleeding from a few other places, so
I wrapped them all up, sort of like loose mittens.

I'd called to the others while I was bandaging. A few fellows
answered back. They was mostly fine. We lost three men in that
collapse, and one of them I saw his hand, glove knocked right off

it, sticking up out of the dirt. The only part of him above ground. But the rest of us did all we could do—started heading up. We had to lift a few beams that'd blocked the tunnel, and I gouged one of those empty fingernail holes good. Nearly screamed. End of the day, I don't think the broken ribs hurt as much as the durn fingernails.

I knew I was sore all over, and my side did pain me something awful, but I kept on—wasn't no other choice. Once we were on the surface a doctor came and figured I had the broken ribs, plus my ankle had swole to the size of a ham. That was the start of my back trouble, too, I reckon. (Wasn't 'til later that I near broke it, and after that it never stopped acting up.) I hadn't felt any of it, though, not before I saw daylight. Can't say we ever mentioned sitting down and waiting to be rescued. We all kept climbing and digging and cursing—I don't hold with cursing, but sometimes I felt like saying "Amen" at the way those other fellows could string a good one together—and bleeding and sweating and praying. Still and all, it was them aboveground that got to us; we heard the yelling and tap-tapping on the rocks above. Took half a day for them to dig us out. Leta was there with all the women, with food and water and tea for the ones trying to get us out. I drank a pitcher of tea and nearly threw up.

Rain blowed onto the porch, hard, stinging droplets more like shards of ice than water. Water ran over to my boots. Drops dinged into the bucket by my feet—buckets cost a heap less than a new roof. Lightning flashed and thunder cracked almost at the same time, and I saw the lights flicker in the sitting room. Leta must've taken the children in there. I stood, feeling a sharp slap of rain with every heavy gust, and tried to imagine just laying in the dirt and coal and lumber and not getting up. And I realized I hadn't known Jesse Bridgeman at all. Just knew a name and a face.

Tess MY KNEES STUCK up over the old washtub, my elbows hanging over the side. It fit pants and shirts and drawers a lot better than it fit me. The sheet was hung across the kitchen from cupboard to cupboard so I'd have privacy, but Papa and Jack knew not to come back there anyway. That washtub was confining, and a waste of good water. (At least it was warm since Mama had boiled two pots to add to the water straight from the well.) Men-folks would bathe in the creek, but me and Virgie and Mama had to bathe in the washtub.

I tried to wash up as fast as I could, keeping my shoulders underwater, which meant my legs hung out. But I scrubbed the lye soap over them, laying the goose bumps to rest. I took time between my toes. Then I got soap under my toenails and had to kick them underwater to shake it loose.

I could hear the Grand Ole Opry on the radio, just a hum. I couldn't hear good with all my splashing, plus the radio was at the front of the house.

"Turn it up louder, Virgie," I yelled.

Mama stuck her head around the sheet a few seconds later. "Don't yell so, Tess," she said, frowning. "And keep the water in the tub."

Her head disappeared, but the music got louder. I heard a banjo, a bow dancing over the strings…Uncle Dave Macon playing "Rockabout My Saro Jane." I scooted up, shoulders above water and legs mostly below it, soaping and rinsing in rhythm. Uncle Dave'd break up the fiddling with clogging, yelling and whooing as his feet stomped fast and hard. I moved on to my head, rubbing the bar over my hair, then running my fingers through it. Mama always said to rub especially hard behind your ears. I did and dunked my head.

When I came up, he'd switched songs, calling out, "If they beat me to the door, I'll put them under the floor / Keep my skillet good and greasy…" His voice was like the twang of that banjo.

I was nearly rinsed off, the water cool and cloudy, when

I heard the first bolt of lightning. My hair didn't squeak yet, so I checked the light dangling over my head and dunked myself under again real quick. I wasn't sure where my towel was.

Papa was the first on our street to get electricity. Those droplights would be so warm and inviting at night, little balls of light hanging from the ceiling. It seemed like magic to light the house with just a pull of a cord, but in a storm, those lights would pop and fly, with sparks and whole strings of electricity shooting out. No long lines were coming out yet, but the one above the tub sent a spark a foot away from me. The taste of metal stung my mouth. Marianne at school said a man in Jasper was eating cereal at his kitchen table during an electrical storm, and a bolt of electricity came right down the bulb and landed on his head and killed him dead. I wondered if he landed in his bowl.

Electricity was like old Mr. Gordon at church, who had a cottonball's worth of white hair sprouting out of his ears and was prone to catching you by surprise. Sometimes that meant he'd have a peppermint stick in his pocket that he'd give you for no reason, just stick it in your face so quick you were afraid you'd lose an eye. Other times he'd thump you on the back of the head during service, even if you were sitting right beside your parents and you weren't talking at all, just shifting a little from side to side. On the one hand you didn't want to sit close enough to him to get thumped, but if you played it too safe, you'd never get a peppermint either. It kept things interesting.

Normally I wouldn't have worried too much about a storm. We got to move the buckets around to catch the roof leaks when they sprung, and we all tried to be first at spotting them. Jack was probably out there getting to do all the bucket moving—Virgie wouldn't fight him for it.

I even sort of liked the electrical sparks, and I loved the feel of the air when it crackled. And I liked the water. I'd never understood why I couldn't have all of it at the same time, even if that one man happened to have bad luck while he was eating breakfast. But this time I really wanted out of that tub. I was scared, and the feeling snuck up on me like it had been waiting nearby to pounce. Nothing used to scare me. But after that baby, it seemed like I wasn't ever safe. I didn't know from what, but I even checked under the bed at night before we turned out the lights.

I hopped out sopping wet, only spotting the towel draped over a chair after I'd left footprint pools across the floor. I watched the sparks fly off the lights, keeping my head turned toward them as I stepped back to the washtub and wrung my hair out. I was still standing there hunched over when Mama yanked back the sheet again.

"What are you still doing in here, girl? You better..." She stopped all of a sudden, looking surprised, even upside down like I saw her. "Huh—well at least you're out of the tub. Never saw a girl so stubborn about ignoring an electrical storm. Maybe you're learnin'. Anyway hurry up and get in the sitting room with the rest of us... and get out from under these lights! If it gets much worse, we'll go down to the storm cellar."

Leta THE BED WAS COOL, and I pressed against Albert soon as he lay next to me. In the beginning, I hated the smell of the mines on him, hated the coat of dust on his skin. Then it turned into his smell, not the mines', and there was a comfort to it.

We sank into the mattress, with the weight of two bodies and all the tiredness and the work and the bills to be paid. Usually he'd squeeze my leg and I'd nuzzle his neck and we'd fall into sleep without saying a word. All the words and all the moving and all the thinking were used up by dark.

That night we lay there breathing, him not complaining about my cold feet sliding under his long johns. The rain had slowed to a drizzle, making a nice lullaby. But neither of us slept. I could tell by the children's breathing that they'd drifted off already. Albert rolled toward me, lifting my hair away from my ear. His breath came from above me since he breathed better when he slept on two pillows.

"I been thinking about that baby," he said. At night, his

words blew out like smoke curling around my ear. Didn't want to wake the little ones. "You?"

"The girls still are," I said, looking at the ceiling. I could hear the train whistle, and I knew I hadn't answered his question exactly.

"Don't you wonder who could do it, Leta-ree?"

Even when we were courting, he never called me "honey" or "sweetheart." I didn't care for sugary words anyway. But once he heard my father call me "Leta-ree," short for my middle name, Reanne. He didn't say a word about it, but picked it up from then on.

"What's the use in that?" I asked. "Wonderin' don't get any more food on the table than wishin' or cussin'."

He pulled away from me slightly, his mouth still close to my ear, but our bodies no longer touching. "It's likely somebody we know."

I thought about the women parading through my kitchen, picking through women they sat next to at church like they'd pick through a mess of greens looking for mites. "It's poison, Albert. Nothin' to come from that kind of thinkin' but hate. Better to leave it be."

"Don't know how you can do that," he said, turning on his side, his back to me. "Just put it out of your mind like that."

He lay there grinding his teeth. Nervous habit. Liked to drove me crazy.

"Just can," I said finally.

He only lay there, his whole body stiff. I couldn't relax with him like that. "Don't be blamin' me for needin' to get through the day," I said.

Nothing from him, but I could feel him melt a little, body slowly settling into the mattress. Then he rolled back to me, arm against my side. My feet slipped between his calves. Warm. We just breathed for a while.

"Virgie say anything to you about that boy?" he asked against my ear.

"I don't think she cared much for him," I whispered. I could almost hear his smile.

"Why not?"

"Snooty. Bragged he could get all the candy he wanted. He thought that'd win her over."

Albert shifted and stifled a laugh, maybe a groan. The ribs he'd broke in No. 5 a few years back had never healed up right, and it hurt him to lie on his left side. Didn't have no hospital payments for that—hoped eventually U M W would get back on its feet and there might be some union insurance up at Norwood.

"Might be a boy with free candy now, but he'll be a man with rotten teeth," he said. "Eat nothin' but soup by the time he's forty." That idea seemed to please him, and he got silent.

"She's gone end up with one," I couldn't help saying. "Got to sooner or later."

"Wouldn't you rather it be later?"

"Why'd you let him walk her home then?"

"Don't know," he said, sighing. "Couldn't rightly say no with him asking so politely, just walking her back from church. Seemed nice enough."

"Then why're you lookin' forward to him gummin' his meals?"

"A walk from church is one thing. Her bein' sweet on a fella— fallin' under his sway — is somethin' different. You don't know what's behind the toothy smiles and combed-back Sunday hair."

"No, you don't."

"That don't scare you?"

Albert WHEN I FIRST saw her, Leta had her back to me. We were in Townley, where she's from, on land owned by neighbors of hers. They were clearing out a field that hadn't been used in a few years, burning all the brush in a great rush of flame you could see for a mile. It was October. I'd come with a second cousin, Emory. Fuzz, we all called him, after some rabbit hunt from when we was kids. I'd only been in the mines a few years then, still smooth-faced and easy-moving.

I walked up to the fire to warm up, along with a dozen or so others, and there was a girl standing by herself, wrapped in a shawl. Don't remember the color. Something cheerful. She was replaiting her dark hair, and the firelight was throwing all sorts of colors on it. The waves of hair fell past her waist. That hair was like nothing I'd ever seen, and my mouth went dry at the sight.

I couldn't believe she was alone. Townley was as rough a place as Carbon Hill, no work but hard work, and beauty was a rare thing. But I wasn't going to question good luck—I walked over. There must have been six other single fellows around that fire, and as far as I was concerned, they must have been blind or slow-witted.

When she turned toward me, I was glad I'd hustled over. Virgie's always been almost too pretty, nearly unapproachable— there's a chance that's my own wishful thinking. Leta wasn't less beautiful, but she had this kindness in her face, a wide-openness. She made you want to make her smile.

"Evenin', miss."

"Hello." She continued her braiding, her fingers working quickly and hypnotizing to watch.

I nodded toward the fire. "Ought to stay plenty warm for a few more hours yet."

"I'd say so." She'd meet my eyes for a second at a time, long enough to give me hope that she'd look a little longer next time.

"I'm Albert Moore, here with my cousin Fuzz, that is, Emory Beasley. We call him Fuzz. He's from around here. One of the Beasleys."

"I went to grammar school with Emory," she said, acting as if I hadn't tripped all over my tongue. Before she could say her name, an older man strode up, taking long, fast steps until he reached her side. He situated himself almost between us.

"Son," he nodded. "I'm Rex Tobin."

"Hello, sir." I was slightly taken aback, wondering if this was an older husband.

"See you've already introduced yourself to my daughter."

I hoped he took my smile as being friendly, not relieved.

"Yessir. Albert Moore."

Leta hooked her elbow through her father's arm. "I didn't introduce myself, Daddy. Leta Tobin."

"Pleasure," I said.

It took a month of calling on her at home until we went walking by ourselves. That night I stood and talked more to her father than to her. She was embarrassed, she told me later, that she'd let down her hair, which she'd thought was slatternly. But a spark had flown into it, and she'd mussed her braid trying to put out the spark. I mentioned that spark in my prayers that night.

Lying next to her in bed, I could feel her hair falling across my arm. Cool and heavy. I couldn't see her face. Just the slope of an ear and a chin and the soft spot of a cheek in the dark. All shadows.

I wondered how I really saw her that first night and how much was me shaping that memory, patting it down until it was tidy. For years I thought of her sweetness as written there in the darkness of her eyes, the softness of her mouth. Remembered—imagined?—that from that first night, I knew her small hands would mend a pain in my neck as sure as a swig of whiskey, that the crook of her elbow would fit a baby like God had carved it purely for that purpose.

I'd been so sure of that always, sure of the rightness of it all. And that all of a sudden seemed like some made-up magic thing Tess would come up with. Did God really work like that, steer your woman into your life? Match you up like bookends? Did he steer that woman to our well or help Jesse Bridgeman remember where he kept the bullets for his gun?

Maybe she was just a beautiful girl with a pleasing way about her. No hand of God pulling me to her, no future written on her face. It made me cold there in our bed, layered with quilts and warm with our bodies, to think that it could have been noth-ing but blind man's bluff.

"Leta," I called to her, real quiet, hoping she'd turn to me, that I'd see her face.

"Um." She'd breathed out her answer, not even managing a real word.

"Leta-ree." She shifted that time, tilting her head enough that I could see her lips just barely smack together before she answered me.

"Y'alright?" she said.

Her voice was enough then. Didn't need her face. My mind emptied, lay flat and calm. I settled, easing closer to her. "Fine," I said.

Virgie INSIDE MY HEAD, I repeated how I would approach Lola Lowe. "Hello, Mrs. Lowe," I'd say. "We just thought you might like some apples."

I thought about saying that Mama thought she'd like the apples, but that would be an outright lie. She'd be pleased to get the apples anyway, and that might get us some goodwill. I was pretty sure she'd just say "thank you" and ask us in and we would see whether or not her new baby was there.

I was holding the basket tight enough that it cut into my fingers.

"You want me to knock?" asked Tess.

I'd said I would do this. That I would talk and handle things.

"I'm fine," I said. I made my back ruler-straight and fixed a smile on my face and rapped twice.

Lola Lowe said, "Leta Moore's girls," instead of hello when she opened the door. Even though she wasn't really fat, she was soft all over with loose skin hanging. The backs of her arms shook when she moved. I tried not to look at them. Children lay around, outnumbering the furniture, standing, sitting, draped across the floor playing jacks. I didn't see the baby.

They lived in a clapboard house set up on cinder blocks, all of them packed in nothing but a big sitting room and a kitchen. If I'd put my head to the outside wall, I could've seen through the holes between the planks. Not that there was much to see—a stove, two rockers with the seats fraying, a table and chairs, and a small iron bed in one corner. I guessed the kids slept on the floor.

It had taken Tess and me an hour to climb the tree and get enough ripe apples to fill the basket—it'd really be another week before they started dropping to the ground ready to eat.

"Hello, Mrs. Lowe," I said, holding out the basket. "We brought you some apples."

"Right nice of you," she said, just standing there looking at us, no smile at all. She didn't look overcome by goodwill. We'd never come by before, and Mama and her weren't especially friends. Nobody was good friends with Mrs. Lowe. She mainly stayed in her house with all those little ones. "Y'all here to see Ellen?"

Ellen was in Tess's class. She only had one dress, worn thin like paper, with more patches than dress. We should've figured Mrs. Lowe would want to know why we were dropping by.

"No, ma'am," I said. "We just had some extra apples and thought y'all might like some."

Still no smile.

"And we ain't seen your new baby yet," said Tess. "But I heard he's precious." She grinned when she said it, dimples showing, tilting her head a little in that way that made her curls shake. I'd said I would do the talking, but I couldn't do what Tess did. She could turn on charm like pulling the light switch, the right words coming out so bright and easy. Adults were always patting her head, laughing at her, whispering to Papa and Mama how clever she was, what a cute little thing. And it wasn't like she even had to pull the string—it just happened. My hands were clammy and my mouth was dry and my shoulders hurt from holding so stiff, and I'd rehearsed what I wanted to say all the way over, and then Tess just turned on her light.

And I was so glad she did that I could have cried.

Mrs. Lowe looked at us awhile longer, then she stepped back and swung the door open wide. "Come on in."

I stepped through first, followed by Tess. Lola Lowe'd had half as many husbands as she had children, and they kept on dying. Her fifth was in Kentucky trying to find work. One keeled over of a heart attack, one choked on a chicken gizzard, one got smacked by a car walking home from town one night. I couldn't remember the fourth one.

Mrs. Lowe took the basket, carrying it over to the kitchen, which was really just one corner of the room with shelves and the table and stove. "Y'all want your basket back now? I can dump out the apples."

It was only an old strawlike thing with the edges chewed up. "No rush, ma'am. Just keep it until the apples are gone," I said.

"Have a seat," she said.

There were four cane-bottomed chairs around the table, so I pulled one out. Tess did, too. Mrs. Lowe pulled out the third one, which had a piece of twine tied in a loop around two of the legs. She noticed me looking down.

"The boys kept resting their feet on the wood bar and it finally broke in two," she said. "String does just as well holdin' the legs together. Sorry we ain't got a sofa."

"We don't have one neither," said Tess quickly. "Just rockers. And my brother's just like that, always tearin' everything up. Boys are nothin' but trouble."

Mrs. Lowe smiled at that, probably not so much at the words as at the way Tess shook her head in such a serious, grown-up way.

Then we sat and looked at each other, and I tried to think of anything else I knew about sofas or chairs or apples. It was a different kind of quiet than at our house. When none of us were talking, it was comfortable, peaceful, like at night after the birds and crickets are asleep. This kind of quiet made me want to jump up from the table and run clear to Jasper.

"Did you say you wanted to see the baby?" asked Mrs. Lowe.

"Yes!" we both answered, too loud and too fast. She likely thought we were there to kidnap it.

He was alive and well, it turned out, a little chubby and more than a little red. Mrs. Lowe held him just like Mama used to hold Jack, and I thought how every woman seemed to know where to put their hands and how to fit the feet and knees and elbows against them so everything was tucked in snugly. Mama had told me to never let Jack's neck snap back and never let his head jerk. It did once or twice accidentally, and I prayed for his brain not to jostle too much and run out his nose.

"His name's Franklin, Frankie we call him." Mrs. Lowe tipped him down so we could see his face better. "Ain't he a big, jolly one? Only four months."

He was big, but awfully quiet. I couldn't remember Jack ever being quiet. When he wasn't crying, he'd coo and gurgle and make silly sputters. But Mrs. Lowe only smiled at her boy—she had a chipped front tooth, I noticed—and didn't seem to mind him keeping to himself. I guessed she appreciated a quiet one.

"Can I hold him?" I asked.

"Sure," she said, already holding him out to me. I eased one arm under his back, cupping his head like Mama told me, and scooped him toward my chest. Then I wasn't sure what to do with him. "Would he like me to sit or stand?" I asked Mrs. Lowe.

"Don't matter," she said. "Just rock him a bit side to side."

So I did, walking and bobbing around the room. I hadn't held Mrs. Stanton's baby or Mrs. Torrence's when we stopped by their places—we went to those two first because they were closest to school. (For those first two visits, I'd felt sick to my stomach all the way there. At least by the time we got to Lola Lowe, I'd gotten over the nausea of practicing a good hello.) Mrs. Stanton was even out on the porch rocking her George, so that time we only waved hello and walked close enough to ooh and ahh a little at how precious he was, even though he was frowning and wrinkled. We didn't stay more than five minutes at either place, and we didn't have to go inside. This was a more sociable visit, which really meant it took more work.

"He's good," I said.

"Yep. Not colicky or nothin'. Sweet as pie."

I sat down again and swayed back and forth in my chair. Frankie seemed equally happy. Tess stood behind me and stroked his peach-fuzz head.

"Your mama doin' alright?" asked Mrs. Lowe.

"Yes'm," Tess answered.

"Did you know we went to school together in Townley?"

"No, ma'am," we both answered. Mama had never mentioned knowing Lola Lowe when she was a girl. But Mama didn't talk much about being a girl herself.

"Met her when I was about your age," she said, nodding to Tess. I figured then that she didn't know our names, but it was too late to tell them to her. "She had the longest braids I'd ever seen."

"Our hair won't grow that long," said Tess. "It gets to our shoulders and just stops growing."

Mrs. Lowe went on like Tess hadn't spoken. "She was a real pretty girl. Real sweet, too. One of the few girls I thought highly of in school. 'Course, she went on to high school and nearly finished, and I left after grammar school to help my mama. Married my first husband not a year later."

She must've been barely older than me when she married.

"But your mama brought me a pound cake when I got married. Nobody else brought me nothin'. Thought real highly of her. Tell her I said hello."

A girl barely able to stay on her feet wearing nothing but a rag of some sort pinned around her bottom wobbled over to Mrs. Lowe. Pee was leaking down her leg, dripping on the floor. Her face was all screwed up and she was starting to whimper.

"Lord have mercy!" said her mother, scooping her up, but holding her away from her body. She snatched a stained sheet—probably a clean one—off a stack of laundry in the corner and lay it across the table where we were sitting. When she started to unfasten the baby's diaper, I scooted back my chair and turned to face the other way. That pee'd run right through the sheet onto the dinner table.

I watched Mrs. Lowe wrestle a cloth around the baby's bottom, digging for safety pins in the pocket of her used-to-be-flowered dress, and I didn't see an ounce of temper in her face. She looked as calm and mild as she had since we walked in, never mind the peeing or the staining or the crying. I'd been thinking she was the most likely of the women on the list because she had the least money and the most children. So she'd be stretched thinnest, I'd figured. She kept herself apart from the other women—maybe not by design, but she did it just the same. Of course from the minute we laid eyes on the baby I knew I'd been wrong, but I was beginning to feel ashamed of myself for even thinking it. My tongue felt thick and my temperature'd shot up like when the teacher called on me in class or when I'd walked home with Henry Harken. I told myself I was being bashful and silly like Ella said, but the feeling just sunk deeper. My stomach curled up in a ball as I sat there watching the baby in my lap eat his fist.

It would have been easier for me to understand—and forget about—the baby in the well if it had been Mrs. Lowe that put him there. I'd have known that having kids didn't make you lose your mind—just having a houseful of them. And it wouldn't be as if a woman who'd sat in our kitchen sipping tea had done it. Lola Lowe was barely a real person to me. At least until I walked into her house and saw her smile at her children. I started to see the problem with my plan—I was going to get to know all these women if I talked to them long enough. And then they'd all be real.

A yellow-haired boy with hair down to his eyebrows put both hands on my knee. Snot ran thick and yellow from his nose; smudges had dried on his cheeks. I had a handkerchief in my pocket, and I jostled the baby around a little so I could pull out the little square and hand it to him. (Mama always said a lady should never be without a handkerchief.) He looked at it like I'd handed him purple galoshes, so I wiped his nose for him, then gave him the cloth.

"What's your name?" I asked.

He mumbled and drug his sleeve across his nose so that I couldn't understand him. "What was it?" I asked again.

"Mark."

"After the apostle," his mother called, looking over her shoulder.

"I'm Virgie."

He stared at me. I pointed at Tess. "That's my sister, Tess."

"How old are you?" asked Tess.

He looked at his mother. "Six," she answered.

One year younger than Jack, and he wasn't half my brother's size. He looked like he was barely out of diapers. "Can you hold up six fingers?" I asked, holding up six of my own behind the baby's back.

"Six," he said. "I'm six." He didn't let go of the handkerchief I'd given him, didn't move his fingers at all. "Apples," he added, pointing at the basket. "I like apples."

"He likes everything," Mrs. Lowe said, talking out one side of her mouth with a safety pin in her teeth. "Don't have a picky kid in the bunch."

"What're we havin' for supper, Mama?" Mark asked, flapping the handkerchief. He didn't really seem too curious. His nose was running again.

"Blackberries and bread."

His expression didn't change.

"I love blackberries," Tess said.

"They're better in pies," Mark said.

"I like 'em plain," she said.

"I used to."

I'd heard Papa and Mama both say about one person or another who couldn't find work that they'd starve if it wasn't for blackberries and bread, and why didn't Mama bring them by some real food.

The little girl on the table started howling then, probably not liking the cold air on her wet rear end, and the baby in my arms seemed to catch her bad mood. He screwed up his face and mewled, so I stood up and started pacing. The door opened then and Ellen walked in, looking surprised to see me and Tess. She tugged at her one dress, and I saw the thoughts flash across her face as clear as if they'd been spelled out in a bubble over her head like in Little Orphan Annie. She realized how we were seeing this—her mother changing a diaper on the kitchen table, her brother with dried snot on his face, our basket of apples the only food we could see in the place. The stove wasn't lit, and I knew they had no firewood or coal to burn in it. It was one thing to be poor as Job's turkey, but it was something else to have somebody from the outside stick themselves in the middle of it. She said hello without looking us in the face, held out her arms for her baby brother, and crossed the room as soon as I handed him to her. We only stayed another few minutes, but Ellen never met our eyes once.

We didn't really talk on the way home. I felt dirty and sad and glad that I'd left that boy my handkerchief.

Tess   IT WOULD'VE MADE more sense to think that Lola Lowe had a cradle full of eggs and that that houseful of children had hatched out in one bundle. To think of each of those ten big-eyed, all-knees-and-elbows kids tucked in her belly made me ache. It was much nicer to think of them packed safely inside an egg, plenty to eat and a warm body keeping them snug.

"Why would somebody have so many kids?" I asked Virgie. We'd sat down on the porch steps when we got home, and nobody had noticed us yet. I was trying to get a sulfur butterfly to land on my finger, but he wasn't having any of it.

She shrugged, hands crossed in her lap.

So I kept talking. "'Cause I don't know why you'd have 'em if you can't feed 'em."

"I don't think she planned on not feedin' 'em," she said.

The stupid butterfly landed on her shoulder. She didn't notice, and I didn't tell her.

"I bet they haven't had anybody call on them in ages," I said. "Bet they was glad to see us."

"Hush up, Tess."

"What?"

She jerked to her feet. "Can't you ever just sit and not talk? You're givin' me a pain in my head!"

She'd yelled. That took me aback. Virgie never lost her temper—she clammed up cold and hard and far away. Even that one time when I dipped my finger in ashes and drew big eyebrows and a mustache on her while she slept, she only flung herself out of bed and stomped off without a word. But she was almost shaking this time.

"I was only talkin'. Don't take my head off," I said.

"So quit talkin'."

"You quit listenin'."

"You're such a baby."

"You're a nag."

"I said quit talkin'."

"You can keep on sayin' it all you want!"

She sighed and stalked off toward the woods, and happy as I was to get in the last word, I was still confused. And that won out. "What's the matter with you?" I yelled after her just as she reached the edge of the yard.

She stopped but didn't turn around. "I don't think it was such a nice thing we did today," she said.

I dreamed a dream more sound than picture that night. Mrs. Lowe's baby Frankie was screaming underwater, but instead of a voice, he had a stream of bubbles pouring out of his mouth. I was only up to my knees in the water, and I reached down and plugged my finger in his mouth. He smiled and smiled, sucking away, and I didn't make any move to pull him out of the water.

5 Jonah

Jack SOMETIMES I WAS ALLOWED TO GO CAMPING WITH
boys from school. Not overnight—not until I was ten or
twelve—but long enough to roast marshmallows and sit around
the fire.

There was a group of us, and Paul Kelly was always the
center of it. A big boy, three years older than me, he could shoot
any squirrel or bird he aimed at, and he always built the fire.
I'd seen him wrestle high school boys and beat them. Once he ate
a roach on a dare.

One night he bet he could hold his breath for the time it
took him to get the fire going. And he did—it was only seconds
before sparks from his flint caught on the little pile of leaves
and twigs. He never even turned red. Paul Kelly. He was the one
who always talked about niggers. I'd heard the word at school,
but not like Paul said it. He said he hated them. Must've said it
twenty times with that fire lighting up his face.

It would be dark and still and with that fire shining on him
and him built up in my mind already, he seemed like John
the Baptist (who ate locusts himself) or some other prophet who
could call down all sorts of things from heaven.

In church we learned about Cain and Abel. Abel tended the
flocks and Cain worked the soil, and the Lord preferred Abel's
offerings of fat firstborn animal sacrifices to Cain's offerings of
vegetables. (Even as a teenager, Tess would keep on about that pas-
sage all the way home from church—"Do you think God would

like squash? Do you think Cain got in all that trouble just because God was allergic to green beans or some such?" And eventually Papa would tell her to hush because she was being sacrilegious, and he'd try to keep his mouth from twitching. But Cain was jealous that the Lord favored Abel, and he killed his brother. The Lord heard Abel's blood cry out to him from the ground, and he cursed Cain to wander ceaselessly across the earth. And to make sure that Cain wasn't killed before he got in a life's worth of wandering, God put the Mark of Cain on him.

So the Sunday school teacher, a mousy man with a woman's hands, told us that's how colored people got made—God put the mark of the cursed on them. The mark of the criminal. Sentenced to never find peace and be no good. I had the Bible to back up Paul Kelly's fondness for "nigger," and it gave the word a kind of righteousness. There was ugliness to it, too, I didn't miss that, but church was full of ugly things—blood and crucifixion and thorns and swords and ears lopped off—that were part of God's perfect plan.

Tess   THE COLORED MAN banged on the door when we were all asleep. Our bed was in the front room, and Virgie and I both sat up from the shock of the noise. Then she threw a blanket around her shoulders and went to the door, even though she wasn't allowed. I hopped up, too, and peeked around the doorway. I heard Papa getting out of bed as Virgie called out, "Who's there?"

"Virgil, ma'am. I work for your daddy." He did—I remembered him coming by before. Sometimes the colored men came by for Papa to get them out of jail, because the police were always arresting them for gambling or vagrancy if they were walking around wrong. Police would get money out of their supervisors if they wanted those Negroes to show up for work the next day.

Virgie opened the door, and Papa showed up with his shirt just half buttoned over his undershirt. "Somethin' happen, Virgil?"

"Yessir, Mr. Moore. Jonah's done got hisself put in jail."

He seemed careful not to look at Virgie or me, even though we were right in line with the door.

"Jonah?" Papa seemed surprised, and it took me a second to realize Jonah was Mr. Benton. "What for?"

"Said he was drunk and disorderly."

"Jonah?" Papa said again, quiet-like. He went back to Mama and said something to her, then came back carrying his boots. "I'm comin', Virgil. Just wait right there."

Virgil stood on the porch, turning away from the house, while Papa leaned against the wall and started to pull on his boots. He stopped when he saw Jack come shuffling out, wiping his eyes. The moonlight from the doorway fell on him and made his nightshirt shine. Jack frowned at Virgil and said, "Why's a nigger at the door, Pop? I hate niggers."

Before I could blink, Papa hauled off and whacked Jack so hard on the backside that I could hear the breath gush out of Jack's mouth. Then he snatched him up by the arms and pulled him off the floor, to eye level. Jack was so stunned he didn't move—didn't even cry.

"Where'd you learn to talk like that?" Papa asked, hard, like a stranger.

Jack didn't say nothing.

"Don't you be talking about hatin' people," Papa said with a shake that snapped Jack's chin. "God don't allow for hatin' people."

Jack was closemouthed, still, and watery-eyed, and his bare feet hung in the air without even a twitch. Mama'd come to stand next to me at the bedroom door; her forehead was crinkled up, but she wasn't saying nothing. Papa looked at her, then set Jack down real gentle on the floor, lifting his fingers and looking where he'd left red marks on Jack's arms. He looked like he might be sorry, but he didn't say so. Instead he nodded toward Virgil.

"Tell Mr. Virgil you're sorry," he said.

"I'm sorry, Mr. Virgil," said Jack, dark in Papa's shadow.

"Thank you, sir," said Virgil to Jack, sounding solemn and uncomfortable and confused all at once.

Papa patted Jack's head, met Mama's eyes for one second, then shoved his feet in his boots and went out to Virgil. "Be back before long," he said over his shoulder.

When the door closed, Mama came and knelt by Jack, who'd started sniffling and wiping at his eyes. She smoothed his hair and hugged him. "Now, don't cry, son. You're a good boy and your papa ain't mad at you. But you know better than to talk hateful like that. That ain't the kind of boy we raised you to be."

Sometimes Mama did that—soothed over the hurt then made it sting even more. I'd never seen her mad at any of us, but disappointing her was worse than a dozen slaps from Papa, even with a belt. And sure enough, Jack had a steady stream of tears running down his face by the time she stopped talking. Mama picked him up, groaning a little at his weight, and carried him back to his pallet. She'd tuck him in, kiss his forehead, make sure he didn't cry himself to sleep. To me and Virgie she said, "Go on back to bed, girls. Only a few hours 'til daylight."

"Papa didn't get much sleep," said Virgie, still looking at the door, her forehead wrinkling up.

My sister, even when she's in heaven with her own puffy cloud, will find something to worry over.

Mama looked back at the door, too, rolling her shoulders a little after plopping Jack down. I watched her and Virgie watch the door for a little while, and when I yawned, I tried to make it quiet. It seemed like if anybody ever spoke, it might be something worth hearing.

Mama's face was in the shadows, so I couldn't see her expression.

"Your Papa'll be alright," she said. "Takes more than missing a few hours of sleep to hurt him. But," and then she got quiet like she was talking to herself, which meant we shouldn't really hear it but she couldn't help saying it, "I'd think he'd get tired of running over and bailing those people out all the time."

Me and Virgie didn't say anything. We climbed into bed, tussling over who had more covers, and finally settled down.

"She doesn't want him helpin' Mr. Benton," I whispered to Virgie. She swatted at my face because I'd said it too close to her ear, which tickled her a little and annoyed her a lot.

"She just doesn't want him tired out," she said. She never could stand the thought of Mama and Papa disagreeing.

"You think she minded him whippin' Jack?" I asked, staying a little farther from her ear.

She turned over fast enough that her elbow caught me in the side. "He said 'hate,'" she said, like that was that. And I guess it was.

"Do you think the woman was a colored woman?" I whispered next. She knew who I was talking about.

"Why do you think that?" she whispered back.

"More likely, ain't it? Mama says they're different from us, don't have the same morals." She said the Negro men lived with more than one wife, sometimes with whole families in different camps. Sometimes when Virgie and Jack and I passed near Nigger Town, kids would holler at us, and I'd holler back and call 'em chocolate drops, and then we'd all run. Nobody hollered if there were adults with us. Somehow it would make it easier to think it wasn't so much a woman that did it as a colored woman. Then nothing much would have changed after all. It'd be meanness already set off to the side and held apart like the Negroes in their little piece of town.

Virgie was quiet for a bit. "Papa says everybody's the same covered in coal—can't tell black from white. And he likes Mr. Benton."

I thought for a minute, and Virgie started sniggering. "And in all the commotion over getting him out of the well, don't you think somebody would've mentioned if the baby was colored?"

She thought she was so smart. And I wasn't exactly sure how that worked, to tell the truth. I knew pigs had pigs and hens had chickens, but then again, sometimes the mama might be speckled when the baby wasn't...or just the opposite. The cat we kept in the barn had a beautiful smoke-colored kitten in her litter one year, making all the everyday brown ones look lots less cute. The Hudsons had a pretty gray tomcat.

"Well, the daddy could be white, couldn't he?" I finally whispered.

She didn't answer that.

"And that'd be a good reason to kill a baby."

"Time for sleepin', not talkin'," said Mama from her bed. And we shut up.

Virgie TO PAPA, GOOD was something you could hold in your hand. Hard and solid like coal rock. You could weigh it, measure it, see its beginning and end. You were never to hate anyone. You were to call all grown-ups "ma'am" and "sir" when you answered them. You were to help Mama without her asking. You were never to disobey Papa or Mama. If you went by those rules, you were good. If not, well, I didn't know about that. None of us did really, even though Jack and Tess might get whipped for sassing Papa every now and then. I'd hear him talk about men who left their families—just picked up and took off without a word. Or there were women who wouldn't take in their husband's mama when she got too old and feeble to look after herself. These were unforgivable things.

There was something comforting to that, knowing what he wanted, what he expected, and knowing what would disappoint him. But it meant lots of times there was no point in talking to him, because he knew his own mind so well that he didn't need to know yours.

And there were more unforgivable things for Papa himself. There was an old colored man, Old Romy, who'd come to the door every so often and say he was hungry. He used to work with Papa in the mines when Papa was young. Every time Old Romy came by, Papa would go get him a chicken and wring its neck, even if we hadn't eaten chicken for weeks. Nobody could come to the door asking for food but that Papa would see that they got some. Nobody could ask for anything, really, that Papa wouldn't give it to them. Right after everybody'd lost their jobs and businesses, our cousin came to the door asking for a gold pocket watch that belonged to Papa's father. That cousin said he was going to take a mess of jewelry to Birmingham to sell it, and he'd take that watch for Papa and bring us back the money he got. Papa gave it to him, thinking we could use a refrigerator or new shoes and clothes more than we needed a watch. The cousin never came back—he moved to Tennessee with all the money he got from the kinfolks' jewelry. Papa wasn't even mad about it. "You're here to be givin', not takin'," he'd say.

He never would take anything. All in all, he held himself to a different measuring stick than he did everybody else.

Mama never seemed to concern herself with good and bad unless it happened under our roof. She didn't care for whining, but still and all, if we were determined to claim being tired or sickly, she'd do the work herself with no more than a "Well, sit yourself down then." I'd never heard Mama say she was tired or sore or frustrated, even though she kept on working after Papa was rocking and smoking. One time I saw a bright red blister across the top of her hand, pulled tight like the skin would burst any minute. I asked her about it and she said she had bumped her hand against a skillet the day before. I thought back over all those hours that I hadn't noticed it, that she hadn't favored her hand or flinched from the fire or even said "ouch."

Sometimes it seemed like instead of the coal Papa and Mama had been put in the furnace, only instead of burning, they'd hardened and toughened to something that wouldn't budge.

Albert WE TOOK THE CAR. Virgil said he hadn't been in one before and since it was dark I let him set up front. Dropped him off a few blocks from his house on my way to the jail.

It wasn't the first time I'd come at this time of night, and it always seemed strange to me that such a nothing kind of building could turn somebody's life upside down. It was just a stone box, with a couple of steps leading up to the door, three windows down one side, none in the front or back. Flat roof. I pulled up right by the door—wasn't no other car around. The police chief walked to work.

"Should've brought you some coffee, Ted," I said, stepping in after he answered my knock. "Ain't your deputy usually pullin' nights?"

He sat at the desk, an over-big contraption that made him look like a boy in short pants behind it. Ted Taylor wasn't a bad man, but not a particularly good one, neither. He knew I'd pay to get Jonah out, just like he knew Jonah hadn't done nothing wrong. Likely he hadn't said "sir" enough when Ted asked him where he was headed.

"My sorry deputy's sick with the flu," he said. "I been here the past few nights."

I could see Jonah sitting straight-backed in his cell, looking more ready for a church service than jail time. He didn't speak to me, didn't smile even. Barely nodded. I did the same, giving my attention to the sheriff. "Wife and kids makin' it alright?"

"Well as can be expected. My oldest went to look for work in Tupelo. Your'n?"

"Doin' right well."

"Glad to hear it. So I expect you're here for him," he said, jerking his head toward Jonah but not even looking at him. Ted was several inches shorter than me, but with a chest so wide you'd think his elbows would have to bow out. His stomach was a little smaller than his chest, but his buttons always looked near to popping. I thought he was one of those men who was so mad he couldn't grow higher that he'd decided he'd just grow wider.

"Yep," I said. "One of my boys came and told me you'd brought him in on some sort of charges."

"Could smell the whiskey on him all the way down the street."

I walked over to Jonah, who was still sitting and staring

toward the door. "Can't smell nothin' now, Ted. Seems alright to me."

"Must be wearin' off."

"He give you any trouble?"

"Nah. Meek as a lamb. Tried to tell me he was out trying to find wood to burn in the fire. Not unless he thought he'd find it at the bottom of a bottle."

Jonah didn't say a word, which was the best thing.

"Reckon he might have been out lookin' for wood," I said, casual-like. "Cool night tonight."

Ted ignored me. "You let one of 'em get away with the least little thing, you end up with a whole pack of 'em roamin' the streets, makin' it where it ain't even safe for women and kids to be out on the back porch at night."

I'd had enough going in circles. It was too late at night for the normal hemming and hawing. "What's this gone cost me?" I asked.

"No tellin' what he coulda got up to if I'd left him alone."

"How much, Ted?"

"Four dollars."

I sighed. "He's one of my best men. Ain't never had any problems with him. Now you know he's never caused a lick of trouble in the ten years he's been here. I ain't one of the big bosses. This is money comin' out of my pocket."

"S'pose you could get him for two dollars." He finally looked at Jonah. "But you consider this a warning, boy."

For the first time, Jonah looked over at us. His jaw worked and his tongue slid over his front teeth. But his mouth was soon still, and his face turned blank and calm.

"Yessir," he said in a voice as empty as his face. "I'll do that."

I could tell Ted wanted to find fault, wanted to hear some crawling and cowering in Jonah's voice. I could see Jonah's jaw muscles still tensed up, though, and I didn't care to think what he might say next. I didn't care to pay four dollars, neither.

"Mighty decent of you," I told Ted. "I best be headin' on

with him, then, so I can go on and get back. Might even work out good for Leta—I sure got plenty of time to do the milkin' before I leave for the mines."

Ted shifted over my way then, leaning against the bars of the cell. "That reminds me—I got some more news you might be interested in. 'Bout that baby."

I waited for him to go on. Ted would always keep talking if you just kept quiet. "Doctor said he didn't drown after all," he said. "They cut him open and he didn't have no water in his lungs. So looks like there wasn't no murder."

I couldn't wrap my head around that quite so fast. "You sayin' she threw a dead baby in there?"

"Yep." He looked pleased with himself. I'd have sworn his face was even rounder and redder than usual.

"And he's only findin' this out a month after we found the baby?"

"Shoot, he knew the day after. I just ain't seen you since then."

"So what did kill him?"

"Don't know." He looked less puffed up. "Could've been anything. But no bruises on him, no blood. It don't look like he was shook or beat or cut."

"So what're you doin' next?"

"Not much to do. I'll ask around, but I got my money on it bein' some delicate-minded woman who lost her head when her baby died. Nervous condition, maybe. But ain't nothin' to charge her with, really, even if we did find her, 'specially with your water bein' alright. We could prob'bly fine her if you felt that strong about it."

"No," I said. "No, I don't care 'bout that. It just don't make no sense. If she wasn't meanin' to kill the baby, why throw it in our well at all?"

I could tell Ted wasn't losing sleep over it. He'd got to tell me something I didn't know, and that was all the pleasure he had to get out of the thing. He went on and took my money and let Jonah out.

When we closed the door behind us, Jonah rolled his neck around and cracked his back like all of us had a habit of doing. Years of bending over left you with a fist always closed around your backbone, and that fist grabbed on like the devil when you'd been sitting for a while. Other than that cracking, we didn't make much noise, scuffling along through the dirt to the car. He never talked much and didn't expect me to chatter, neither. We could work for hours loading cars and digging into seams without a word. When one of us had a notion to say something, there was a reason to it.

Once we were pulling onto the road, I felt his eyes on me.

"Sorry for draggin' you out, wakin' your family," he said, clearing his throat. "I do thank you. Wouldn't have called on you if there'd been money to spare. You got my word I'll pay you back next week."

At least paychecks were every two weeks by then, which made things easier. Used to be once a month when I started, 'fore I married Leta. That kept most fellas borrowing from the company during that last week or two before payday, and they'd all but hand over that check when it finally came on account of all the interest. Striking hadn't gotten us much—not any more money—but it got us that same money split in half and paid separate.

"Ain't no hurry," I said. Would have been an insult if I'd said he didn't have to pay me.

"I wasn't drinkin' none. Thought you should know."

"Didn't think you was."

"My wife got busy with the two sick ones today. She didn't get no chance to bring wood in, and wasn't until we headed to bed I realized the fire was about out. Thought I'd just get some limbs out in the woods to tide us over—didn't want the children to get cold, 'specially them bein' poorly an' all."

We rode on, both of us looking straight ahead.

"He give you trouble before?" I asked.

"Nah. Never ran across him 'fore tonight."

"He sees mostly the good-for-nothin' colored, I s'pose. Don't know the difference between you and them."

"You see a difference?" He didn't say it like he was trying to be smart, I didn't think. I gave him the first answer that popped into my head.

"There's a difference. I know you walk the chalk. Not like some."

He didn't answer, staring out his window. I figured he was pleased. Then he said more in one chunk than I'd ever heard come out of his mouth.

"I got a cousin in Birmingham, always talkin' 'bout uplift. 'Bout how we Negroes oughta do what the boss tells us, work real hard, not gamble or drink up our pay, and then we'd have somethin' worth havin'. Well, I ain't had a drink since I got married nine year ago. Wife don't like it no more than your'n does. And not drinkin' or playin' cards still don't make money magic itself into my pocket when there ain't none. Boss pays you seven dollars a week, and food and rent and clothes for the children cost seven dollars and fifty cents a week, ain't no use blamin' sin for bein' at rock bottom. Plenty of fellas at rock bottom who didn't have no fun gettin' there."

I could see him look at me, but I kept on looking at the road. I didn't have much of an answer.

"You ownin' land, don't s'pose you'd know much about it," he said. "Ain't complainin', but it sits different with us."

I was still as a stump, thinking. He fidgeted for the first time that night. "You ain't mad that I spoke my mind? Didn't mean no offense."

"Didn't take none," I said. The street lamps hardly lit the road worth anything. "I figure I know somethin'. I know Ted Taylor wouldn't cart me off to jail for walkin' down the street. Know I get to be 'Mr. Moore' and you never get no kind of handle in front of your name. I know no shack rouster gets sent to a white man's house to see if he's really sick. No supervisor would so much as look wrong at Leta. Know I've worked next to you long as Tess has been alive and I ain't never seen you lazy or drunk."

We rode on, both resting from all those words, shucking the meaning out of them and sorting it.

"You're sort of an odd egg, Albert," Jonah said. "A good'un, mind you. But an odd one."

We'd pulled up even with where his street hit Main, but before he pulled the door handle, I called his name. He looked back.

"You heard what Ted said about that dead baby," I said. "You heard anybody say somethin' worth repeatin' about it? About its mama?"

He moved his hand off the door. "Can't say I have."

"Seems to me that a woman who'd do that would stand out. That it would pain her somethin' awful. You ain't noticed any, well, you might say, disturbed women?"

"Ain't they all disturbed?"

I chuckled. "Any woman that seemed troubled by some-thing? Negro women? Or white women, too, if you noticed any."

"Now, Albert, you know durn well I ain't spendin' time around no white women. And if I am, they's gone be troubled for sure. As for Negro women..." His tone changed, sounded harsher than I was used to. "They got their own reasons for bein' troubled."

"You don't have a notion of who did it?"

He shook his head, and I believed him. I didn't have any notions worth an Indian nickel myself.

"I got some thoughts on it," he said, surprising me.

"Yeah?"

"It's a sad woman that would do that, Albert. Not a mean one. Take your own dead child and toss it in a well belonging to good people—that says somethin' to me. That she's, you might say, a little crazy, but that's nothin' next to the size of the sadness."

He stopped talking and didn't start back again. Finally I asked, "Why you say that?"

"I figure she gave up on this life, and if this life don't matter, that little body didn't matter a whit. She'd already moved on to thinkin' about the next life. One where the baby didn't care about that body so neither did she."

I understood that. It didn't answer none of my questions about who and where—it being my well—but he'd done a better job getting inside her head than I'd come close to. I hadn't expected that of him; I admitted that to myself right then and there. It didn't make me proud. I couldn't figure just what it made me. "There's good sense in that, Jonah."

And somehow I opened my mouth yet again before his hand got to the door.

"You knew Jesse Bridgeman killed hisself?"

Jonah nodded.

"Been on my mind. I passed that man on the street at least once a week, always saw him on the way to church on Sunday. I never saw that in him. Feel like I just looked at some shell of him not meant for nothin' but to be throwed away. But I never knew it for a shell, never knew to peel it back or crack it to see what was underneath."

He smiled, a flash of white I rarely saw in the mines, and I looked straight at him and met his eyes. They were deep and dark almost like Leta's and the children's, I thought, and it gave me a start to see them looking back at me. What shook me most was how clear they were at nearly three in the morning, no red in them, and I felt a shiver inside like I did when Leta would explain something in a simple way that made me know her eyes took in whole worlds mine never blinked at.

Jonah's smile made him look older, not happier. "Shoot, I wouldn't know nothin' 'bout that," he said.

I thought about that on the way home. And about how we'd used up a year's worth of words.

Tess SO THERE WAS no water in that baby's lungs. The doctors cut him open because Chief Taylor needed to see for sure how he was killed before he started carting women off to jail. And he didn't have a bit of water in his lungs. Not any. Meaning that baby wasn't breathing when he got thrown in. He was dead before he hit the water. And that set us to rethinking our list.

"What does it mean, Virgie?" I swung my book satchel from two fingers; she carried hers over her shoulder like a handbag. We'd gotten good and warm by the fire before we left, and the walk to school would just give us time to lose all the heat and be ready for the warm stove.

"I've been thinking about that," she said. "It means she wasn't a murderer, for one thing. I'd been thinking we were looking for someone wanting to get rid of her baby, somebody pushed into it by meanness or tiredness or misery. But maybe she wasn't desperate at all. Maybe she was something else."

"Like what?"

"I'm not sure."

"So she threw a dead baby in our well." Crunch, crunch— leaves fell apart under my feet. "That don't seem any more sensible than throwing in a live baby."

"But it's different," she insisted.

"How?" I answered back just as stubborn. I didn't understand why she wanted to divide up crazy into different sections. We'd been looking for a crazy woman and we still were.

"I don't know." She caught my arm and looked down the road to school. The boys usually played around until the bell rang, and sometimes the little kids' parents would stand around the road talking. "I hope nobody's out this morning." She chewed her lip while she started down the road and then pulled me in the opposite direction. "Oh, let's just go the long way. I don't feel like saying hello to everybody."

It beat all how Virgie thought it was a chore to wave and answer back to people. But I followed her into the trees toward the creek, where nobody'd call out to us but the squirrels. Virgie loved the woods, liked being around trees more than she did people. I didn't care much for being in the middle of all them branches and trunks and briars. I wouldn't have set foot in the woods by myself. They seemed darker than they used to, and anything could be hiding. Jack had gotten me thinking about why we didn't ever see fairies in the woods. I figured something ate them. Some sort of lizard, maybe, or one of those sharp-toothed possums. I leaned toward possums with their red eyes and rat tails. They could hang upside down and snatch those fairies right out of the air, ripping their wings off and chomping them like popped corn. The wings would be the tastiest part. If you were evil.

It was a big thing for me to realize about all the bad magic creatures that must be out there to fight against the good ones, and before long I had a head full of them.

"Maybe we never knew she was pregnant," said Virgie, as I kept an eye out for red eyes. "Maybe she hid it."

"Hid carryin' a baby?" That got my attention. Soon the solution dawned on me. "So we're lookin' for a big, fat woman?"

She frowned and stepped over a rotten log. "She could've worn a corset."

"But it'd be easier to hide it if you were big. We should think about a list of big women."

She didn't stop frowning, just started chewing her lip again. "I was thinkin' our list was too simple. Maybe we shouldn't be accountin' for babies. And maybe we shouldn't be thinkin' of who's big as a house. We should be figurin' what kind of woman would throw a dead baby in a well."

"A crazy one," I said.

She ignored me. "Not one that did wrong by her baby. She prob'bly loved him."

"She could've killed him ahead of time. Clubbed him on the head."

I'd dreamed of bruises the night before. Not my own. Just pale, pale skin and purple blotches. Water dripping from

everything, making the bruises shine. I couldn't remember more
than that.

Virgie shook her head. "Papa said the chief said there was
no sign of that. Not bruises or nothin'. Just as likely he died from
bein' sickly."

It'd rained enough to fill up the creek to the edge of the
bank, and the planks we walked across were wet. The water nearly
touched them, splashing over them from time to time. We both
hiked up our skirts.

"I'd rather hop across the rocks," I said. "It's more fun."

"All we need's for you to fall in," she said, halfway across.
I think it was looking around to give me a scowl she borrowed
from Papa that upset her balance. Or maybe she stepped on a leaf
or something. At any rate, Virgie toppled over into the creek
with the same slowness a glassful of milk has when you knock it
off the table.

The creek was no more than waist deep at its highest, but
she got soaked good. She managed to keep her head above water,
so her curls didn't get wet, and her right hand held her satchel in
the air. But every inch below her neck was sopping. She didn't sit
there long; before I could even say anything, she was standing
and wading to shore. More like stomping.

"Ohhhhh," was all I could say. "Oh, Virgie." But then I got
a good look at her, water streaming from the bottom of her dress,
and I couldn't help but smile.

"This isn't funny," she said. "I'm gone be late—I'll have to
run home and change my clothes." But she was fighting a smile
herself. She almost laughed, then it turned to a spluttery cough,
and I saw she had goose bumps.

"You'll catch cold," I said, worried then. "Run on home. I'll
tell your teacher."

"Not in front of the whole class!"

"Okay, I'll tell her real quiet." She decided to believe me
and took off running back toward the house. She got almost to

the road when I yelled her name. "You should've went across the rocks," I told her; she didn't even look back.

I tiptoed on across the planks without any trouble—it was faster than going across the rocks, and I didn't have extra time if I had to go to Virgie's classroom first. I started running on the other side of the creek, thinking I'd slow down when I got back in view of people. (I moved better in water than I did on land. My legs were a little too long for me and my knees were always bloodied from tripping over nothing more than my feet. It seemed like I had more than just two of them.)

So Virgie thought the Well Woman wasn't evil. But if she wasn't evil, she had to be crazy. I couldn't see no other reason to it—no mama like ours could do such a thing. I could hear Virgie's voice in my head, though. If it's so plain, why doesn't she stick out? Evil or crazy must look different than we thought.

Virgie I WAS ONLY half an hour late. Mama helped me pull off my wet dress and under things. That was after I burst open the back door—still standing on the porch so I wouldn't drip on the floors—and announced I fell in the creek.

Mama looked up from the breakfast dishes and blinked at me, then she was right beside me with a towel before I could say another word.

"Take off your shoes and leave them here," she said first. Second she said, "How come you fell in and not Tess?"

Back in the bedroom, towel wrapped around me and not wearing a stitch, I stood while Mama hunted for bloomers and stockings for me. "I don't believe you've ever fell in the creek before," she said. "Hardly ever even scraped your knees."

I just stood there.

She seemed more puzzled than anything, not the least bit mad. She held my hands in hers and then held the back of her hand to my forehead to be sure I was warm enough...but not so warm as to have a temperature. Then she kissed my forehead and whacked me lightly on the rear end as I turned to the door.

I did not enjoy being wet or mussed or late, and I sank into my seat as quietly as possible. Tess must've said something to Miss Etheridge because she didn't say a word to me, and normally you'd be called to the front of the room for being late. Being tardy twice would get your knuckles rapped with the ruler. Well, Miss Etheridge never used the ruler, but Jack's teacher had left welts the year before when Jack lost track of time digging for crawdads before school.

Three seats away from the potbellied stove, I could feel its heat already. Too close to it and you'd be too warm, turning groggy and stupid with the coziness of it. Three seats away was perfect.

Miss Etheridge's eyes flickered to mine, and she smiled enough to let me know I wasn't in trouble. I wondered how old she was. She only had a few lines around her eyes. She was pretty enough, slender and neat, with penny-colored hair. Ella and Lois thought she was a bit standoffish, but I didn't mind that. She was friendly in her quiet way, always glad to stay after school to go over an assignment. And when she read aloud, she was beautiful, her eyes bright and her cheeks pink. Her voice turned into something new and strong and fascinating when she had somebody else's words to read instead of her own.

I asked her once if she enjoyed being a teacher, and she said, "I do, Virgie. I enjoy it quite a bit." Then she asked me if I thought I might want to be a teacher myself someday, and I answered something about thinking I might enjoy it. I really meant that I knew I'd have to do some sort of work, and I thought teaching would be better than nursing. She said I was well able and smart and a few other things I appreciated being called, but all the while I was thinking about how she looked when she read Shakespeare or Emily Dickinson. My cousin Naomi read all the time, but it had never caught fire with me. I wondered if it might if I was a teacher, if it was something in the training.

"Quite a bit." Really, she loved it in a way that lit a bulb in her face. Loved it in some deep, unfamiliar way that was worlds apart from drawing water and washing floors and sewing until your head ached from the bad light.

Of course, she'd have to quit if she decided to get married. And if she kept teaching for too long, she might never marry because she'd be an old maid and nobody would want her. An educated old maid was the worst of all, bottom of the list. Aunt Celia said no man wanted a woman who cared more about books than she did about him. When I was learning long division, the numbers all swam together and I hated it. Aunt Celia said then that it didn't pay to be too smart, that it wouldn't serve me well anyhow. I figured out long division anyway, partly because that made me mad, and partly because when I repeated it to Papa, he said, "It don't pay to be too stupid, neither."

I wondered about Miss Etheridge and how she filled the rest of her day after school was over. What did she do at home with no one to look after? Could you fix a pone of cornbread or fry a chicken for just one person? Or maybe she ate every night in a restaurant, a napkin in her lap and her handbag beside her, and the only thing she had in her kitchen was a pitcher of tea. Sometimes teachers lived with older women who rented them a room. I wondered if she slept in an attic with no windows and the sound of mice running across the floor or if her bedroom window let in the sun and she woke up looking at dogwoods every morning.

Leta WHEN I STRAIGHTENED from stirring the clothes, I saw a woman's boots with the soles coming off. Turned out Lola Lowe was attached to them. She'd never been by the house before, so it took me aback. But before I could even wish her a good morning, she said, "Your girls come by to see me."

That jolted me. "Virgie and Tess?"

"Ain't got no other girls do you?" She didn't smile when she said it, but I didn't take offense. It was her way. If I had such a mess of children, I wouldn't bother too much with politeness, either.

"Reckon not."

I didn't want her to feel unwelcome, but I couldn't leave the clothes. The fire had got going strong and the clothes were boiling, all but chaining me there to the pot. I found myself wishing she'd come a few hours earlier when I'd have welcomed a break.

It took twelve trips from the creek to fill up the iron wash pot sitting at the edge of the hackberries, and after six trips my arms felt like they might pop out of their sockets. Then there was the fire to be stoked underneath, which at least didn't take much strength. While the straw and twigs lit up and teased the bigger logs into burning, I'd sort through the clothes, making piles of the darks and lights and whites. Only needed to boil work clothes, sheets, and anything really dirty. That meant about everything of Jack's.

But once the wood was going, I couldn't afford to waste it by taking a break, no matter how my arms screamed or my face burned or my throat begged for a gulp of cool, dry air instead of the steam pouring out of the pot. The clothes were tossing around, overalls and shirts and socks bobbing over and through the foam. It was the dirtiest load, in need of the longest soak. I'd do sheets separate. The dresses and the rest of the clothes— ones not needing boiling—I'd scrub over the washboard as the others boiled. The clean, sudsy dresses were piled on top of an old blanket, waiting to be rinsed. I looked at Lola, then looked at my piles of clothes, then looked down at the clothes still cooking and gave them a swirl with the old broom handle. Lola spoke before I figured out what I wanted to say.

"No need to stop," she said. She was standing over the soapy pile. "These done?"

"They're done."

"And this the rinsin' tub?"

"It is," I said, nodding at the silver circle filled with clean water. "But don't you be doin' that, Lola. Just pull a chair out from the kitchen and visit with me a spell. I'll take a rest before rinsin' time."

The wash took a whole day's work once a week. It would be nice to have another pair of hands, even if I didn't want to admit it. If the sun was bright, I might be able to finish the ironing before bedtime. But if it turned cloudy and cooler, the ironing would have to wait until tomorrow. I liked to wash in the creek on account of the heat from the fire, but without the girls to help, it wasn't worth the hike there and back.

Lola made an impolite, horselike kind of sound. "I sure as Sam Hill ain't gone sit here and yammer while you work," she said. "I got time—Ellen's mindin' the little ones."

So I kept on stirring while she started dunking clothes piece by piece, drenching them then wringing them out, finally draping them over the clothesline.

"I'll leave you to hang 'em as you like," she said.

We went on like that for a while, no sound but water sloshing and wood crackling. I pulled a pair of overalls out, shook them until the steam died down, and looked them over. I used the tips of my fingers to hold up first one leg, then the other, then smoothed out the bib to where I could see it without any shadows or folds. Mostly clean. No smell to them. I added them to the washtub, which Lola had almost emptied.

"I'll work on scrubbing these," she said. "You get to hangin' when you finish up."

By the time I finished dipping out the sheets, the fire had died down of its own accord. I did as she'd told me, not seeing any sense in commenting or arguing. If she was rinsing, then I ought to be hanging. We got into a good rhythm by the time she started rinsing the second batch of clothes, handing me a piece at a time to pin up. After the heat making my face pour sweat ("perspiration" I always corrected the girls) and the steam making my hair wooly, I welcomed the easiness of hanging. Nothing but snapping and tucking and smoothing.

"Good girls you got," Lola said. "Pretty."

"Nice of you to say so," I said. I looked over and noticed the basket by her feet then—our old straw basket. Lola saw my eyes fix on it and waved one wet hand toward it.

"Girls left this for me with apples in it. Nice of them."

"You didn't have to bring it back. But I thank you."

I did wonder what possessed the girls to take her apples. I hadn't gone by her house in more than a year. Last time I went over I took her some eggs, and I could barely remember even visiting with her. But the last year had been a hard one, and we'd been giving away all of our extra. Between kin on Albert's side and mine, plus whoever happened by the door seeing if we could spare anything, I hadn't even thought to make a visit.

"They wanted to see my new baby." Lola had both hands back in the water.

Now that was more unusual than apples. The girls weren't baby crazy, hadn't ever been ones for doting on dolls or making cow eyes at little ones. And they didn't even know Lola. "Can't imagine what put that in their heads," I said, more to myself than to her.

The bag of clothespins slapped against my hip as I inched my way down the line. My face had already dried, but I could taste the salt on my knuckles when I'd stick one wooden pin in my mouth while I clamped another one on the line.

"I figured they were worried about Frankie," Lola said.

I only looked at her, clothespin between my teeth.

"I couldn't think why they'd come by at first," she kept on. "Thought maybe you'd sent 'em to say hello, but they didn't even know we'd growed up together. I asked Ellen if she was friendly with them, and she said not particularly. Then I thought about that dead baby. Thought they might be feelin' kindly toward babies right now. Maybe needed to see a healthy one."

If the girls had gone by Lola's because of the baby, I thought it was more than needing comfort from the sight of a healthy child. I thought Lola figured that, too. She kept rinsing, her head toward the clothes, her hands as regular as if they were set to music.

"I do keep my children fed, Leta," she said just as I was getting lost in a breeze tussling my hair and whipping my dress. "I care for them right. I'd take the last blanket off my own bed and the food off my own plate for them."

"'Course you would."

"You don't think they're bad off?"

The breeze wasn't as relaxing as it had been. I jostled the pins in their bag, not fishing the next one out yet. "Ain't nobody well-off right now," I told her. "You're doin' the best you can, same as everybody."

"Didn't want you or your family thinkin' poorly of me."

I wanted to slap the fire out of Tess and Virgie. I wanted to tell Lola nobody thought ill of her, though that wasn't true. But there was worse things than being poor. I wanted to tell her I thought she'd handled a hard life with not one lick of luck as well as anybody could have. Her father was a drunk, and her mama never had anything for those kids. She did her best to keep them from him, but Lola'd still come to school with welts across her legs and arms and who knows where else even when she was a little bitty thing. There wasn't anything new about it—I could name a dozen women who had the same story—but it didn't make it any righter just because it wasn't the first time or the first woman. I thought she'd really loved that first boy she married, but then he died not long after her first baby was born. And ten children later, she still didn't have no one to lean on what with the dull-witted fellow she'd married the last time not able to find a job within two hundred miles…and even if he did, she'd never see a penny. I thought for Lola to still be standing, still as good-hearted as she was when we'd played ring-around-the-rosy at Tess's age, was a sign she was made of a rare, precious thing. Of course you didn't say such things.

"I ain't got a bad word to say about you, Lola. Not one."

She might have smiled, but she was looking down, and I

went back to my hanging. I didn't think I'd ever mentioned anything about Lola to the girls—nothing I hate more in this world than gossip—and I wondered what they'd thought of her. Maybe them poking around a bit wasn't a bad thing. Virgie was nearly grown, and she'd been so busy helping around the house, she'd hardly seen the insides of any others. Not other than kin and her own friends. Let her and Tess see how blessed we were by their daddy's work and backbone. Tess had a way of seeing the world as nothing but a playground full of goodies. It made her a happy child quick to smile, but I worried about what kind of adult it might make her. She'd complained one time I sent her on a picnic with just a cold baked potato. She thought it was shameful. I wondered if Lola and her children made her think about that baked potato. I had noticed her talking a little less about magic things at the bottom of the well lately, living a little more in this world than one inside her own head. I hoped that was good.

If my girls wanted to see what the job of living was costing some of these women, I didn't think it would hurt them none.

Virgie HENRY HARKEN MET me after church twice more. I had less and less to say, and he tried harder and harder to buy me candy.

The last time he walked me home, he wanted to stop by and say hello to Dr. Marshall, whose office was across from the bank. Everybody knew he'd had to replace the bank's stained-glass windows three times because he kept backing into it while he was trying to park. We used Dr. Grissom, so all I knew about Dr. Marshall was his driving problems.

"His car's here, so he must be inside," said Henry.

"Y'all use him?" I asked.

"My papa's friends with him, so, yeah, we always do."

"I hear he's a real bad driver."

Henry laughed. "He keeps sayin' 'whoa' instead of stompin' the brakes."

That was the first time Henry ever made me laugh. And he was interesting for that second. But I still didn't like him too much, and I didn't see any reason to work on changing my mind. There was another boy at church who'd started sitting next to me—Tess and I sometimes sat in the pew in front of Mama and Papa—but a lot of times he was late and there wasn't space for him. Those times he'd wait in the back and walk me to the car. But the car was as far as it ever got.

Papa didn't even comment on that boy, and I figured it was the short distance. It stood to reason that the farther a boy walked me, the more serious he was. A nice short trip to the car suited Papa fine. Every now and then a boy might walk me home from school, but Tess would walk with us, and Papa didn't even know about that usually. I'd tell Mama and leave it up to her whether or not she thought it was worth mentioning. She usually didn't, and I was glad. Because as much as Henry had spooked me that first time he showed up at church, soon enough I didn't fret about walking with a boy at all. I relaxed when I realized it didn't mean a boy loved you or wanted to marry you—it meant he thought spending five minutes with you might be a nice way to pass the time. Or maybe he liked looking at you and wanted to look a little longer. Walks were easy, natural things where nothing much was expected of me. Boys loved to talk, and there wasn't much to listening. I could nod and say, "Hmm, I didn't know that," and boys were perfectly happy. Or if I wanted to say something—anything—they were pleased as punch with that, too. It was hard to go wrong once I realized they only wanted to interest me.

So all that walking served its purpose, and in a few weeks I got to where it seemed normal for this boy or that to show up by my side. For some reason Henry asking me (or maybe asking Papa) that first time had given the all clear to the others, and I was grateful to him for that, for somehow pushing me into this thing that had so terrified me.

And I was grateful to him for introducing me to Dr. Marshall.

The doctor answered his door when we knocked that Sunday afternoon, and suddenly I was staring at a tuft of white hair and a big, wide smile with the straightest teeth I'd ever seen. I liked him right away. He shook my hand like I was a grown-up man, with a firm grip instead of taking hold of my fingertips. He said I was lovely and what was I doing with "this Harken fellow."

"I didn't stop by so you could bad-mouth me," Henry said.

"Just thought I should warn her," Dr. Marshall said, looking at me. "He cleans up nice, but this one's trouble." Then he asked if we'd like to look around the office, but I said I had to be getting home for dinner.

"Virgie Moore," he said. "I didn't put it together at first— y'all found that baby."

"Yessir," I said, and I repeated what I'd heard said over and over after anybody mentioned finding the baby. "Isn't it the most terrible thing?"

But he was the only person who didn't come back with the normal response: "It sure was."

Instead he said, "Not the most terrible."

Neither Henry or me answered him, and his smile popped up again, not as big, and I thought how the lines in his face suited him. I couldn't imagine him as a young man.

"I probably shouldn't have said that." He shrugged. "But there's some damn long, drawn-out ways for babies to die. Some awful things to happen. Bein' buried in a well ain't close to the worst I can think of."

"What's the worst you can think of?" asked Henry. Part of me thought he'd watched too much *Frankenstein* and was interested in ghoulish things. And part of me wondered what Dr. Marshall would say.

No smile this time, but the doctor thought on Henry's question for a good while.

"Well," he said to Henry, "I don't know about the worst, but being alone, really alone, is right up there on the list. At least that baby's mother left him with people who'd care about him, who'd do the right thing by him."

And then, without him even looking at me, much less asking me a question, I answered him. The words came out of my mouth smooth and easy and like I talked with grown-ups I'd never met all the time.

What I meant to say, I thought, was that we wanted to know who'd done it.

I said, "We want to know his name."

Dr. Marshall acted like that was just what he'd expected me to say. Like in all the other conversations he had with girls who had babies found in their wells, the girls said exactly that same thing.

"That's it," he said. "That's just the thing."

Tess   I WENT WITH my cousin Emmaline to the Baptist brush arbor. Uncle Bill and Aunt Merilyn sat behind us, but they didn't watch us nearly as close as Mama and Papa did. Plus the brush arbor meant we were outside, with just poles around us, and a roof made of saplings and brush all woven together. It was a homemade tent, pulled straight out of the woods. That right there made their meetings better than ours—you felt wind on your face and sometimes a moth would fly right past you aiming for one of the lanterns hung around the pulpit, which was really only a tall, narrow table with a little shelf near the bottom. Moths would hover around those lanterns, swooping in under the tent all the time the preacher was speaking, like they'd been called to God themselves.

Never mind that lanterns seemed like a bad idea because just one misstep from someone and the whole church service could go up in one whoosh. God's presence was supposed to take care of that.

The good thing about the Baptists was that they sang a lot of the same songs we did. When I went to Methodist meetings with Emmaline, I had to mouth nonsense words to look like I knew what I was doing.

This particular Baptist preacher I didn't care for too much. He was too bony for one thing, with cheekbones that looked like you could slice yourself on them. And he sounded angry, shouting every word. I thought that might have been because he hadn't gotten enough to eat. But his bad mood caught hold of his sermon; he preached about how this earth wasn't our true home and we were only here for a brief time before we passed along to our true home. He talked about not being tied to money or earthly things and how we should shun this world and love the other. I wondered if he was right. I never liked sermons about this world being just a train stop. It had always seemed like a pretty nice place to me, with magnolias and chocolate cake and baby chicks. But it could be that I'd missed something important, that really the earth was a place as full of hatefulness and danger as the preacher said. That the Well Woman was only the beginning of me seeing what was important. Maybe the fairy-eating possums counted for more than the magnolias.

Plenty of other people must have thought it was a real humdinger of a lesson. A handful of women and a couple of men hustled forward, wiping at their eyes, crouching down on the ground in front of the preacher and waiting for him to hug them and pat their shoulders. I'd never seen so many people come forward. I wondered if they all wanted to be baptized, which I thought would be interesting since we'd have to take the lanterns down to the creek. The moths would probably come with us.

But none of them needed to be saved apparently—they only felt overcome by their sins and wanted to be prayed for. The preacher started up "Amazing Grace," then bent down to comfort—or scare, I wasn't really sure—the people who had come forward. Several of the women were crying, and one was bawling so much that her collar was wet. She didn't look the least bit familiar.

"Who is she?" I whispered to Emmaline. Aunt Merilyn and Uncle Bill didn't even glance at me.

"Don't know," she said.

The other men and women were surrounded by clumps of people shaking their hands, folding them in their arms, sometimes kissing their cheeks. That one stranger woman didn't have nobody holding on to her. People would walk past her, pat her and smile at her, but nobody stayed long enough for her to get her own clump going.

Aunt Merilyn must've heard my question. She leaned forward and tapped my shoulder. "I think she's from Brilliant," she whispered. "Moved in with a sister somewhere around here. I forget who."

Well, since she'd gone and broken the rules herself about no talking in church, I decided I'd break them again myself. "She don't have nobody, Aunt Merilyn," I whispered over my shoulder. "Nobody's staying with her."

Aunt Merilyn, bless her heart, didn't even answer me. She looked at the woman awhile, glanced at the other sinners who'd come forward, and hopped up out of her chair and took off toward the front. That caught me by surprise, but I'd pick moving around over being stuck in a chair any day. Plus there was the woman's feelings to consider. I followed Aunt Merilyn, and Emmaline followed me.

The woman was still crying when we got there, and Aunt Merilyn had sat beside her and was smoothing her dark hair back from her face. I wondered how she and Mama learned to comfort people in just the same way. She even alternated stroking with her palm and then her knuckles like Mama did. It wasn't helping the woman much. I couldn't see her face because of how she kept bawling, her shoulders hitching and her breath hiccupping.

"Lord have mercy on me," she said in between gulps and sniffs. "I don't deserve to be forgiven."

"God forgives you anyway, sugar," said Aunt Merilyn. "He loves you."

It didn't seem like a good time to introduce myself.

"He couldn't," said the woman. "Not now. How could he?"

Aunt Merilyn tsk-tsked and kept on smoothing the woman's hair and patting her back, and the woman quieted down a little and didn't say anything else. Aunt Merilyn shooed me and Emmaline back to our seats. I thought to myself that I'd found another person who'd agree that if there were fairies in the forest, there must be an ugly something that ate them.

Albert "YOU HEAR ABOUT those terriers?" I asked Bill Clark.

The paper that morning had a story about two rat terriers killing a pile of seventy-two rats, plus a few field mice the farmer hadn't bothered to count. That was a mess of rats.

"What do you reckon you do once you got seventy-two rats in a pile?" he asked, flashing his teeth.

A big man, a head taller than me, Bill could smile and make you forget all about his size. That grin was part playing-hooky and part tying-the-cats-tails-together. And I thought that smile was one reason his businesses did right well—he had a furniture store, too. He carried good merchandise, priced fair, and he was an honest man. But mostly, everyone loved him. If the stacks of magazines and the fancy cakes didn't get your feet to tapping, one great bellowed "How you?" from Bill would.

"Get ready for the cats to come," I said.

He laughed, deep and slow, not one to rush amusement. The few boxes spread in front of him weren't opened, and he held his pocketknife loose in one hand. "Good to see you, Albert. Been more than a week."

We were in the back of the store, with my kids running wild in the front. They never got tired of coming—the girls'd kiss their uncle on the cheek, then head off to stare at the shelves. Shoes covered the left wall, next to bolts of cloth. Toward the back, cookies sat on shelves as long as two men put together. They were chocolate-covered; yellow-, red-, and green-iced with coconut topping; plain sugar; dipped in sprinkles. I could always find

Virgie there. Tess would be by the soda cracker barrel, looking like she wanted to jump in, and Jack would be looking at knives.

"Leta keeps seein' Merilyn in the daytime 'fore I'm back," I said to my brother-in-law. "Finally decided I'd best come over here if I wanted to catch you."

"Leta here?"

"At the house."

He had a little piano for his daughter to play, and even though I didn't have an eye for such things, I knew Merilyn's dresses were at least a little more fashionable than Leta's. Leta never mentioned it. I couldn't have afforded a piano, but then again, my girls weren't so musical, so I didn't lose much sleep over it. His family had plenty, but he wasn't la-tee-da. Lord, Walter Bankhead had built a house that cost $20,000 in Jasper. For that money, he better have contracted with God Almighty for streets paved with gold and some pearly white gates.

"Looks like you're doin' good business."

Bill stopped moving altogether, his back still to me, and finally hung his head and let out a gust of breath. "Can't make it another year at this rate. Gone have to close up."

I wouldn't have been more shocked if he'd told me at night he turned himself into a possum and hung from his tail. "That don't make no sense. Not ten minutes goes by that somebody's not gettin' somethin' rung up at the cash register."

He ran a wide, wrinkled hand over his head. "They're not payin'."

I understood then, and I felt ashamed for begrudging him that piano. "How much you lettin' everybody run up on credit?"

"Much as they need. I'm not gone tell somebody he can't feed his children just because the mines are closin' up."

"How much you figure you're owed?"

He ran his tongue over his teeth.

"You know I ain't sayin' nothin' to nobody," I said.

"Figure a few dozen owe me two or three hundred apiece. A few thousand altogether."

"Merilyn knows you're doin' it," I said, sure that she did.

"'Course. She'd string me up if I wasn't. You see her turnin' away a man trying to buy groceries?"

I didn't bother to answer. "How bad is it?"

He shrugged. "Oh, it won't mean no food on the table. We're still better off than most. I'm plannin' to close the furniture store next month—maybe hold on a little longer. General store here might make it to spring."

"Can't think of no way to help you." Those kinds of numbers he was talking were too big to imagine. Any help I could give wouldn't be much more than candy money for the kids.

"Nah—I wouldn't ask you to. I shouldn't have even brought it up, only it's weighin' heavy on me lately. It feels pretty good to say the words out loud."

"Your family know?"

"Not the whole of it."

"I'll be prayin' for y'all, hopin' that things turn around." Things turning around for him would mean things turning around for the whole town, of course, so there were plenty of prayers being directed along those lines even without me.

"It'll all work out," he said. "I got other ideas for what might come next." His smile was back and his hands busy for the first time since he brought up the store. I knew he wanted me to ask about those other ideas of his, so I did, and he slit a couple more boxes without looking up.

"Not quite ready to say yet," he said finally. Well, that lifted the mood. It was pure Bill Clark, leading and teasing like you would a horse with a sugar cube. He wanted me to press him for what was on his mind, and I wasn't going to do it. "Bill, you was born to torment people. I never seen anybody who liked to tell half a story and then just wait for people to froth at the mouth."

"More likely I'm waitin' for you to help me with these boxes." He nodded toward a stack three boxes high lined up against the wall.

I shook my head at him, and crossed over behind his inventory-sorting table. He waved a hand toward a few medium-size cardboard boxes on one end, and we each bent down, knees cracking like dead leaves, and grabbed one.

"How's Tess doin'?" he asked, shirt pulled tight across his back.

"Reckon she's better."

"Must've been hard on her. Merilyn told me she hadn't quite shook the nightmares."

"They're better at least." We set down our loads and went back for more.

"I 'member Merilyn always rubbed the girls' ears when they had bad dreams. Swore it calmed them."

"Leta's done that. Gave her warm milk, too. Somethin' must've took—ain't heard her yellin' or moanin' lately."

Bill always kept a notepad in his front pocket, tucked in with a blue fountain pen that sprang a leak fairly often. Wasn't uncommon to see him with a bright white shirt, ironed smooth as a sheet of paper, and a blue stain oozing down his chest. I could see a blue speck already. After three boxes apiece, I stood back while he slit the top of one and started pulling out handfuls of white socks. His lips moved as he pulled out pair after pair, and soon he flipped open that notebook.

"Seventy-five pair," he said. "Ought to be seventy-five more black ones."

He opened the next box, big fingers prying the flaps apart after his knife did its job. "People might cut back on their bread or their coffee or even their shoes, but you just about got to buy some new socks pretty regular," he said. Black socks piled up next to the white pile. "You know you was lucky the well is stream-fed so it didn't go bad. This ain't no time to have to be diggin' a new well."

I hadn't spent much time thinking of it from that side. "You think somebody was hopin' to turn the water?"

His glanced over, knife in hand. "Didn't say that. Didn't

mean it, either. I don't figure it means anything other than some woman lost her mind."

"And in a month nobody around here's noticed a crazy woman wanderin' around missin' a baby?"

"Even so." The next box was jammed full of buttons. Looked like a rainbow got hammered to smithereens.

"Must be some reason they chose our house," I tried again. I wouldn't have minded hearing more than two words worth of thoughts.

"Nah. Don't need to be a reason when a mind's troubled."

When I left to go collect the children from the front of the store, he was still sifting through rainbow bits. Funny, I thought during the few steps I had between leaving Bill and gathering up the kids, that he wasn't more help filling in pieces to the puzzle. For a businessman, more education than me and more money, he didn't seem to see much of a puzzle at all.

I headed on back home with the kids, dragging them away from the soda crackers and penny candy and the rows of buttons. They ran a little ahead of me most of the way, and I liked following their little footprints in the dust.

I smelled supper the minute I walked inside, and Leta must have heard the screen door creak, because she called as soon as I had both feet inside. Hot yeast rolls and thick slices of tomatoes and hunks of Vidalia and a pot of white beans and some fried squash. She'd outdone herself.

No man could have a better-looking bunch of kids. Sometimes sitting down to eat supper—even though Leta made fun of me for eating like somebody might snatch the plate away from me at any second—I'd forget to take a bite for looking at the children. I'd think all of a sudden that Tess's hair was blacker than it used to be or that Jack didn't used to have that many freckles on his nose or that Virgie had a way of chewing on her lip that reminded me of my mother. You'd think I'd have learned my own kids after all those years, but I was always finding something new.

And the dinner table was about the only time I ever saw them all together and staying still.

There was something perfect about a spoon of thick heavy beans and a bite of sweet onion. That mix of hot and cold, soft and crisp. Leta was a great cook, good as any woman I'd ever known, but the real mystery was how she knew what should fit together, what mix of foods made the right mouthful. Beans and onion. Squash and tomato. It was the different tastes together, the ones that it didn't make no sense at all to stick on the same fork, that your tongue really remembered.

6 Picking Cotton

Jack IN 1934, AFTER HE HAD TO CLOSE THE STORE,
Uncle Bill ran for the state legislature and won. Toward the
end of the Depression, he tracked down the addresses of miners
who'd moved on, and he wrote more than fifty of them letters.
They'd say, "Dear Tom: You owe me $375.00 for your grocery bill.
If you'd pay me $150, I'll be willing to cancel the debt."

Just a short, simple letter with a different number and name
on each.

I saw that list of names and addresses written out in Uncle
Bill's chicken scratch on lined sheets of Aunt Merilyn's station-
ary. He typed the letters, and he kept the list of names to check
through as he got back responses.

Some never wrote back. Some sent him $5 at a time, saying
they appreciated his understanding and would pay him back
in installments. One man wrote, "You fed my family when they
would have starved. I'll pay you every cent I owe." It took him
five years, but he did.

That man was the only one who got a blue circle drawn
around his name on Uncle Bill's list. I'd see it every time I passed
that sheet of paper tacked on Uncle Bill's rolltop desk, right
next to his Ships of the Navy calendar. I still remember his name,
can still see it with the blue cutting through the top of the "t"s:
Norman Bett.

Uncle Bill would call out that name when he got a payment—
"Here's one from old Norman!"

I don't know if there's anyone left who knew Norman, who could pick him out in some faded, dog-eared picture that sat for too long in a shoe box or the bottom of a drawer. But his name is carved into my head, more than just a bunch of letters strung together.

His name hasn't faded at all.

Mama's sister Emmaline died at eighteen, and Aunt Merilyn named her youngest daughter for her. That daughter's granddaughter named her youngest daughter Emmaline. When the family and friends packed into a tiny maternity-ward room in Boston, Massachusetts, in 2004, text-messaging the good news while they waited their turn to tug at the fingers of a dark-headed baby, they were also touching some part of a girl who died quietly on top of a handmade quilt in 1906.

Tess WITH SCHOOL CLOSED for cotton picking, we usually helped out at the house, maybe walked up the mountain or took our time collecting the mail if we were lucky. Mama'd have plenty for me and Virgie to do—probably have us scrub the floors—and Jack would catch frogs or fish, something that wasn't work. But we never picked cotton—it was hard work, Papa said, not for children, and the people living on the farm took care of it.

But in front of the fire, one night that fall, Papa crooked his finger at the three of us after he got our attention by whistling high and quick. We were sitting knee to knee not an arm's length from the fireplace, heat sponges with heavy eyelids. (I wondered if being drunk was like being too close to the fire. I'd heard people say whiskey burned their throats. And when I went over to Marianne's house one time, it turned out her father kept some homebrew in the butter churn on the porch and somehow it got knocked over and when Marianne and me went outside, the cat had gotten into the mess and was zigzagging all over the porch. It nearly hit the wall. I didn't mention that to Mama and Papa. But that was how I felt when I tried to walk from the fire to bed. It seemed to me that sometimes the police might mistake somebody good and warm for being good and drunk.)

We all jerked at Papa's whistle, and we started to spin around to face his chair. But he held his hand up and slid out of the rocker, his knees cracking as he eased down to the floor. He made a face.

"Y'all gone have to heft him up," Mama said, not looking up from her mending.

"I'll heft you," said Jack right away, looking pleased to be eye to eye with Papa. Papa snatched him up and threw him over his shoulder, Jack laughing and wailing and kicking.

"How 'bout I heft you?"

I remembered Papa holding my wrists in one hand and Virgie's in his other, lifting us off the ground 'til we were over his head. He could do it until we got off balance—down, up, ground, sky, Papa's knees, Papa's grin. He said he needed to get his exercise so he wouldn't get tired and drop his shovel.

He set Jack on his feet, and Jack was as red as a sugar beet from the heat and the being upside down. "Listen here," said Papa. "I've got a deal to make you. If y'all want to go pick cotton tomorrow, you can keep the money from whatever you pick. I'm gone help the Talberts, but we won't be able to get it all. Last season a quarter of it sat there and rotted."

"You don't ever let us pick cotton," said Virgie. Which all of us already knew, so I don't know why she bothered saying it.

"It wouldn't hurt you to try it once," he said, looking at Mama.

"You can see what a day's like for little girls and boys who do have to pick it," she said.

She and Papa looked at each other and I hoped I could remember to ask Virgie later if she knew what that look meant.

"As much as we can pick?" asked Jack.

"Yep," said Papa.

"We don't know how," I said.

"I'll teach you," he answered. "But we need to be out by six tomorrow."

We never got to spend time with Papa alone. Sometimes he and Jack would work in the garden together, or maybe once a year he'd carry me or Virgie to town with nobody else in the car. But a whole day with Papa? I couldn't remember one.

"So we'll eat breakfast all together?" asked Virgie, half to herself.

"It's up to your mama." Papa had his hands on the seat of the rocker, heaving himself back to his feet.

"Sure will. Don't see no reason not to," Mama said. "If your papa's not still on that floor." She smiled a little, just a curve of her mouth. I about never saw Mama's teeth.

Papa didn't answer her, only gave one big push and snapped to his feet. He walked over to Mama's chair as calm as you please and took her needle and sock from her hands. She managed to say, "What…?" before he pulled her to her feet, bent low, and tossed her over his shoulder.

"Albert Moore!" she shrieked. "I swannee, you deserve to be horsewhipped! Put me down!" She didn't kick and pound on Papa's back like Jack did, but she wiggled a little. Her braid twisted out of its ball and hung nearly to the floor. The bottoms of her feet were a strange sight from that angle, tiny, with dirty heels and toes and pale arches.

Me, Jack, and Virgie whooped and jumped up ourselves. We'd never seen Mama off the ground before. "Albert!" she called again. Then he turned and winked at us, bent down again, halfway sitting, and in one movement he pulled her into his arms, sat in her chair, and tugged her into his lap. She really started wriggling that time, tugging at his hands around her waist. "The children, Albert," she said, her face pink.

"You can sit on his lap, Mama," piped up Jack. "We don't mind none."

Mama huffed and stopped struggling. She gave that same half smile to Papa, and pretty soon he took his hands from around her waist, resting them on her hips. She was up like a shot, across the room before Papa even got out a laugh. His laugh was dry and deep, like the sound of rubbing your hand over his whiskers.

"Masher," Mama said. She walked back over, looking like she'd bolt any second, making a circle around him to collect her sewing. He just leaned back and grinned. Socks and threaded needle in hand, Mama stopped and turned toward us, looked down at Papa, and ran her hand through his hair. For just one second, she left her still fingers there, but then she moved them quick, glaring down at him until he got out of her chair.

The next morning we headed out to the farm, walking instead of driving because it was bright and fine, even with the sun only beginning to peek out. The farm had sections of watermelon and corn, big chunks of land for them, but it was the cotton that was ripe for picking. Every plant had a very strict schedule.

Once we were in front of the cotton, it was almost all we could see—rows and rows of it, with the plain wood house and the dirt yard where the Talberts lived stuck there like an after-thought. I saw two hats—both straw and wide-brimmed—moving down the rows. Papa must've, too, because he hollered, "We'll start on the far rows," and with that, Mr. and Mrs. Talbert popped out from the cotton. Short and stubby, Mrs. Talbert looked like a mushroom with that hat.

"We'll meet up with you somewhere near the middle," yelled back Mr. Talbert. "Least I hope we do."

That was all we said to them. Papa took us to the other side of the cotton field. He took hold of the first plant and pulled a stalk toward us. It was a cloud on a stick, a little dirty, but soft looking and puffy. It would be like picking a pillow. Papa explained how to pull the fluff out of the prickly boll, prying it out in one twist. He popped it in Jack's sack, saying that one was for free. He assigned me and Jack to opposite sides of the same row and told Virgie to take the next one with him. I wished I was on the row with Papa. But then as soon as I had time to be jealous, he and Virgie were both back on our row.

"Take care and don't get the brown part in with the cotton," he said. "Shouldn't be nothing but white when we take it to the gin."

I'd wasted my time worrying about Virgie getting to spend more time with Papa than I did—he was off down their row, tossing cotton in his sack, before any of us had even opened our sacks.

"Y'all alright?" he called back. He picked so fast his hand was a blur.

"Yessir," we all said, even though none of us had picked any. I wrapped my finger around my first boll. It didn't feel a bit like a pillow; it was tough and sticky, and it fought to keep its piece of fuzz.

"Ouch," said Jack next to me. "It bites."

We went a few more feet, stooped and slow, wedging our fingertips under the cotton puffs and trying to get more softness than sticker. The sun hadn't cleared the tops of the rows, and my fingers already felt raw. I checked for blood and didn't see any. I heard rustling from Virgie's row, but she didn't say anything.

"Doin' alright, Virgie?" I looked over, shoving the hair around my face back toward my ribbon.

"Tryin' to get the hang of it."

"My fingers hurt," said Jack.

"We've hardly gotten past where we started," I said. I stood up all the way and tried to retie my ribbon. "And my hair's already coming apart. Virgie..."

She was knocking my hands away before I finished my sentence. She tied one tight pigtail, almost hurting my head. But I knew it would stay. "There," she said. "And don't look towards the end of the row. It only makes it go slower. Just look at one plant at a time. Then you'll lose track."

We went on like that, awkward and fumbling, until I finally did see a drop of blood on a piece of cotton. My fingers were

bright red, tender, and scratched in several places. I felt proud.
I stuck the bloody cotton on the finger that was dripping
and pulled the ribbon out of my hair to tie it around the cotton.
I couldn't do all that work and stain the cotton.

The twigs and rocks cut into my knees even through my
skirt, and my back ached.

"Virgie," I called over the cotton. "Did I tell you about that
woman at the revival?"

"Nuh-uh," she said.

I stood up, but I could hear her still rustling, so I tried to
pick while I talked. "This woman nobody knows came down
front and cried and cried and when me and Aunt Merilyn went
down there, she said she'd sinned and God shouldn't love her
anymore."

"You went forward?"

"No, not like to repent. Aunt Merilyn went to comfort her,
and I went with her. But doesn't that sound sort of odd to you?
Her talkin' about God not lovin' her?"

"Did you recognize her?"

"Well, no. But she was sittin' down and I couldn't tell much
about her with her all hunched over." I wiped my forehead, and
a little shower of sweat rained down.

"Recognize her from what?" asked Jack, his sack of cotton
forgotten. "From puttin' that baby in our well?"

"Hush, Jack," I said. "You're too little to talk about this."

"I am not."

"Yes, you are. Quit interruptin'."

"I want to know who did it," he said.

"You'll end up with lots more cotton than Tess will since
she's busy runnin' her mouth," said Virgie.

That made him smile, and he went back to picking.

"We don't know her?" asked Virgie.

"Aunt Merilyn says she's somebody's sister from Brilliant."

"But it doesn't make any sense that she'd come to our well
then. Why would somebody we don't know pick our well?"

We thought on that for a while. A gnat flew in my eye and I dug it out tangled in a little ball of sleep.

"She was passin' by?" said Jack. Neither of us answered him, but I couldn't think of a better answer.

"It can't be her," Virgie finally said. "That woman could have been upset at yellin' at her little ones or havin' some bad thought about her neighbor. Could be anything."

I couldn't argue with her, and I knew part of me just didn't want to let go of the notion that the Well Woman wasn't somebody we nodded at every day. Soon I stopped thinking about it and didn't have nothing but cotton on my mind and in my hands and even in my mouth. The sun shone midmorning, and I still couldn't seem to lose track of time. I'd never seen a slower moving sun. We weren't talking, only picking and stooping and tossing. I knew Negroes used to sing in the fields while they picked cotton. I couldn't figure out why they'd do that. I didn't feel a bit like singing. The back of my dress was wet with sweat. Jack's hands were bleeding, I'd noticed. Virgie hadn't seen. He had cotton wrapped around them as a bandage.

I stood and stretched, arching backward. Jack threw down his sack then, looking very serious. "I don't think I'm much cut out for cotton picking," he said.

"Baby," I said.

He looked at his sack like he wanted to pick it up again, then stuck out his tongue at me. "You keep on going, then, smarty. You won't have any fingers left."

I looked at him and looked at my fingers. I'd have loved to prove him wrong, but then he'd get to sit and relax and cool off while I kept sweating and bleeding, and that didn't seem fair at all.

"I don't care for it myself," I announced.

Virgie was just a shadow and a hat from the other side of the cotton. (She didn't want to get sun on her face, but I wouldn't let Mama put a hat on me. She said if I wanted to be ugly and wrinkled by high school, she wouldn't stop me. Then it was too late to say I'd changed my mind.) "I don't like it much, either," said Virgie soon enough.

We stood looking at one another for all of ten seconds, picked up our sacks, and went to find Papa to tell him that we were through with picking. He didn't seem surprised. And since he didn't mind none, we plopped ourselves down under a pecan tree, comparing bloody fingers and feeling like nobody ever deserved a nice warm patch of grass more than we did. We went on and took out the biscuits Mama had packed for us, figuring it was close enough to lunchtime. Papa used to make the best sausage, and I missed it. Empty biscuits weren't the same. He had a smokehouse set up against the barn, and the sausage came from it. I knew there was more to it, that you took pig parts and stuffed them in another pig part, but I didn't care to hear about it once Papa started explaining it.

We'd all taken just a bite or two when we looked up and saw a strange boy and girl standing in front of us. We didn't even see them coming. Neither of them was wearing shoes, but it was a nice day, and I didn't care for shoes myself.

"Those sausage?" asked the boy. Not even a "hello."

"Yep," said me and Jack at the same time.

"You belong to Mr. Moore?" the girl asked.

"He's our father," Virgie said. It was written plain across her face that she thought it was a rude question.

"We live here," said the boy.

About then I saw they had sacks like ours, only stuffed full of cotton.

"You been pickin' cotton, too?" I said. "We did it for the first time just now."

They looked at us like we were simpleminded when I showed them my fingers and Jack stuck his out, too. Their fingers were calloused and tough like Papa's, and they were much browner than us, even Jack, who was brown as a nut. But even being that brown, something was off with their color. They had circles under their eyes like Papa when he'd worked double shifts and come up tired and short on sunlight. And their hair wasn't blond or black or brown, but like it hadn't been painted with any color at all.

"You never picked before?" the girl asked. I noticed then that her dress was made from a bleached-out flour sack same as our dish towels. "We always help Mama and Daddy."

"The Talberts?" asked Virgie.

They nodded, and the boy wrinkled his forehead at our cotton sacks.

"You might get a dollar for all that," he said, not looking too sure about it. "Maybe less. Ain't got but a few pounds in there."

"We can both pick three dollars a day," said the girl.

Pretty soon they stopped looking at our sacks, though, and went back to looking at our biscuits.

"You eatin' lunch already?" asked the girl. "We don't stop for lunch. Work from can to can't."

She shook her head at us when we didn't say anything. "When you can see to when you can't. Light to dark."

We each only had one biscuit, but we should have halved them and shared, really. We didn't. And even though I felt guilty about them not having any lunch, mainly I wanted them to go away so I wouldn't have to taste the guilt along with the biscuit. And it went away real fast—as soon as those children got out of sight. They turned around and walked back to the cotton rows and didn't even say "nice to meet you." None of us said anything about them. We swallowed our last bites and licked our fingers, alright with tasting a little blood and dirt and cotton if it meant getting those last crumbs. I dabbed at the crumbs on my skirt with my wet finger, and Virgie swept hers into the grass. Then the guilt came back up like heartburn.

I'd never had somebody ask me for food. People came to the door often enough, but really they were there for Mama and Papa. They decided who got a few eggs or a plate of beans or a whole chicken. It had been like that as long as I could remember, with people coming to the door, and you for certain gave them something.

Me and Virgie and Jack were supposed to be the kind of people who helped out. But we didn't give those Talbert children nothing. That pained me, not just from the guilt, but because it took something so simple and confused it. I hated that, even though I wasn't supposed to hate.

Ever since that baby died, pieces didn't fit together as well as they used to. Some things were convoluted before, of course. Papa was the strongest man in the world, so of course nothing could hurt him, but he was cracked all over from the mines. God was good, but he might decide to send you to hell. Getting baptized in the river cleaned your soul, but I still had to take a bath on Saturday nights even if I'd just been swimming.

But usually I tried to ignore it when the pieces didn't come together quite right, even when something big and heavy poked at the edge of my mind and tried to shove its way in. Especially then. When I went over to Missy Summerfield's house for lunch one day—Mama said I could—I found out they had more than a maid. They had a polished table nearly as wide as our kitchen with a red and white china bowl full of oranges in the middle. Seven oranges, so many of them that they might mold before the Summerfields got around to eating them all, and somehow I didn't think they would miss the oranges even if that did happen. We only got an orange in our Christmas stocking.

I'd also been over there on Sunday afternoons when Missy's older sister had boys calling, and Missy would have me upstairs while she powdered her sister's back so she'd stay clean and sweet-smelling during a whole afternoon of beaus. I was fascinated by that powder drifting through the air when Missy patted the puff against her sister's back.

The other thing that I liked about Missy's—and that I'd figured out on a visit before I saw that bowl of oranges—was that they had chicken or pork chops or some thick slab of meat with every meal. So I never minded being asked to dinner. Everybody got served by the maid, a thin Negro woman with a white kerchief on her head who said "Miss Missy" when she was talking to Missy. That struck me as funny. The day of the oranges, I thought they must live the best lives in the world. I was thinking about asking for an orange for dessert when the maid asked me if I'd like a slice of fresh tomato. I said, "Yes, ma'am."

Missy corrected me right in front of the maid: "Don't say 'ma'am' to her. We don't do that."

Papa always told us to say "ma'am" to any grown woman, and I thought it was right rude not to. But I knew Missy's parents had told her that being a Negro cancelled out being a grown-up. So one of us had parents that told us wrong, and of course I knew it must be the Summerfields but I figured she felt just as sure it was mine. After that I tried to stay away from the maid when I was visiting Missy because I never figured out whether I would still call her ma'am or not. That was the easiest way, but something pushed at me, nagging me that there was more to it. I ignored the push.

Some other big, heavy thought shoved at me after those Talbert children left, or maybe a bunch of thoughts stuck together. A picture in my head of Lola Lowe's bunch of children eating just blackberries and bread. Whatever it was, it was too big to fit in my head. We told Papa about the children when he came over an hour or so later for his own sausage and biscuit, and I realized I didn't even know their names. Just called them those Talbert children, and that seemed almost as bad as hogging my biscuit.

But Papa wasn't mad at us for not giving them any. "I'll bring them somethin' special," he said. "Don't you worry about it no more."

And sure enough, we had enough for breakfast the next morning, but he'd given them the rest of that sausage. I wasn't even sorry not to have more of it, and the not-feeling-sorry made me feel more Christian, like I might still be good after all.

Albert I'D BEEN THINKING about those boys in Scottsboro.

Back in March, nine Negro boys were headed from Chattanooga to Memphis, and they ended up with two white girls in a railroad car. Two white girls in men's clothes. The girls said the Negroes raped them, and wasn't long after they got hauled to jail at Scottsboro that eight out of the nine of them got sentenced to die. Jury only held off on a twelve-year-old, and that wasn't from lack of trying. I'd heard the colored fellows at Galloway talk about it, about how those girls were selling their bodies but just embarrassed to be caught with colored men. Most of us white men—me included—figured the girls were honest, and the boys weren't fit to live.

I'd always thought that all that mattered was how a body treated people. Colored man, white man, polka-dotted man, I was gone treat them fair and kind. And that was that. Laws and such didn't concern me—they was only fences and cords arranged just so, and I couldn't see why it mattered where they were set up. I'd even mostly fall into wherever the cords pointed me. Because inside them, I was acting right.

Tess and those biscuits. She hadn't acted at all, hadn't shared with those poor Talberts. But she'd thought on it, felt guilty about it, known she should do something different. It made me wonder about the difference between doing and thinking. I'd never have figured Jonah to work out a problem I couldn't, to see inside that woman's head so clear. Now Bill, him being so successful, him I would've thought to have all kinds of insight. I'd never have considered it being the other way around. It shook me up to keep hearing Jonah's words in my head over and over when I was trying to make sense of that woman and her baby.

Long as I didn't do nobody ill, separate lines and separate churches and separate lives didn't matter much. Probably mattered to those Scottsboro boys, all wrapped up in those cords I didn't care about. And me, I was feeling tangled up a tad myself.

Leta   HARD TO BELIEVE droppings had anything to do with a rose. On a fall day with a strong wind, the petals would fall in dainty red designs, and I'd have to snatch them up before I spread the manure. Sometimes Tess would see me with the wheelbarrow down at the animal pens, and she'd hurry out and scoop up the petals, wanting to dry them or toss them in the air. She loved them. I wasn't so attached, but if I left them on the ground, it'd allow for black-spot fungus. So I saved the petals from the shovelfuls of horse manure—the best kind of manure. I'd fertilize the roses good at the start of warm weather and at the end of it, carting a wheelbarrowful and spreading it thick, then chopping it into the soil.

I picked off the dead flowers, looked them over for traces of brown on the stem. Bugs and rot got to them easier if anything dead stayed around. Didn't want to overprune them—roses could go rotten from too much attention just like children could. Usually I'd fit them in wherever I had a hole in my day, a quick check for dead leaves, maybe give them a can of water. But on fertilizing days, I'd spoil myself a bit along with my roses. Most everything I did had to be done in a hurry, but this I didn't rush. I laid out the shovelfuls dead even, smoothed them out like I was making a layer cake. I looked at every bloom, every stem to check for disease or bugs. I leaned in to breathe in the rose air. They were all red but for one dark pink one. I let Virgie talk me into that one.

My papa couldn't grow roses worth a flip. He struggled even with the vegetable garden. One time he grew radishes as big as oranges, completely hollow on the inside. He said the problem was they grew so fast that they didn't have time to fill up. He'd worked the mines when he was younger, but by the time I came around, he farmed full-time, so you'd have thought he'd get the hang of it.

My mother had started the rosebushes, planting one special for each of us. She'd planted me a pink tea rose before she died, although I couldn't remember her doing it. But the bush itself was one of my first memories. I was so fond of it that the same year I started school, I started taking rose clippings and tending them in a bucket. Since my older sisters had only barely managed to keep their own roses alive, I took over when I was eight or nine.

Funny how even with sunshine falling straight on them, the petals are always cool.

Now when I was a little thing, I did like pink. I was the youngest, so my sisters took care of most of the housework, and that left me free to tend the roses. They coddled me a bit, too, me being the baby, and they'd try to keep from laying any work on my shoulders even after I was old enough. So I had years steeped in my roses from morning until night, talking to them when I wasn't tending to them. I had names for them that I never told my sisters about—Esmerelda for the flashy bright pink one desperate for attention; Beulah for the solid, strong red; Virginia for the delicate white one that'd wilt with too much sun. I'd prick my finger on them and we'd be blood sisters. I'd put rose petals in my pillow case so I could smell them while I slept.

It was an odd attachment that puzzled me: the grown-up married me looking back on it from a distance. I had three sisters who doted on me, but I told my secrets to the roses. They were so beautiful, and they pulled you in every which way—the smell of them, the look of them, the softness of them. And they were the only part of the house that still had my mother printed on them, or at least I felt that way then. I suppose their smell and feel became hers in my mind. Janie, two years older than me, would sit with me—she couldn't remember Mama much neither, so we'd imagine her together. (I did have the one clear memory of her lying dead on the bed, but I mostly kept it covered and put away.) We were always wanting Merilyn and Emmaline to tell us stories about her. But since they were busy cooking the meals and running the house, we were on our own a lot. We'd collect fallen petals and try to make a carpet, pushing each petal into the ground after we softened it with a little water.

I was lucky to have those years, so fanciful and pointless. My last year in grammar school, though, Janie got typhoid. She'd been tired and poorly, but when she showed Papa the rose-colored spots on her sides and belly, he nearly knocked over his chair snatching her up and yelling for my brother to hitch up the mule and go find the doctor.

Later on, I heard that the bad sewage in town was to blame. Some of the business houses and hotels downtown emptied directly into the storm sewers, giving off an awful smell. You'd walk past a manhole, and you'd swear you'd been picked up and set in an outhouse. Plenty of children fought off the runs and dysentery, but that summer was the first my papa could remember that typhoid caught on.

At any rate, we all took antityphoid serum, which I guess we should've had anyway, and I could hardly sleep for the ache in my arm. I shook with fever for the next couple of days, cold under all my blankets, and wondered if I'd got the typhoid. But they told me it wasn't sickness, it was just from the serum. It turned out our oldest sister, Emmaline, had got it, though—you didn't hardly ever see her without Janie right at her heels. Emmaline dressed us all in the morning, packed our lunch buckets, put cold rags on our heads when we had fever. She was busy every minute, and looking back, she should have had a beau already instead of minding us. But she was always there, first up in the morning and last in bed at night. She gave us lemon juice and honey for sore throats. And she could do four or five cartwheels in a row.

Janie got better bit by bit, but Emmaline died. I woke up one morning and Papa was standing in the doorway telling us all she'd died in the night.

Her rosebush was the white one, Virginia. I cut off ten long stems for the funeral, even trimmed off all the thorns, meaning to lay them in the casket. But my nerves on end, I picked them apart as I stood listening to the preacher. Emmaline was blurry to me even by the time I had Virgie—I remembered she was pretty, but I could hardly picture a single feature. And all we had was one family photograph with her in it, a square no bigger than a lady's compact, taken before I was born. She's not even smiling, though I do remember her having a crooked, catchy smile. Of course, nobody wanted to hold a smile long enough for those photos to take, so if you judged by that little square, we were sure enough a sober, grim-faced family.

Roses last long into the fall, too, another thing that pleased me as a girl and as a woman. My jasmine smells as sweet, but once there's a nip in the air, it falls to pieces. Still and all, I've always loved the scent of it drifting into the kitchen. I never let the girls touch the jasmine, which I planted right near the lavender bush so the smells would mix.

Papa was sort of lost with all those girls, but he was a kind man. His fingers always had dirt under them, not coal stain like Albert's, and he had a fine singing voice that we'd wake up to in the morning sometimes. Once he built a trellis for me when I wanted to try climbing roses, and the only thing I really remember from that afternoon is when Papa tried to fix my pigtail. He did an awful job, his big fingers clumsy with the ribbon, and the pigtail stuck off to the side of my head. I left it in anyway.

Albert hadn't ever tried fixing the girls' hair as far as I knew. I was sure he'd do a pitiful job of it. Much as he loved my hair, loved touching it, brushing it off my face. Covering his hands with it, even, when we were first married and it was a strange new thing for him to wake up with a pillow-full of hair all around him.

I still let it down at night, of course, but I didn't think he'd had much time to notice my hair in a long spell. A boy might stare at some young girl's hair, but there wasn't such staring between a man and his wife.

I used to love Albert's shoulders. I'd push as hard as I could at the muscle, seeing if I could make it give. If my hair was fascinating to him, the hardness of his shoulders (arms and back just as solid) was a new world to me. You could look at a man's shoulders all day long and never know they felt like that.

I stepped on a rock just sharp enough to make me look down and notice the filthiness of my feet. Covered in dust and—I lifted one behind me—black on the bottoms. Tess would love to see me, love to be able to tell me to go wash my feet. If I could remember, I'd let her catch me before I cleaned up.

All the softness of my roses rubbed off soon enough. Emmaline's dying started it. Then Papa took sick the year after Albert and me married. It was different than when Emmaline died: Then nobody came to call, keeping their distance from the house. With Papa gone, both his house and our house was full up, with the dinner table piled high with casseroles and chicken and pies and cakes. It took me months before I could taste sugar without feeling queasy.

I worked my way down the row of roses, curving around the east side of the house. Before I moved on to the section under the kitchen window, I sized up what I'd already done, making sure I'd fertilized them all even and smooth. I had, but I hefted the shovel again and spread a little extra manure on Virgie's bush. It had been planted last, after she asked for a pink one for her birthday. The blooms were smaller than the rest, and I worried that it wasn't getting enough sun, maybe catching too much shade from the eaves.

That same year Papa passed away, Robert, the only boy among us, died in the Great War when he was nineteen. That made two out of the five of us children gone. Funny that the roses never made me think about dying, even though we always cut bunches of them to take to the cemetery.

Instead I found myself drifting off while I pruned them, and I'd feel Emmaline standing next to me, calm and quiet. Sometimes I'd fancy I felt Papa standing behind me, that I'd feel him tug my hair, trying to make me jump. Or I'd imagine Janie scampering down the steps, begging to help me with the cuttings. Ideas not fit for anything. I kept them out of the house, but they could creep up on me outside.

I always hoped that I'd die in summertime, or fall maybe.

All my papa could talk about his last few weeks was how much he wanted to taste a pear, crisp and juicy. It was January, and the closest we could get was some pear preserves on toast. With your teeth about gone and your stomach not handling much, I could see how fruit would be on your mind, how a taste of sunshine and breeze might hold you over when you're wrapped up in blankets, sore from not leaving the bed for so long. When you pass away in the summer, they can bring the summer in to you. Pears and nectarines and peaches and tomatoes, as much as can fit on your bed stand. They could leave a big enough pile so you could feed yourself for days—you wouldn't even be much trouble.

Albert WE WAS LUCKY to have a cage. In the push mines, those men had to crawl on their knees or even their bellies to get to the mine face, not making a red cent for all that time and effort. We had the one trip down.

The wire cage took me down, and I could imagine Ole Sol operating it in the next life, taking you past the coal and down into the fire below. But every morning we stopped at the midpoint— somewhere below land but a little above hell. I stepped into the dark, stooping over right away so I wouldn't hit my head, and headed toward the last room, lights bobbing ahead of me and around me and behind me. Carbide made for underground lightning bugs, with no man recognizable from more than a few yards away unless you could tell him by the height of his lamp.

The light from my own cap spread out in front of me. It flashed over the roof made of coal and rock, shored up with timbers, pillars of left-behind rock and coal shooting down from the ceiling to hold it up as the coal was cut out. As section foreman, I'd made the marks on the walls myself yesterday evening, then the coal-cutting machine had come through the room after we'd cleared out, ripping cuts in the seam with that circle of dull teeth. It struck the first blow, riled up the coal, let it know who was boss. Then came the men drilling holes for the dynamite, holes about six or eight feet apart all the way along a wall of rock.

The shooters would come and put the shots in, and everyone would back out. It'd blow, heaving coal and rock and dust. Time to time the coal might get in a lick of its own, taking a roof or a few men with it as it blew apart. But not lately. The drillers and the shooters had been doing their jobs fine and by the time my boots were walking where theirs had been, the blasting powder, smoke, and coal dust had settled.

I'd done plenty of loading, worked side by side with plenty of the men filling up the rooms. Now I didn't have a room of my own, and I didn't get paid by the tonnage. Got paid hourly, which suited me just fine. Most of the men worked in pairs assigned to one room, and I'd put in plenty of time with Jonah over the years, tagging my number—72—to the side of the car when we finished her up. The bosses would add up those circles of "72"—brass checks—and those checks turned into dollars on the paycheck once the coal got weighed.

Supervising, though, I'd go from room to room checking on the pace of the work, seeing if all the supports were steady, if the equipment was running like it should, who'd hit a snag, if the men were getting along. Some days it was just as hard on the back as loading. Safety was big and I'd need to keep an eye on nearly a hundred men spaced out in dozens of rooms, some no bigger than the storage space under the house. I'd get a shout from someone saying the air seemed stale, smelled off, and I'd check the ventilation. Or a pump would break down or a shovel handle break or sometimes some argument would break out. But mostly I was walking and bending and poking and prodding, in one room and out the other, saying hello occasionally, usually just nodding. Checking the seams and timbers and haulage system and listening and smelling for things I hoped I wouldn't hear or smell.

I'd made my way into one of the larger rooms and noticed a crack in one of the posts near the ground. I was glad it was a big room—I could get on my knees with my back straight up, cap not even brushing the ceiling.

I always was wearing off the knees of my overalls, but Leta never did say a word about it.

The four-by-eight post was solid enough, and the crack didn't look to be spreading. Not deep, either—could hardly wedge a thumbnail in it. While I was still on my knees, one of the boys came up to me, a good-natured, slow-moving Negro. Red his name was, and I never knew why. There wasn't a red spot on the man. I moved around to the other side of the post, running my hand down it, waiting for him to speak.

"Mr. Albert," he said.

"What's the trouble, Red?"

He didn't waste no time, I'll give him that. "Figure I saw some matches on B."

I straightened up as much as I could, knees cold and stiff from the ground. B's given name had enough letters and sounds that it was more trouble than it was worth to say. By the time you got to the end of calling it, the whole roof could've caved. I hadn't ever had trouble with him or anybody sneaking in matches—the fellows here stuck to the rules. I couldn't think what had got into the boy.

"Say anything to him?" I asked.

"No, sir."

"Where's he got 'em?"

"Pants cuff."

"Get on back then," I said. "I'll go see about it."

Red nodded and turned around and started making his way back to the deeper room they was in. I took off behind him, stooping into the same hunched-back walk he'd started. Some of the Birmingham mines had men to check miners for matches before they set one foot down the shaft. Every man among us smoked, and every man missed his cigarettes below ground, but trying to sneak a smoke was plain foolish. Plenty did it anyway, especially if the air was thick with smoke after a blast—that was the time to work in your cigarette. But it was still stupid, particularly because some fool would usually sneak off somewhere, and you didn't need to be heading off to some nook of the shaft and striking a match. Some of the smaller mines weren't so strict, but Galloway had too much money invested in the whole operation to have patience with a man's weakness. If a man was caught with matches, he'd be fired that same day.

B was working hard, at least. It took him a second to see me—he'd been moving over to give Red room to settle back in.

"Need to talk to you, B," I said. Red wasn't looking at B, just staring straight at the coal he was aiming for.

"Yessir?" B leaned on his shovel.

I watched him for a few seconds and took my time. I couldn't see his pants legs good without aiming my light straight at them. "You know about bringin' matches down here," I said.

"Yessir."

He'd know Red snitched on him no matter what. I thought about saying I'd seen the matches myself, but that wouldn't hold water. I'd followed right behind Red. But then again, Red was a grown man—I'd leave him to patch over any hurt feelings.

"You got some matches in your cuff there?" I said, pointing.

B didn't answer.

"I ain't gone turn you in for that," I said. "But I'll cut you loose here and now if you lie to me."

"I do got some, Mr. Albert," he said.

"You stark ravin' mad or just stupid?"

He didn't answer again, only looked down toward about my knees.

"Pull 'em out," I said.

He reached down, hiked up his pants leg, and fished out a pack of matches from between the stitches of the cuff.

"Hand 'em here." He did, not ever getting his eyes up to my shoulder, much less my face. I couldn't figure him. I'd known him for a couple of years, and he'd never taken a step wrong at work. Sure, I'd hardly said five words to him apart from "good mornin'" and "afternoon to you" and "I'd move on down a ways," but this kind of stupid was hard to hide.

"What got into you, B?" Nothing. "Ain't gone hurt none to answer me."

Wasn't no easy thing to have a dead-serious conversation hunched over halfway with lights stuck on your head glaring at each other. We couldn't look each other in the eye, so aiming a stern look at him didn't do me no good.

"B?"

"Plumb forgot," he said finally.

"Forgot you had matches?"

"Yessir. I went straight home without changin' yesterday. Wanted to try and catch me a rabbit or squirrel or somethin' before dark. I jus' stuck 'em in there soon as I got home. I swear I wasn't intendin' to smoke. Don't even have a cigarette."

"You sayin' you didn't recollect those matches one time between gettin' out of bed and when I walked over here?"

"No sir."

Well. Didn't know what to say to that. I knew he might be lying straight to my face. And as for not carrying smokes, paper to roll and a little pouch of tobacco could be anywhere on him. It put me in a mind to check his other pants cuff. But the thing was he had four kids hisself, none much more than knee-high, and he'd been lucky to get this work. If I pulled him off my team or told the supervisor, he'd have nothing. No land, so no food. Never find more work with half the town already heading up to West Virginia and Kentucky trying to find something, anything, and still not making enough to send something home.

"You hear about what happened over at Sipsey?" I asked finally, and it caught him off guard enough that he looked right in my face, blinding me for that second before he moved his head.

"Sipsey?"

"A fellow over there a few years back got to one of the back rooms and snuck off by hisself for just a few puffs, nobody else around. He lit up, least they figure that's what happened, and the match caught carbonic acid and blew him clean out of his boots. Couldn't even recognize him. The room next to him caught fire, too, burned up a couple of other fellows. Nothin' but cinders. Three families left with no man. You ever heard that told?"

"I don't recall it."

"Just want to be sure you understood there bein' the rule is all."

"Yessir."

"I'm gone take these," I said, holding up the matches.

"Nothin's gone come of it. But if I ever get wind of this again, I'll have you leave that second, not even give you time to get your things. You understand?"

"Yessir." He put a lot of effort into his nodding. "Honest about it bein' an accident."

I left the two of them shoveling. Red never did say a word while I was in earshot. I walked back to the supervisor's office near the elevator. Just a chair and a desk in there, with the door next to the board where we hung our tags when we went on shift. I knocked to get his attention, and he waved me in.

"Found these," I said and tossed the matches on his desk. His one giant eyebrow raised up on his forehead.

"See who had 'em?" he asked.

"Just found 'em. I didn't want nobody to pick them up."

He let that go. I'd been in that supervisor's office a couple times myself in smaller mines. I'd done about everything but dynamite. Started as a boy sorting the coal from the slate for the tipple. I knew my way around the pit mules by the time I quit grammar school for good—poor blind creatures that must've thought they were born and raised in hell. We didn't use them no more once the electric cars came around, with the chains hauling the cars up to the top. I'd run the cutting machine, which was good money, but you had to get hold of the machine first. I was a second-shift tipple boss for quite awhile at Moss and Mc-Cormick. Galloway had the tipple at the surface, but we also had the new chute on the Frisco line, right off 78, that we only got in '29. The fancy-looking wood and concrete outsides covered up more chutes and belts than I'd ever seen.

When I stopped for lunch I swung by Jonah's room and saw he was still eating. So I nodded and walked over. Took a swig of water before I sat down.

"Not too bad today," Jonah said.

"Passable."

The trick was to not hold your sandwich but one place. I once saw a man waste a few sips of water trying to wash his hands off, and he never did live it down. Might as well have worn a dress. I unwrapped my biscuits, saw the hunks of onion in the bottom, and two hard-boiled eggs. With just a thumb and one finger, I slid a piece of onion in the biscuit (Leta'd already cut it open) and picked up the sandwich. Finished it off in three bites, then started on the next one.

Jonah and I squatted a few feet apart, resting on the balls of our feet. You didn't want to break too long. Sitting down just made it harder to get up.

"Ham'd be mighty good," Jonah said, looking from his biscuit to mine. I nodded, smiled partly. Mentioning who had meat and who didn't could be a touchy subject with some of the men, but we knew each other's buckets as well as we knew our own.

"Ain't forgotten about payin' you back," he said. "Comin' straight out of my paycheck first thing."

"I ain't even thought about it," I said. I had, of course—dollars weren't so common that I didn't miss two. But I wasn't worried about getting it back. I really wanted to talk to him some more about how he imagined the woman with the baby. I found myself needing to hear him say more. Even stranger, I'd like to have asked him if his oldest daughter was seeing boys yet. See what he thought about handling the boys calling. I didn't want to interrupt his eating, though, and nobody hardly talked while we worked. Distracting.

Jonah made a surprised sound, and I looked up, my mouth full.

"Baked apple," he said and held it up. The juice was running down his fingers, and I could smell it. My biscuits weren't quite as tasty then.

I tossed the last bit—the one with black fingerprints—to a mine rat skulking against the wall. They always came out at lunchtime. Saw one riding on the edge of a car one time, resting against a pile of coal, watching us all like we was scenery from a train window. Handy animals, even if they were filthy. Couldn't blame 'em. And they paid you back their snack. When they got to moving, you knew there was trouble. Those rats could feel the shifting and shaking of the shafts sooner than we could. When they started running, so did we. And they got a full lunch of everybody's black-stained last bite. I didn't hold to superstition, but there wasn't no need to spit on common knowledge. It kept you alive. Mind the rats. Steer clear of any mine where a woman had been. Mind your flame. A lamp would flicker out if you hit a pocket of dead air, and you best back out fast, keeping low to the ground, if you didn't want to be just as dead.

Tess MAMA HAD A way of mashing up butter and sugar in the sweet potatoes that made your toes curl. The potatoes were still steaming, and the sweet butter juice would run out on your plate.

"These are good, Mama," I said. "Real good."

Everybody nodded and um-hmed. "Can I have another?" asked Jack.

Mama got up and pulled him another out of the warmer. Sweet potatoes weren't hard to come by.

"I could eat these every day," I said. I wanted to make myself clear.

"They're as good as a pie," said Virgie, and Mama looked down like she always did when we complimented her too much.

"Sure are," said Papa. "I been thinkin' about baked apples, Leta-ree. Think we might could have some sometime?"

And we all knew we'd be having apples the next day.

7 Telling Stories

Jack POP ALWAYS DID LOVE JOHN LEWIS. FOR MOST OF
the miners, he fell somewhere between Jesus and Roosevelt. And The Great Man came to Birmingham in 1933, drumming
up support for the UMW after Roosevelt had given it a second wind.

> *In nineteen hundred and thirty-three*
> *When Mr. Roosevelt took his seat,*
> *He said to President John L. Lewis,*
> *In union we must be.*
> *Hooray! Hooray!*
> *For the union we must stan'*
> *It's the only organization*
> *Protects the laborin' man.*

That was the song they'd sing late that year after the eight-
hour day and five-day week became law and after scrip was
banned.

Pop drove to see Mr. Lewis that day in Birmingham. I was
supposed to go with him, to get a sense of the power of Lewis
and his ideas, but I'd come down with some flu or something,
hardly able to get out of bed without my knees buckling.

Pop was gone all day, and by the time the sun started dipping behind the trees, I was feeling clearheaded enough to get
impatient. To wonder what I'd missed. I lay there listening for
his car, and, finally, just as Mama was turning the lights on, I could

hear him coming up the road. He came straight to my bed—probably kissed Mama first, but I didn't see that—and he started telling about the speech before he even had his hat off his head. I could see Lewis, a big man with bushy eyebrows that threatened to take over his whole face. He towered over the crowd, talking to them like he was some Old Testament prophet. Pop built up the suspense of it all, standing over my bed, shaking his fist in the air, his voice deep and rumbling and not his voice at all. Then, he said, in the middle of Lewis's speech about the power of the masses, a man in the front row threw a raw egg that smashed against Lewis's temple, running down his face. Mr. Lewis hardly paused, only wiped off the egg with one huge hand and continued with his speech. When he finished his remarks, with the applause still full throttle, he walked off the stage and punched the egg thrower in the face.

When Pop stopped laughing, he wiped his eyes and reminded me that I should always turn the other cheek. He swiped at his face and added, "Mostly."

I'd get Pop to retell that story year after year, to any new boy that I happened to bring home for supper or any new girl who I happened to be talking to at church. And eventually I would have sworn I had been in that crowd: I had watched that egg sail through the air. I had heard the wet smack it made against Mr. Lewis's forehead. I had cheered and clapped until my hands hurt when Mr. Lewis decked that drunken egg thrower. (I'd surely gotten just a whiff of whiskey even from where I was standing.) I'd listened to Pop good enough to make his story mine.

Albert I KNEW IT was likely that we didn't know the woman had even had a baby. Nobody'd mentioned any missing baby; for a couple of months, everybody'd been checking their neighbors' kids—with all sorts of excuses handy—to be sure they were all accounted for. There was talk about it being some young girl still in school wanting to keep the baby a secret, even though Tess would tell anybody who'd listen that the woman was too tall and broad to have been some young thing. Wasn't the sort of talk I wanted to listen to. And it wasn't the kind I could forget. It rattled around in my head without ever shaking loose.

I waited on the porch for Virgie to come home from the basketball game.

"You're back in one piece," I said.

"Yessir."

"Did you win?" Guin wasn't never as good as Carbon Hill.

"We did."

"By how much?"

She screwed up her face, looking closer to four than fourteen. "I don't know."

I wanted to ask her what she thought of that Olsen boy, whether he had tried to hold her hand, whether he had stared at her hair.

"I been thinkin', Virgie, about you goin' to the game with the what's-his-name Olsen. This one time with all you girls together was alright for a special occasion, but I don't want you seein' boys like that again. Not for a while longer," I said.

"Alright," she said, sounding happier than I expected. She nearly turned to walk away, then stopped and cocked her head. "Why not, Papa?"

"You're too young yet. No need to be runnin' around with boys."

She still didn't look upset, running her fingers through her hair and tucking it under like she always did. "Yessir."

"So if any other boy asks you, you just tell him not until you're in high school."

"But he didn't really ask me proper, Papa. I told you that. It was just a group of us, remember? Ella and Lois talked to him, not me."

I did know all that. I'd given her permission. I was just regretting it.

"I know what it was," I said. "And I don't want you doing it again."

"But you said…"

"I know what I said. I'm sayin' somethin' different now."

"We were only…"

"I didn't figure you to back talk," I said.

"No, Papa, but…"

"Listen to me!" I yelled, and I slammed my open hand against the wall hard enough to make the floors shake. Virgie jumped, and I heard Leta call my name in the bedroom. I felt all the temper run off me and pool around my feet. Never raised my voice to Virgie—never even spanked her. She never needed it.

"I don't want to hear any more. I know about boys, Virgie," I said. My face was turning red, but it was too dark for her to tell. This was Leta's place, not mine, but I'd speak my mind enough for her to understand. "Not one of 'em's good enough for you."

"I don't want one, Papa," she said, and I realized she was pink, too. A fine pair we were. "I don't like Tom or anyone special. I just enjoy being with my friends. And they go with boys. So to do things with them, it'd be nice to have an even number."

"I don't want you gettin' mixed up with some fellow at your age."

She looked a little afraid of me, but she answered anyway, quiet and calm. "I won't. I promise. We're only havin' fun, Papa. All of us."

Leta turned to me, her hair falling on my arm cool and smooth, when I lay down a few minutes later. I knew my yelling and slamming walls would have woken her. But she didn't say anything about that. "Don't worry for nothin'," she said. "That's an old soul inside that young body. She ain't gone do nothin' foolish."

I sighed and bent my leg so that it touched hers. Couldn't sleep. All wound up.

"And she don't care for any of them anyway," she whispered. "Pickiest girl I ever seen."

"Don't want her goin' with that boy. She's too young."

"Alright," she said. "Sets fine with me."

I thought she was drifting off, but she spoke again, her voice sleepy and thoughtful.

"I wonder if she had a nice time," she said.

I hadn't asked.

Virgie I CALLED FOR Aunt Merilyn twice before I finally pushed open the back door. I caught the screen door with my elbow so it wouldn't slam, then looked around the kitchen and called her name once more before I stepped all the way in.

"You in here, Aunt Merilyn? It's Virgie."

No answer. The butter churn sat in the middle of the kitchen, a chair beside it. I could smell the cream. Aunt Merilyn's blue-flowered dishes were stacked in the basin, bits of eggs on them. I could see the unmade beds in the back, sort of embarrassing, all personal with their sheets hanging out. Aunt Merilyn wasn't much for housekeeping. She'd clean when she had the time, but she'd gladly set it aside to chat, have a glass of tea, run to the post office. She went there most every day and stayed nearly an hour. Mama said if it weren't for women congregating at the post office, we'd find Aunt Merilyn down at the henhouse, desperate for clucking.

Mama had a strict schedule with her work, each thing done or put away as soon as it had served its purpose. Dishes done soon as we finished eating. Beds made soon as we finished sleeping. And nobody sat back down on her beds after she'd made them. When women came by, she might wipe her hands on her apron and talk for a minute, but if they wanted to visit for any length of time, they best trot along after her while she folded clothes or swept the floors. Her sisters all teased her for having a cleaning sickness.

I had closed the door behind me and got back to the road when I saw Aunt Merilyn ahead. Small and quick like Mama, she barely kicked up any dust as she walked. Her hair, dark and chin-length, shifted and bounced; her arms swung, a stack a letters in one hand. She was all movement—backward, forward, side to side, every direction appealing to her.

She waved when she saw me, both hands flapping happily, letters and all. "Virgie, dear! Get on back to the house and I'll feed you some tea cakes."

I turned myself around, climbed back up the steps, and waited on the porch for her. I realized I hadn't seen any of my cousins inside, and they weren't with her. She had two girls, Naomi and Emmaline, both pretty and popular. Big talkers, both of them.

"'Afternoon, Aunt Merilyn. Where is everybody?"

She shrugged, hugging my neck before she pushed open the door. "Out and about. Girls went with me to the post office, then wanted to run around town by themselves. Lord knows where the boys are. Off snatchin' the legs off bugs or throwin' each other in the creek or some such. Your uncle's at the store."

Uncle Bill's store seemed like no work at all to me. Instead of darkness and dirt, he spent the day surrounded by fabrics and trinkets and sweets. I'd never even seen him sweat.

We stepped into the kitchen, and Aunt Merilyn didn't seem at all embarrassed by the mess. She let out a little "hmph" that sounded more pleased than frustrated as she set down her letters and glanced over at the sink full of dishes. The next second she started opening cupboards, pulling out an empty saucer from one shelf and a towel-covered plate from another.

I could have found my way around her kitchen as easy as our own. Mama and Aunt Merilyn saw each other nearly every day and Papa and Uncle Bill got along like peas in a pod. Uncle Bill had a great, bellowing voice that could shake the walls when he sang, and their youngest daughter loved to play the piano. They were the only people I knew with a piano. Sometimes Tess and I would come over after supper—sometimes all of us would come— and listen to Emmaline playing while Uncle Bill sang. They didn't even have a radio.

"I been meanin' to talk to you for weeks now," Aunt Merilyn said. "Your mama told me you and Tess went by to see Lola."

"We did," I said. "We didn't stay long." She slid the plate of cookies in front of me, and I picked one that was almost a perfect circle, just barely brown around the edges. Then I realized something strange. "How come Mama to know that?"

"Lola came by the house. Brought back y'all's basket. Your mama didn't tell you?"

"No." She hadn't said a word. "When did she come by?"

"Lord, I don't know. I wasn't there. Last week, I reckon." She shook her head like there was a bee on it. "But you're gettin' me off track. You ever been to her place before?"

"No, ma'am." I looked over at the not-quite butter. "You want me to churn that for you?"

"It'll keep," she said.

"Or I s'pose you want to be startin' supper…" Mama'd probably be starting ours, and I'd rather have been elbow-deep in cornmeal than talk to Aunt Merilyn about Lola Lowe.

"It'll keep," she repeated. "Virgie, why in the world did you go over there? And why take Tess with you?"

I hesitated. I could have said we were being neighborly. I could have told her we knew the Lowe girls from school and wanted to visit.

"Virgie?" she prompted.

"We thought her baby might be the one missing."

She didn't look too surprised at that, just reached for a tea cake. Her other hand stayed still, almost touching her chin; she had a habit of relaxing her hand and curling her fingers toward her in a way that seemed like a fan. (I thought it looked elegant, and I practiced it at home in front of the mirror.) She took a nibble of the cookie, then held it as she talked.

"Thought that might be it. I could've told you it wasn't so. She's a good woman. Has it worse than most, but she does all she can for those kids."

"I know." I watched the tea cake bob through the air as she nodded.

"Did you ever think about her realizin' what you were up to?"

"No." I thought about her expression, our conversation. She hadn't seemed like she guessed anything. "Do you think she did?"

She lay the cookie on the table and brushed her hands together. "You asked to see the baby."

"She mentioned that to Mama?"

She nodded. "Your mama wasn't dead sure—Lola's not one to get wrought up—but she thought Lola was feeling like she needed to stand up for herself."

I wondered if we'd turned her off the taste of those apples by making her suspicious of our coming. I hoped not.

"You been to see any more killers lately?" she asked, eyebrow raised.

"No, ma'am." I caught myself before I started chewing my lip. "We know his mother didn't kill him for one thing. But also we ran out of women to check. We saw all the babies we thought it might be."

The front door swung open, and my cousin Naomi sailed into the room, sky blue dress—with navy blue piping around the collar and sleeves—swirling around her knees. She caught the screen door with her empty hand; the other one was holding a thick book. She had Uncle Bill's moss-colored eyes, and hair a little darker than mine that fell in curls around her face. Her curls were obedient, though, falling in perfect curlicues, not with a mind of their own like Tess's. But that was all about Naomi that was tame.

"Somebody's supposed to be finishin' the churnin'," said Aunt Merilyn before Naomi even opened her mouth.

"Who?" Naomi answered right back, eyebrows all furrowed together even as her mouth turned up at the corners.

"Same person that's gone have to cook her own supper if she don't get busy churnin'," said Aunt Merilyn, poking Naomi in the side as she passed. They both giggled. Aunt Merilyn and her girls were all sassy and full of opinions, teasing each other all the time and entertaining each other something crazy. Tess was sort of more like them, really.

Naomi pulled out the chair next to me and slid the churn between her knees, pushing her skirt down and tucking it under her thighs. "I'm sorry, Mama," she said, sincere. "I lost track of time."

"Well, help yourself to some of those tea cakes." Aunt Merilyn never seemed bothered enough by anything that she didn't want you to have some of her tea cakes.

"Hi Virgie," Naomi said, grinning at me. "How's everything with y'all?"

"Pretty good."

Naomi propped her book on the table, opened it, and unfolded the corner of a page. Once the book was situated, she grabbed the wooden paddle of the churn with one hand and started lifting and lowering it. She didn't start reading, though; instead she looked at me like I was the first page.

"I won't be rude and read it while you're here," she said. Even without smiling, she always looked like she'd just heard a joke. "I just like to have it ready."

"That girl don't never go nowhere without carryin' a story with her," said Aunt Merilyn, finally at the basin washing her dishes. In water turned cold, I was sure.

Naomi was still staring a hole through me, but she seemed to be working hard at the churning, the paddle moving steadily and the cream sloshing inside. "So you're seein' Tom Olsen?" she asked.

"Are you really?" asked Aunt Merilyn. "Leta didn't mention any such thing."

"I'm not really," I said. "We went to the basketball game with a group of friends."

"I thought Henry Harken was sweet on you," Aunt Merilyn said. Then she added, "Churn."

Naomi had stopped churning. She was always doing that, especially when she was reading. I'd come into the house before to find her caught up in her book, her hand still around the paddle, but completely still. Sometimes she wouldn't even have heard the front door open. Eventually Aunt Merilyn would walk by, tap her on the shoulder, and say, "Churn." Then Naomi's arm would get to working again.

"No, ma'am," I said, figuring to keep it as simple as possible. "I don't think Henry's sweet on me."

"Everybody's sweet on Virgie," Naomi said, churning.

"They are not," I said to Aunt Merilyn. And to Naomi, "You're trying to embarrass me."

She just smiled. "Maybe."

"Well, they should be," said Aunt Merilyn, turning to me and getting excited enough that she started talking with her hands even though they were wet. A spray of droplets shot through the air. "And you have all the fun you can leadin' them around by the nose. No boy's more fun than a lovesick one."

I'd never heard Mama talk like that. "They're not lovesick," I said. "And how is that fun?"

"You know how you train a tomato vine to follow the stake?" asked Aunt Merilyn. "Well, you're the stake, honey."

Naomi, who didn't seemed shocked at all, reached for a tea cake. "She's big on talkin' about how they're tomato vines."

"Churn," said Aunt Merilyn.

Naomi frowned but lay down her book and held the cookie with one hand while she churned with the other.

"Does she talk like that around Uncle Bill?" I asked softly to Naomi.

"Shoot, you tell Papa about him bein' a tomato all the time, don't you, Mama?"

Aunt Merilyn shrugged.

"And he doesn't mind?" I asked.

"Oh, he usually tells me at least the tomato vine produces

something. But the stake only sits around doin' nothin' until it rots."

"And you tell him…" Naomi trailed off and Aunt Merilyn finished, "That it's a lot easier to stomp a tomato flat."

Then they bent over giggling again. I laughed too, still trying to imagine the picture in my head of Uncle Bill and Aunt Merilyn talking about love and tomatoes. Mama and Aunt Merilyn looked so much alike, and even our houses were built similar, but once you walked through their door, it was a different thing altogether. I sat there and thought about all of them circled around the piano, the whole family making one smart remark after another, turning the conversation into a game of checkers with everybody trying to queen each other.

I stayed around alternating the churning with Naomi until the cream had turned to butter and was ready to be spooned into the mold. That was the best part.

The butter mold, shaped like a miniature churn, pressed a daisy design in the top of the butter. Mama and Aunt Merilyn had the same one, and I loved making the smooth, round slabs of butter. I turned the wooden mold upside down, pulling the plunger all the way up so Naomi could spoon in globs of butter with her wooden spoon. She packed in spoonful after spoonful, scraping the spoon on the edge of the mold so it was full to the brim. Then I turned it right-side-up on a plate and eased the plunger down, pressing the butter out with a satisfying sucking sound. It looked so cool and delicious there, like a custard or some shell-less pie—I and most everybody else had snuck a mouthful of it as soon as we were tall enough to reach the tabletop. I'd walked in the kitchen once when Tess was small and in the middle of the table sat the butter pretty as you please… with three little mouth holes bitten out of it. Tess was the only one I knew who kept on eating after the first bite.

"You should come to church with me Sunday," said Naomi as she took over the mold. I started spooning. "You'd like the minister."

"Which one?" I asked. Uncle Bill was a Baptist and Aunt Merilyn was a Methodist. Both those churches only met two Sundays a month, so they just swapped out. But Aunt Merilyn ended up making casseroles and pies for two congregations' worth of sick people.

"Methodist this coming time," Naomi said. "But this is a young one coming up from Birmingham-Southern."

That was a Methodist college. "You sayin' you like him?"

"He's a minister—'course I like him."

But I thought I'd heard something else in her tone. And she wasn't looking me straight in the eye, which, for Naomi, was fairly unusual. I thought I saw the chance to get in some teasing of my own, which, for me, was fairly unusual.

"But do you like him as maybe more than a minister?" Before she could answer, I added, "To go to a dance with?"

She and her little sister could go to dances—the Methodists and Baptists didn't know it was wrong. I'd never had much desire to go anyway because all the little kids went up to the gymnasium where they held dances and pressed their noses to the windows and came back telling everybody who was dancing with who and how close they were standing and where their hands were. No, thank you, I didn't need to learn to dance.

"He's a good five years older than me," she said.

"He's twenty? Twenty-one? That's not too much of a difference."

She shook her curls, and I worried some hair would fall in the butter. Mama made us brush ourselves off and tie our hair back before we set foot in the kitchen. Aunt Merilyn didn't care so much.

"All I'm sayin' is you should hear him preach. He'll for sure make you laugh, and the time flies by." She pressed out a perfect white circle and admired it. "You'd think a minister would be boring, but ... " She stopped talking suddenly.

"You're dreamin' of marryin' him," I said, surprising myself, but taken aback by the look on her face.

She didn't answer right away. "He probably thinks I'm a little sister or something. Probably not the kind of woman he'd marry." She sounded wistful.

"You're gone dance with the preacher and date the preacher and marry the preacher," I said, singsong, giddy from butter making.

"Am not," she said, focusing way too hard on making another mold.

"You ready to get married?" She was only in her first year of high school, and she hated stockings even worse than I did. It seemed like you should make your peace with stockings before thinking about promising yourself to a boy for the rest of your life.

"Not now, of course. But someday." She waved the mold toward me. "More butter."

I thought about the basketball game, which I'd dreaded and had ended up not minding so much at all. I'd dreaded the walks with boys, too, and those were sort of nice. I still dreaded marrying some boy and spending all day washing and cooking and tending children and waving from the porch while everybody else drove off.

"It don't scare you to think of it?" I asked.

"Scare me?"

"Being a wife. Forever. And havin' kids. And not just being plain old Naomi anymore."

"It seems fun, doesn't it?" she said. "Havin' a family of your own?"

"Mold," said Aunt Merilyn as she walked by without looking down.

"I was!" said Naomi. "You can't be remindin' me when I'm already doin' it!"

Tess THE PART OF COTTON PICKING that we did like and that didn't make us bleed was when our porch got covered in white. After great sacks of cotton were picked and baled, Papa and Mr. Talbert hitched up Horse and hauled the bales to our house in the wagon. It collected on one side of the porch, getting higher and higher every day, finally spilling over into the middle of the porch until we had to cram the rocking chairs in one corner. The whole porch would become a big bed, soft and springy, sucking you down deep inside it. It was a white playground, catching in your hair, rubbing against your skin. Jack and me loved to climb on it, leap on it, run and do belly flops on it.

I was going to ask the Talbert kids if they wanted to come jump on our cotton.

"But they wasn't even nice," Jack said. He was nearly running to keep up with me, his bare feet kicking up dirt behind him. Since he was a boy, he was allowed to take his shoes off after he got in from school.

"They just didn't know us good," I told him.

"I don't like them." He stopped then, hands on his hips, daring me.

"Oh, don't be a pest, Jack. You said you'd come. We'll get them, then we'll come back and I'll boost you on the cotton as much as you want." His special favorite was when I laced my hands together, then he stepped in them and I hoisted him into the bales.

"As much as I want," he repeated.

"Yes," I huffed. We started back to walking.

"Still don't understand why you're stuck on those ugly Talberts," he mumbled, but soft enough that I could ignore him.

So I did. Then I managed to collect a whole handful of crab apples along the way without him noticing. I waited until we passed the last of the crab apple trees, then I pelted him with them all at once. Right in the back of the head. It made him yelp.

But by then we were just at the edge of the Talberts' place, and there wasn't much he could do but yank at my hair real quick. The boy and girl were outside the house, watching us walk up the road. The boy was sitting on the porch steps, whittling a block of wood that was still mostly a block. The girl was sweeping off the porch—not aiming for her brother, which seemed like a real waste to me—the whirls of dust flying over the sides to the yard below. The broom handle came up past her head.

"Mr. Moore ain't here," said the girl, with the straw still scraping against the porch floor.

"I wasn't lookin' for Papa," I said. "I don't think we got introduced proper last week. I'm Tess."

"Lou Ellen," she said, not smiling, but resting the broom.

"And this is—"

"I'm Jack," he interrupted before I could finish.

"This is Eddie." Lou Ellen waved her hand toward her brother, but he didn't look up from his shavings.

Lou Ellen and Eddie, I said inside my head. Lou Ellen and Eddie. I tried to pay attention to Lou Ellen's face while I got the feel for her name—she had a pushed-up knob of a nose and it was pink and peeling, even as suntanned as she was. I liked her nose.

"Listen," I said. "We got all the cotton piled up on our porch—they're takin' it to the gin tomorrow. We thought you might like to jump on it with us. You and your brother both."

They were quiet a little too long, so I threw in, "Last day for it."

"Jump in the cotton?" asked the boy, not only looking at us, but putting his stick down.

Not the boy. Eddie. He was close enough that I could see the wide gap between his two front teeth. I could've stuck a pencil in there.

"Sure," Jack said. "You ain't never done it?"

It was clear by their faces that they hadn't. All that picking, and they hadn't ever gotten to the good part. It was like raking leaves and not getting to jump in them. "See," I said, very patiently, "the bales pile up on the porch, higher than me." I held up my hand cotton-high. "You can climb on it, jump on it, roll around in it. It's like playing in the clouds."

"It's real fun," said Jack. "Real fun." He seemed a little more kindly toward the Talberts now that he realized what they'd been missing.

"And your parents don't mind none?" asked Lou Ellen.

"Shoot, no," he said.

"We do it all the time."

"And it's taller than you are?" Eddie asked.

"Yep," I said. "And all the prickly parts are out."

I tried to think of what else I could say about the special-ness of it, but I must have said enough. Lou Ellen leaned the broom against the wall. "Let me go ask Mama," she said as she nearly ran in the house, looking back over her shoulder like she wasn't sure we'd stay put.

They did get permission, so the four of us hightailed it back to our place and didn't stop until we got to the top of our steps (which meant Jack didn't have a chance to stop and pick any crab apples to get me back).

"Now what?" Lou Ellen asked. "We just jump?"

"No, it's more than that," I said. "You have to do the story."

"The story?"

"You do it, Tess," said Jack. "You're the best at it."

That seemed like it might be easiest. Lou Ellen and her bro-ther obviously weren't going to be any help. "Okay," I said, "before you jump on the cotton, you have to decide who you are and what you're doin'."

"We know who we are," said Lou Ellen, looking nervous, like they'd made a mistake in coming with us.

I was about done with being patient. And I'd noticed that Lou Ellen had a habit of holding her mouth open with her tongue, pointy and sharp, worrying the outside of her mouth. It made her look like a nervous animal.

"Just let me finish," I said in a teacher voice, trying to ignore Lou Ellen's wiggly tongue. The tip of it sliding on her upper lip, poking at the corners of her mouth. "Let's start with the cotton. It could be clouds and we could be angels playing our harps in it or we could be birds flying in it or we could be building snow-men and have a snowball fight...or anything."

"We could be boll weevils and eat it," said Eddie.

You could tell he hadn't never played pretend.

"No, that's no good," I said. "You got to think on it more than that. It's not cotton, it's something more…different."

They all sat there for a while, looking at the cotton like it would shape itself into something all on its own. Then Lou Ellen said, "You ever seen where the creek runs fast over rocks and bubbles over?"

We nodded. "Well," she kept on, "it could be fast water. The top of fast water and we could be the fish swimming in the current."

We all thought that was a fine idea. So we flipped and wiggled upstream and downstream and Jack got caught by a hook and tossed hisself off the porch onto dry land. He lay there opening and closing his mouth until Eddie pretended to throw him back in the cotton-water.

Lou Ellen and me was swimming, flapping our tails and moving our fins a lot like we would flap our wings if we were chickens. As we floated in the water, her shirt got pulled up and I saw a long red mark on her side, rough and bubbly next to the rest of her pale skin.

"Did you hurt yourself?" I asked, pointing.

She looked down and tugged at her shirt, sliding off the bales. "I poured boiling water on me when I was little. Hit the pot handle and it dumped off the stove. Burned me good."

"Wasn't your Mama watchin' you?"

She gave me that look again that told me we spoke a different language. "She was workin' with Papa. I was in charge of fixin' supper."

Then she fell back hard on the cotton, her skirt flying up along with her legs, flapping her arms to make a cotton angel. Her bloomers were made of flour sacks, too, and her shirt hitched up again to where I could see her puckered side.

"Papa has scars," I said, words just falling out of my mouth. It hadn't occurred to me kids, little girls, could get them. Scars came from piles of dirt and big chunks of wood falling on top of you or sharp things swinging and slicing. Dangerous dramatic things that didn't happen to me.

"Yeah, my papa does, too," she said. "You don't got none?"

"Uh-uh."

"Not one?"

I wanted to come up with one, something to match that cooked skin or the thick white stripe on Papa's shoulder. I looked down, studying my feet and legs, moving up to my arms and hoping desperately for some new mark to jump out at me. Some sign of a big adventure I'd forgotten about. What I saw was the wide V leftover from when I tripped and fell hard on a rock in the yard. Exactly in the middle of my arm, just below the crook of my elbow, it seemed no more strange than a freckle. I'd forgotten about the scream I'd let out when I hit the ground—I couldn't remember why I'd been running in the first place—and how I nearly fell again trying to rush up the steps to find someone to fix me. I'd forgotten my arm dripped blood for a whole day, Mama leaning over me in the bed, checking on the bandage she'd wrapped around it and frowning deep lines into her forehead when she saw the cut was still seeping. Me thinking I might bleed on the bed and asking if I should sleep in a chair and Mama just brushing hair off my forehead and smiling.

I held out my arm to Lou Ellen and pointed. "I fell on a rock just out there by the steps," I said.

She studied my arm more carefully than I'd studied her side, running one dirty finger over the mark.

"That's nice," she said. Her tongue was peeking out again, curling against her upper lip, and I thought, no, not like a nervous animal. She looked thoughtful, clever. Like a squirrel wanting to hide a pecan. Eyes blinking and whiskers twitching. "I like it."

"It's real small," I said.

She jerked her head toward her side, then traced the shape of my scar again, nearly tickling me. More like a feather than a finger. "Yours is pretty," she said. "It's like how you draw birds in the sky."

I took my time staring at my own arm, twisting it back and forth. She was right—if I'd fallen on a bunch of rocks, I could have a whole flock on my arm, little Vs trying to flap their way down to my wrist or up to my shoulder.

"Lemme see yours again," I said. But this time she looked nervous, embarrassed. "Please," I threw in.

She moved her hand to her shirt, but she didn't lift it at all. "Just one look," I said in what I thought was a sweet voice. Mama called it my whining voice, and the only thing it ever got me with Virgie was a quick hair pull.

But it worked on Lou Ellen. She tugged her shirt up a few inches and I got another look at her scar. Tough and raised and still angry, not looking like a thing of the past at all.

"It doesn't hurt?" I asked.

She shook her head. "You can touch it."

So I did, and it was no warmer than my finger. Not slippery or slimy or dry like a snakeskin. It felt more like the seat of a car than it did a girl. It didn't feel alive. It felt different from anything I'd ever touched, and I wanted to snatch my hand away at the same time I wanted to keep it there for as long as she'd let me. But I gave it one more poke with the pad of my finger and laid my hands back behind me on the porch.

"Nobody else has one like that, I bet," I said. "I never seen one."

She put her shirt down. "You think it's ugly?"

"No," I said. I didn't. "I think it looks like a ribbon. Not a silk one, but one of those wrinkly kinds of ribbons. Taffeta or something."

She shrugged and turned her face away so I couldn't see if she was pleased or not. I waited to see if she wanted me to explain more about the kind of ribbon, but she didn't ask.

We went back to playing.

With the last bits of sun slinking off and the moon already settled in the sky, only Lou Ellen and me were left, sitting with our feet dangling. The cotton was a cliff that touched the clouds and the dirt daubers buzzing around the roof were eagles and the porch floor was a fiery pit where you'd burn to a crisp if you fell. Jack had got mad when he burned to a crisp, so he and Eddie had stomped off.

"This was real fun," Lou Ellen said. "Thank you for invitin' us. But Mama'll be worried if we don't get home soon."

"Is it just you and Eddie at home?" I thought it was odd that I hadn't seen any other kids around the place.

"Oh, I got four older brothers—all grown and left now. Just us two still there. Plus my granny. She's been with us since Granddaddy died. And my Aunt Lou. She moved in this summer."

"How come?" I couldn't see Aunt Celia or Aunt Merilyn up and deciding to move in with us.

"Don't know. She used to live with my granny, and Granny moved in with us after Granddaddy died. That was awhile back. But Aunt Lou—they named me for her—stayed at the old family place until this summer."

"My Aunt Celia lives with my grandma. How come your granny didn't stay with your Aunt Lou?"

"Mama says she likes grandkids bein' around. Papa says Aunt Lou's a trial for one person to deal with."

"Is she a trial?" I wondered just what that involved.

Lou Ellen shrugged. "Well, Granny got my bed and Aunt Lou got Eddie's, so she might be a trial to him. And she is pretty high-strung. At the funeral for my granddaddy, my uncles had to carry her out she was crying so much."

"Did you know him much?" I asked her.

"Visited him some. Why?"

"I ain't never known anybody to die, not somebody I really knew. We go to the cemetery to see my grandma and grandpa on my mama's side, but they've been dead as long as I've known 'em."

"Known plenty dead, but not in the cemetery," Lou Ellen said.

"Where else would they be?"

"If you ain't got money to bury one in the cemetery, you bury it in the backyard," she said. "Mama's done buried three out there."

"Three bodies?"

"Babies. Two of them born blue. One from crib death."

She kept kicking her feet against the bales like it was normal to have babies lying in the backyard. Normal to have death coming up with the grass, up with the sun, up with the water bucket.

Albert THE RACKET FROM the children playing—shrieks and giggling and loud thumps that made me listen close for crying—had died down. I didn't know who all Tess and Jack had roped into coming over, but the house shook from the silliness. But I hadn't wanted to deal with it, hadn't wanted to quiet them or run them off. Not when it was easier to just hide out on the back porch. And stand by Tess's well. She never sat out back anymore, not after all the years we'd had to track her down and pull her away, all turned-down mouth and pitiful voice, from the quiet back here.

I could see why she liked it. You could be alone out back. Leaning against the railing, the wood rough under my hands, I could hear Jack and some other boy whooping around the yard up front, and I could hear Leta clattering in the kitchen—even her clattering seemed steady and purposeful—but I was apart from it. Still caked with the day's work, my shirt stiff with dried sweat, legs complaining under me. But I didn't want to wash up, didn't want to sit down, didn't want to wrap my arms around anyone. Not yet.

What I really wanted to do was have Jonah over for supper and then sit out on the porch and talk. See if he thought Bill Clark made any sense about somebody aiming to turn our water. See if he thought I should just leave the whole thing be, put it out of my mind. I thought I might should.

Bill had a colored man living next door to him for years before the mines started closing and the man moved to Detroit.

Nobody said anything about it. No fuss or whispering or funny looks. So that's what I planned on—I'd see if Jonah would come sit a spell.

I listened to crickets and felt the air cool and still didn't go inside.

"Papa?"

I looked down and saw Tess at my hip. "If you'd been a snake, you'd've bitten me," I said.

She snapped her little teeth at me, an old joke. "What you doin' out here, Papa?"

"Just thinkin'." I ran a hand over her mess of hair, slowly, and it sprang back up as soon as it got free.

"Why are you thinkin'?"

I laughed at that. "Don't insult your Papa. I think plenty."

"I know that," she said, little Leta wrinkles in her forehead. "But what're you thinkin'?"

She seemed as good an audience as any. I tried out the words aloud.

"About havin' Mr. Benton over. Thinkin' on invitin' him to supper some night."

She nodded like we always sat out on the porch and talked about our plans. "I invited the Talberts over to play in the cotton," she said, satisfied-like.

That surprised me, but I just asked, "Did y'all have a nice time?"

"Yessir. They was nice. And they'd never played in cotton."

"Never?"

"No, sir. I had to explain it."

"They gone on home?"

"Yessir."

"Why'd you think to ask them?"

"Just thought it'd be nice."

Unlike her to ask them. She didn't think outside herself too much—not like Virgie, who'd mother any child, grown-up, or butterfly she came across—but maybe that biscuit guilt weighed on Tess more than I'd realized. Maybe Leta'd been right that it would do the children good to see that some people had it a lot harder than we did.

Or maybe I just didn't know Tessie as well as I thought I did.

"Lou Ellen Talbert looks like a chipmunk when she sticks her tongue out," she piped up all of a sudden. "Or a possum or somethin'."

Tessie. I felt something like relief then, which snuck into my laugh, and I pretended to reach for her own tongue, fingers stopping short when she pressed her lips together tightly even as she smiled.

"But I like her," she said once my hand was safely back on the rail. "She's real nice. And I think you should have Mr. Benton over. It'd be nice for you to have some company," she said.

I matched her serious tone. "I appreciate you saying it. I'll take that into account."

She stood by me awhile longer, stepping a little closer, finally leaning into me with her shoulder touching my hip. I knew I stunk to high heaven, but she didn't seem to mind. We didn't say anything else, and I was fairly glad. Leta was the one the girls could share their secrets with, but I wasn't one for long drawn-out conversation that would likely be about dresses or dolls or boys. But Tess didn't like dolls, I didn't think. Couldn't remember her ever asking for one or playing with even a dressed-up corn-cob. I wondered if she thought about boys yet. When did that start? Leta would probably know.

If I needed to know anything, she'd pass it along, surely. And I could enjoy not talking, just standing with Tess, feeling her shoulder against me and hearing the little puffs of her breathing.

Eventually she straightened and turned toward the kitchen door, and I didn't want her to go quite yet.

"Why'd you come out here, Tess?" I called, making her stop with her hand on the doorknob. "You missin' your well?"

For the first time, she looked over at it, cocked her head and made her curls flop, stared for a long second. She took a few steps back toward me, which brought her closer to the well, but she didn't get too close. "No," she said finally. "I wasn't thinking about the well."

"So why're you out back?"

She cocked her head the other way, smiling up at me, and I saw her answer before she said it. Saw it in the set of that pointed chin and in her still-a-little-girl smile that was full of teeth.

"You're out here," she said.

Virgie I FISHED THE hard-boiled egg out of the pot, and Mama tossed the baked potatoes from one hand to the other until she dropped one in each lunch bucket. I didn't dare toss the eggs. Tess and Jack and me each got one egg, and Papa got three in his bucket, along with the biggest potato. I wrapped his eggs in a towel so they wouldn't crack. They went in the food compartment, and Mama would pour fresh water in the other side. We'd already washed and dried the breakfast dishes, and Mama was putting away the last of the saucers. The table didn't have a crumb on it, and all the neatness made me think of Aunt Merilyn.

"Mama, did you think it was fun goin' with boys?"

"Depended on the boy," she said.

"But you enjoyed it?"

"Not any fonder of the Olsen boy than you were of Henry Harken?"

I thought about that. "Yes'm, I guess I like him better than Henry. He's real polite, and he doesn't talk too much—but he does talk enough—and when I smile at him, he smiles back twice as big."

"That's something," she said. "I take him for a nice boy."

Lunches packed and dishes washed, she pulled out the bread-making bowl, a deep wooden circle almost big enough for Tess to sit in. I watched Mama sift the flour, measure out the soda and the buttermilk. Her hands never sped up or paused in the kitchen—they danced from bowl to jar to spoon to basin to dish towel, pouring and stirring and wiping and measuring and testing. I loved to watch the patterns of her hands.

"It seems lots harder than talking to girls, though," I said.

"How do you figure?" That was one thing about Mama—she was good at letting you talk, at poking and prodding you to where you had to find the truth behind what you were saying. She wasn't going to waste much time talking herself, and she didn't always care to tell you how to solve your problems, but she would listen all day long and keep you talking until you knew what you really meant to say.

"You don't know what boys are thinkin'."

"I never have known just what girls are thinkin', neither." She stirred and ground the yeast in a few spoonfuls of hot water. "Smashing the yeast," she called it. If it wasn't smashed good, the bread wouldn't rise.

"Well, no, but…" I had to start over. "With boys you have to figure out why they're talkin' to you and then what they're thinkin' about you."

"Thought you said you didn't care for any of them in particular."

"I don't."

"Then it don't matter what they think, does it?"

I sucked up the sweet, heavy yeast smell. The kitchen was full of it. "But you have to figure out what you think of them."

"Ah," she said. "Now I see."

"See what?"

"What's worryin' you."

"That boys are hard to figure?"

She had her hands in the dough, squeezing and turning. "That you don't know how to tell which ones are worth botherin' with. Flour the counter for me?"

I'd stepped between her and the sack of flour, and she moved the bowl aside, giving me space to scatter a handful of flour on the tabletop. I evened it out with the flat of my hand, and she dropped the lump of dough in the middle of it, rubbing

her hands against mine to coat them white again. She'd make four
or five loaves at one time, enough to last for a week.

"How did you and Papa meet?" I asked as she pulled the
dough apart.

"At a big bonfire. I went over with my papa, and Albert came
up and introduced himself."

"Why did he walk over to you? He liked you right away,
before he even met you?"

"Well, I'd nearly set my hair on fire. Might've caught his
attention."

"What did you think of him?" The flour covered her wrists,
and she'd gotten a smudge on her cheek. She caught the knob
of a drawer with her pinky, pulling out the rolling pin without
leaving a trace of flour behind.

"He was nice enough. Liked his eyes. My daddy liked him."

"Did you think you'd marry him?"

"Land's sakes, no."

"When did you change your mind?"

She turned to the side, both hands still on the rolling pin,
and leaned against the sink. "He asked me, and I said yes."

That wasn't at all what I was looking for. "But how did you
know?"

"Know what?"

"That you wanted to marry him?"

She stopped rolling, holding her doughed and floured
hands bent at the wrist. That moment of thinking only lasted
long enough for her to wipe her forehead with her arm and let
out a long breath.

"He was a good man. Good to me. I liked his company."

My mother wasn't ever a big talker. And she wasn't what
you would call the most romantic soul.

I wondered what kind of soul I was.

Albert THE END OF the afternoon shift was payday, and, like
every other Friday, by the time we stepped out of the cage

into the sunshine, there was already two lines—one Negro, one white—snaking up to the two windows of the office. It was a smiling bunch of men, laughing, scratching, and spitting. Clumps of us stood around chatting, puffing out streams of smoke, and enjoying the feeling of money in our pockets. You never wanted to rush home after payday. The money turned the day sharper and fresher and lifted the dust off you better than shower spray. Negro girls stood a ways off, shifting their hips side to side looking to catch a Negro fellow with money in his pocket. The white women for sale waited for the men to come to them in town. Galloway used paper scrip, but some of the other mines gave out scrip in their own kind of metal coins, dugaloo. You could go to a picture show for a dime, but it'd cost you fifteen cents in dugaloo. I wondered if the whores made that same kind of markup.

I saw Jonah over there in his line, and our eyes met for a second. There wasn't much talkin' between the lines. Below ground, sure, but once you stepped off the elevator, there were clear enough paths in opposite directions. We nodded, a tip of the head so small it wasn't much different than letting out a deep breath. I wanted to ask him about coming over to the house, and the two lines seemed stupid and inconvenient. But I figured I'd ask him later.

The line moved fast, and soon enough I was scribbling my name on a line in the pay book, signing off on twelve dollars and forty cents for the two weeks. I turned around, hearing the coins jangle, stepping in time so they'd play a song. Walking toward me was a fellow I knew well enough, not so's we'd chat, but he was coming straight at me, nearly running. Feeling friendly because of payday, I thought, flush with satisfaction myself. I smiled and nodded at him, ready to call his name, when I realized he was shaking his head. Shaking his head like I was doing something wrong. So until his boots were a couple of inches from mine, I stood there hitching my pockets and listening to my coins, wondering for those few seconds why he looked so unhappy when he had full pockets.

He said, "Your boy's been hit by a truck."

And then I didn't hear nothing. No more coins making music, no more words coming out of his mouth, even though his lips kept moving. I couldn't think to take the smile off my face, only stood there deaf and grinning.

8 The Well Woman

Jack YEARS LATER, ALL I COULD EVER CONJURE WAS the sirens whirring and the taste of dirt. I couldn't for the life of me remember that truck hitting me. I'd been walking to the ball game, and I heard the sounds of tires skidding on dirt behind me, which was different than tires skidding on pavement. I remember thinking the fellows would be so jealous I got to ride in the ambulance.

It was a decade later before I asked Pop why he didn't sue that brick company. People then weren't as litigious as they are now, but even then the common gossip was that he would have gotten a fat settlement just for shutting up. Maybe enough to send his kids to college. Maybe enough even to stop mining.

He wouldn't consider it. Mama wanted him to, but she didn't push. She never pushed. Aunt Celia wanted him to, and she pushed plenty.

What Pop said was, "Ain't no reason to be demandin' somethin' of people. Don't know their story. Best to take care of your own." He didn't mention that the driver never even slowed down after he hit me, and that maybe that was all of his story that we needed to know. But I suspect the world of legality and contracts and lawyers in seersucker suits seemed unreachable to him, undesirable. I wonder if that world seemed any less foreign after I received my law degree.

But at the time, of course, I didn't question him at all. To hear Pop declare something was so was like hearing the voice of God. He and Mama were always a little more than human to us.

When Mama was ninety, she had a bad stroke that left her in the hospital for two months. She could hardly move her left side, just wiggle her fingers, and the doctors in Jasper said she'd never be able to eat on her own again. She choked every time she tried to swallow. Tess was back living with her then, and Virgie came up from Montgomery for a few weeks to help. I came down from Atlanta, and all us kids were back at home for a couple of weeks. We took her home from the hospital with a feeding tube, but she wouldn't let the nurse hook it up. Instead she had us bring her meals to her bedroom and close the door behind us. She said, garbled but firm, to leave her be. I drove down twice a week, and for a few months, she'd hardly make a dent in a plate-ful of food. Then one day she came out before lunchtime and sat herself down at the table. She ate every bite on her plate.

The only time I ever say Mama cry was when I was lying there in the hospital with the dirt from the road still on me. She didn't know I was awake. And I saw Pop's face lined and old and afraid. I got to see the people that were under my pop and mama, and even though it was just a glimmer, it scared me.

That truck knocked more than my teeth loose when it hit me.

Leta   THERE WERE STILL bricks on the ground, and I couldn't help but look and see if there was blood on them. It was a brick truck from Tupelo, Mississippi, was what they told me. Whether the driver was drunk or asleep or just plain worthless, he'd veered off and knocked Jack into a ditch, swerved back onto the road, and left nothing but those bricks behind him. Some-where down the road somebody flagged him down, and he finally stopped, but he wouldn't even get out of the truck. Just gave the company name, said he was sorry, and that he hadn't seen Jack at all. Thought he'd hit a dog.

He should've stopped for a dog.

It was the farthest trip I ever took in the car, with Albert coming by the house from work to pick me up. The neighbors had gotten to me a little before the men at the mines got word to Albert, so I was dressed and ready when he pulled up the drive. Nobody knew much other than that Jack had been hit and that he wasn't moving or talking when they loaded him into the ambulance. And it looked bad enough that they took him on to Birmingham.

Of course to get to Birmingham we went straight down 78, right past where Jack was hit. Which I wouldn't have known if it weren't for the bricks. No blood that I could see after I had Albert pull off the road even though he didn't think I should be looking. But the bricks had dented the dirt. It made a high, long whine build up in my throat to think that what could leave gashes in the earth had left its mark on Jack. But I caught that strange, scared sound by clapping my hand over my mouth, and I swallowed it like cough medicine. Albert and I didn't say a word all the way to the hospital.

Tess PAPA WOULDN'T COMPLAIN to the brick company. He said what's done is done. (His eyes were red, which the mines brung about sometimes, but instead of making them look uglier, it made the blue seem brighter.) He squatted down next to me and told me Jack had been hurt real bad, and for a while all I could think was that his eyes were like sky and roses.

Virgie MAMA AND PAPA wouldn't let us go with them when they drove after the ambulance. They stopped by Mrs. Hudson's and asked her to come over, so we sat around while she tried to make small talk. We couldn't do anything but wait, but that seemed to take up most of our energy; it was exhausting to try to be polite and listen to her. It took a lot of convincing to get her to go back to her own family and let me take care of supper for Tess and me. Finally she did. I made cornbread with cracklin', thinking to give Tess a treat and keep myself busy for a little while, but neither of us could eat much.

I give Mrs. Hudson credit for not telling us much about the talk around town. After she left, neighbors started coming by, asking if we'd heard anything even though they could see for themselves the car wasn't back in the driveway. And they'd say they were praying for Jack and "hope to goodness there wasn't no bleeding inside." Or that "God willing he won't be a cripple for life." Pretty soon we turned out the lights and stopped answering the door.

Mama and Papa drove in sometime after dark, both walking stooped and slow. They managed to smile when we met them at the door. "Don't worry," said Mama. "He'll be right as rain."

No bleeding inside, at least the doctors were fairly sure of it. He broke two ribs, but they hadn't torn his lungs. He broke an arm and a leg and cracked his skull enough to leave a lump and skint his face on the gravel. That list sounded bad enough, but the next day when Tess and I got to skip school to go see him, the words seemed empty next to staring at his face—eyes, nose, mouth, cheeks—all there but shifted around. Swollen and black and blue and purple, his face looked like it had been shaken and not quite fallen back into place. His smile at least was the same, only more gap-toothed.

I had to beg Mama to let me come sit with him for another day or two, and even though she only let me miss one more school day, I pretty much camped out at Norwood over the next two weekends. Mama was there all the time, sometimes overnight. Papa had to work, of course, so he'd drive Mama to Birmingham, drive back to the mine, then pick her up and take her home. And do it all over again the next day.

It was the first time I'd been to Birmingham, and I didn't want to get out of the car at the hospital. I didn't belong. And not only because of the strangeness of the place itself, the size and the noise of it. The people were different. As we drove through downtown, the people on the streets looked like they'd stepped out of a magazine. The girls had the prettiest dresses—the streets one big parade of chiffon and georgette crepe. Pinks and blues and lavenders, like dainty Easter eggs. The men all wore suits with shoes so shiny the sun reflected off them. They moved like they had some place important to be.

"Different, ain't it?" said Papa that first time I stepped down on Birmingham pavement.

The air was full of dust at home, but the air in Birmingham was different. My nose and throat stopped up as soon as I stepped outside. And even though there wasn't a trace of red rock, my white gloves were dirty, covered in some sort of gray grime even when I didn't touch a thing. It was an unreal thing, looking up at the thick cloud hanging over the city where you couldn't hardly see any normal, white clouds, then looking around and seeing satin slippers stepping through those dingy streets. The streets in Birmingham made me think more than Carbon Hill streets did.

I felt like an explorer, walking past more Model As and Model Ts than I'd ever seen in one place. I was like Columbus discovering the Indians. Like I'd taken a wrong turn and stumbled on some other world with a different sky and different air, different land—all paved over, almost no grass to be seen—different buildings that stretched toward the smoke. Tall and thin like pencils, the downtown buildings looked sure to topple over. They blocked out bits of the sky, and I soon found out that at night they blocked out stars. Past the tall buildings, the smokestacks muscled into the city. A few blocks over on First Avenue, Sloss Furnaces spit sparks and flames, fireworks I could see from the street. Every way I looked, something was being made and its leftovers were pouring into the sky.

It made me think of the smallness of Carbon Hill in a way that I hadn't before. I couldn't have imagined this place. Tess was the one good at playing pretend, but I didn't think even she could have thought this up. It didn't bother me much that I hadn't been able to imagine it, but I couldn't stand that I'd never even tried. Carbon Hill had wrapped me up warm and snug, and I never thought of leaving it. I didn't particularly care for Birmingham, but I thought I should have known about it, at least wondered about it. I started running through the other places that were only words—the Grand Ole Opry came through the radio from a giant stage called Nashville, as exciting and unimaginable as Washington, D.C., or England or Montgomery. Those places didn't have any people on the front porches or crickets chirping at night or kids playing in the front yards. All they had was a syllable or two, with nothing behind them. Like Amelia Earhart flying across the Atlantic. President Hoover and Governor Graves. Just ideas, all of them.

Same as nurses. Doctors I'd known, but I'd never met a nurse before, and at first they all blended together in their stiff pinafores and blue-and-white checked dresses, fluttering around Jack's bed. Every inch of them was ironed and starched from their bibs and aprons to their caps, and I wondered how they kept them so white working around bleeding people. Those first couple of days they checked on Jack all the time, partly because something could still pop up unexpected, and partly, I figured, because he was cute. At some point I started noticing that a young, freckled one with thick hair twisted under her cap seemed to be there most of all.

"How do you get it all so straight?" I asked finally, surprising me and her. She didn't answer me until I added, "Your uniforms. They're so perfect. Even the collars."

"Iron 'em while they're wet on a good, hard board, and won't be a wrinkle in them," she said, then leaned toward me over Jack's bed. "And the collars, they'd slit our throats they're so sharp. You've got to put a little soap under the edge so they don't rub your throat raw."

Just like that, with talk about a bloody neck, she turned into a real person. She'd call me by name when she came to check on Jack's bandages and take his temperature (which could mean he had an infection of some sort, she said), and I learned about her three younger sisters in Atlanta. Robin was the first nurse in her family, and she'd given her old uniforms from nursing school to her sisters so they could pretend and maybe get the itch to get trained themselves. "Can't count on findin' the man you want," she said. "Might as well know you can make a livin'."

By the time Jack went home, I'd found out that she was sweet on a law clerk who she met when she stitched up his foot after a nail went clean through it. If he asked her to marry him, she wouldn't be a nurse much longer. She didn't seem too upset about that—with hospital rules she'd either have to give up nursing or give up the boy, and she wasn't about to let him go. The romance didn't interest me much, though. I was taken with her spotless uniform and her little triangle of a cap that always stayed exactly in the middle of her head. I liked how sure she seemed of herself and her job, how she smiled at Jack and laid her hand on his forehead like he was kin, not some boy she happened to be paid to take care of. And I could be like her as easy as I could be a teacher, which had become more than just two syllables long before. A teacher was Miss Etheridge with her soft voice or a dozen other women I'd know by face and voice and mannerisms. And now a nurse was not just a woman in a starched pinafore—a nurse was Robin O'Reilly. In a day, Birmingham and nurses became touchable things and it put me in a mind to reconsider all those other paper-thin ideas that must have as much substance behind them. Somewhere Amelia Earhart, flying airplanes and wearing pants, had as clear a voice as Miss Etheridge or hands as fast as Mama's. The thought was so heavy—too heavy—it made my head jerk.

I could only think of far-off people and places for so long before I'd glance down and see Jack looking up at me. My brother hurt and tucked in bed, that was something I knew. And that something won out over all my new thoughts with no battle at all. With outside the hospital more overwhelming than appealing, I was just fine in Jack's ward. I'd sit on the edge of his bed, stroking his hair, which he always loved. We'd play tic-tac-toe for hours, and when his eyes were droopy but he was too stubborn to close them, I'd sing softly "You Are My Sunshine." He didn't care for the please-don't-take-my-sunshine-away part, which made him think about me leaving, so instead I sang, "No one can take my sunshine away."

Albert I'D NEVER SEEN a smaller thing than my boy lying in that hospital bed. Looked like a breeze would carry him away. Eyes blackened, blood still in his hair, arm and leg fresh in casts. I was there with Leta and the girls that first morning he woke up in the hospital—the only daylight in a long, long stretch that I didn't spend time below ground.

"I'm like you, Pop," Jack said, all smiles, a hole where one tooth should have been. Cheerful eyes staring out of the bruises. "I can take whatever they throw at me. Trucks and all."

I don't know if he saw me struggling to put words together and keep my eyes dry, but he kept on talking without waiting for me to collect myself.

"The doctor showed me his X-ray goggles—with green leather and green glass, too. And people can whack my cast and I won't even feel it. Go on, thump it. Go on."

He held out one stumpy arm toward me, fingers wiggling. I worked up a smile myself and patted the plaster. "Anybody hits you, you'll knock the fire out of 'em with that thing."

"Yessir."

"He'll need to stay here another week," the doctor said. And, may God forgive me, my first thought was that we couldn't afford it. But there just wasn't nothing extra, not even enough for a new winter dress for each of the girls, and I knew about hospital bills. It's why I'd set my own arm with plaster powder when I was younger, and why I still let the Galloway doctor tend to me. Not that I'd have wished that on my boy—he needed to be fixed right, and fixed permanent. But I heard those words and my whole body started to ache, starting at the bones and working out.

"I want him to have whatever he needs," I said. "But I got to ask you—how much is that bill gone run me?"

"You'd need to check at the front desk," he said without

any expression. I didn't answer, and he added with a little more kindness, "It'll run around $75."

That was four months work if it was a day.

"Keep him as long as he needs," I said.

Before we even made it home that first full day after Jack was hit, everybody knew what had happened. And they didn't need the front desk to know what a hospital stay meant. The fellows passed the word along, and almost everybody let me have one of their shifts, whatever they did. That was a chunk that'd be missing from their own dinner tables, and I closed my eyes at the thought of the charity, but it was better than a handout. This way I was working for the money at least. I worked every single day of the ten days Jack was in the hospital, mostly double backing. Those double shifts were a lot of loading—I'd take whatever I could get—and I felt it like I hadn't in years. I'd gotten softer just talking and watching and managing the men. I worked nearly every day the two weeks after the accident—I counted up two hundred and fifty hours that month.

The first week was the hardest, then enough numbness set in to deaden the aches. Sleep was the real weakness, harder to shut out than pain. And it started to win out by the second week, my eyelids drooping, muscles jerking. I missed the car once, slinging coal against the far wall. Nobody said nothing. And I kept on, no pain, the shovel as much a natural part of me as a leg or a hand.

Jack used to fit in the palm of my hand, his neck-to-tailbone no bigger than wrist-to-elbow.

Neck snapping forward, eyes heavy and dry. The fuzzy memory of a soft bed, Leta's back against mine. The thought of scrubbed skin and sun on my face and clothes not stiff with dirt and sweat—it all made my thoughts jumble. Usually I didn't have many thoughts while I loaded, made my mind go blank and still. But those days with Jack in the hospital, my brain balked at the strict schedule, wandering off to dream even if I was awake and shoveling. I'd see Jack chubby and bawling, held up in one hand like a gift. Then I'd see him in the hospital bed. I wondered if that tooth he lost was still on the side of the road. More than once I got it into my head that I should try to find it after my shift was over. Then I'd come to my senses. Did that truck driver have nightmares like Tess when he got back safe to his warm bed that day? I hoped so. I hoped he'd gotten a good look at Jack's round face, seen how small he was across the shoulders. I hoped he couldn't shake the memory of him.

My feet went to sleep every so often and I'd bend my knees a different way. But that only let the air hit them, aggravating the damp that had seeped in. Thousands or millions or more years the coal was here, laying and waiting for us. Us with lives no more than a flicker and a flash. Really only fuel ourselves, burned up quick enough, the moving on to somewhere else as something else, something less solid. Smoke and warmth drifting up.

Fuel for the fire, sacrificed like Abraham offered up Isaac. Held his boy on an altar and readied hisself to slit the boy's throat. Jack again, wiggling in my hand.

"Hand's bleedin', Albert," called Ban behind me. Sure enough it was—I'd scraped my knuckles hard enough on the wall to take the skin off. But the dirt would clog up the blood. I left it be.

Jack grinning up from his hospital bed, proud of his casts and his bruises. I did that to him, made him think pain was a trophy. A friend. It was more of a reminder. A constant nagging whispering to me that it would win someday, that my body— stubborn and weak and hateful and all-important—wouldn't have me keep it harnessed and bridled forever. It would tumble, burnt up as sure as the chunks sliding into my shovel.

I was cold all the time. Sweaty under my arms and my back soaked, but trying not to shiver. One second I'd be digging, then a second later I'd have auger in my hand and be drilling into the coal face. Just like that, the shovel would be out of my hand, another tool there instead. I learned to use whatever I was holding and not be too puzzled by it.

But I started getting antsy about using the blasting caps when I was fading in and out like that.

Wrote a little poetry when I was courting Leta. She never cared much for me saying her hair poured down her back like honey, and I felt foolish for trying my hand at it anyway. Couldn't even write the words down proper. But I liked the sound of some things, liked how they echoed in my ears until I could feel them going down my throat. One bit I always turned around in my head was how alike we were—man and rock—black and buried underground, hardening more every day until we were chipped into bits. I thought about it when I walked into the showers, all of us looking for all the world like we were turning into what we were digging up.

Jonah was next to me.

"You got a sharp mind," I said to him. Then I wasn't sure if I had said it or thought it. So I said it again, making sure it was out loud.

"Heard you the first time, Albert. Just took me aback," he said. "But I thank you."

He didn't seem to be looking at me, but I wasn't bothered. "Ain't never asked you what you thought about nothing outside the mines," I said. "But I thought a lot about what you said about what kind of woman would put her baby in the well. Smartest thing anybody said on it."

He didn't say nothing, and it might have been an hour or the next shift or another day when I thought to finish the conversation.

"Before all this with Jack, I was wantin' you to come over for supper."

"My guess is you might not be thinkin' straight right now," he said. He didn't seem to be sweating at all, and his coveralls was hardly dirty. I wondered how long he'd been there.

"Naw, naw," I said. "I mean it."

He never answered at all. Then he was gone, and Ban was there or Oscar or Red or any of twenty other faces. Ban and Oscar would come over to supper if I asked 'em; they wouldn't think I was off-kilter. I could picture their houses, their dinner tables, their wives putting spoons in the bowls of vegetables. I couldn't see Jonah's house inside or out. Couldn't even think of how many kids he had for sure. But it seemed like he wasn't never there for me to ask—just all those other faces. They'd be next to me for a while, then gone. I'd turned into one of the pillars connecting the ceiling to the floor.

There was talk about the union still wanting a minimum weekly wage. Only a word here and there, never said too loud. Still never knew when the bosses might have ears of their own in the mines, ready to turn in anybody that mentioned the UMW. I couldn't get worked up about it, much as I believed it was a step we had to make for anything to improve much. My mind was filled with wanting sleep, wanting home, wanting my son well, and I couldn't seem to hold on to bigger thoughts of what John Lewis was planning. Wants pushed out the thoughts more and more every night.

I told myself there was no shame walking into the hospital with the coal still under my nails and in the coal tattoos where the dust had settled in the nicks on my hands and arms. I felt some people looking at me, but I had no energy left for it.

Tess   I SAT AND COUNTED the streetcars as they passed by.

Jack wasn't awake, and I kept accidentally catching the eyes of people in the other beds when I looked around the room. Virgie wouldn't leave Jack's bedside, and there wasn't really enough room for us and Mama, too. (At least Mama had a chair. She said it was as comfortable as a bed and she slept real well in it.) A man two beds down from Jack had a black leg that stuck out from his sheet. And next to him a boy about Virgie's age moaned real soft all the time. So I eased myself onto the window sill looking over the street and the streetcar line. It was a big window, wide enough for me to lean back against one side and fold my knees underneath me.

"There's only the one, you know," came a voice from behind me. Aunt Celia.

I turned around and hugged her before I realized what she'd said. "Only one what?"

"One streetcar. Same one keeps coming by on that one track."

I wanted to know how it moved since it looked like part train and part car, but I already felt foolish for having counted up to sixteen of them.

"Jack got an X-ray done," I said. "He said it wasn't a bit like that fancy shoe fitters they have in Jasper where you can see your feet inside the shoe. This one had a screen and you didn't have to look into the goggle doohickeys."

I liked the room better with Aunt Celia in it. It had felt cold before, all white and metal, with pale people and straight-faced nurses who scolded me for trying to make Jack laugh by tickling his belly. Even the nurse Virgie liked seemed nervous about me moving around too much.

We had plenty of visitors, some coming by the house and leaving food and coming to the hospital, too. Not many people had cars, though, so we usually came home to a pile of food left on the front porch, and then we'd have maybe one or two families trickle in to see Jack while we were at the hospital. For the first time since summer, nobody brought up the dead baby. All anybody talked about was how wonderful Jack was and how terrible the truck driver was. They'd go back and forth—after saying "bless his heart" and "he's the sweetest thing" a few times about my brother, they'd start calling the truck driver a no-account and "the worst kind of a man" and "pure evil." Missy and her mother came, Missy's mother wearing a fur of all things. To a hospital. (They didn't have the maid with them, so I didn't have to worry about what to call her.) From one day to the next you could go from being the fortunate ones because you had a porch full of cotton to the needy ones because you didn't have furs or gold bracelets.

"Can I go over there to Sloss Furnaces and see if I can catch sparks?"

"Why would you want to do a fool thing like that?" asked Aunt Celia. I could smell peppermint on her breath, and it was lots better than snuff. They didn't let you dip or spit in the hospital, and I figured she needed something to keep her mouth busy.

"I've never seen it rain sparks like that before."

"You'd burn your hands, probably set yourself on fire, child."

"But I'd catch some sparks."

I wanted to get myself on the other side of that window. I wanted to see where that streetcar went. Nobody would let me out by myself, though, and Virgie didn't want to leave the hospital. The streets had so many lights at night. And everything was bigger and louder. I couldn't hardly take it all in.

"Don't you love Birmingham, Aunt Celia?"

"Nah," she said, the candy in her mouth clacking against her teeth, which she was probably going to rot out by the time Jack went home. "Too much dirt and racket. I get ticked off at enough idiots back home—twenty times as many idiots here to set me off."

"It's so different," I said.

"Ain't that what I just said?"

I kept looking out the window, watching the big monsters of buildings stand guard over the city. "Those sparks from the furnaces could catch the wind and fly all the way to Carbon Hill. They could pick out a nice chimney, sail down like they was dropped off by a stork, then grow into big fires their very own selves." I waved toward Sloss. "Baby fires," I called to the sparks.

Aunt Celia had pulled out her hunk of peppermint and was holding it close to her face. "Spit in my mouth tastes better than this," she said, glaring at it.

I pointed to the other side of the city, hardly hearing her. "And I bet if you climbed those smokestacks at the steel mills, you could snatch a bird right out of the air."

Aunt Celia kept her candy between her thumb and finger and shook it at me like she was dotting i's in the air. "Anybody ever told you, Tessie, that you got a way of paintin' pictures without ever puttin' brush to paper? Might not be pictures that make any sense, but they sure can make you smile."

Sometimes Aunt Celia—even holding a spit-covered piece of candy—seemed like the most wonderful woman in the world to me. I liked the thought of that, of pretty pictures hovering in the air after I talked.

"They call it the Magic City," I told Papa on the way home one night.

He and Mama looked at each other, tired and something else. Something sadder than tired. "Men are sleepin' in the coke ovens here, Tessie," he said. "Miners ain't even got houses to sleep in if they lose their jobs. Company owns it all. Don't care for their brand of magic myself."

But I did. Even with men in the coke ovens. It didn't matter if it was ugly, it was sure exciting.

Leta   WHILE ALBERT WAS working—which was most all the time during that October—I shored up everything around the house. Funny how for once there didn't seem to be enough to do.

Once the children were asleep, I worked by candlelight, not wanting to waste electricity. I was keeping late hours partly to fill the nights and partly to keep Albert from seeing me mending shoes. I couldn't seem to close my eyes for any length of time. I'd listen to the children breathe, needed to listen to them. I found myself propped up on one elbow, not wanting to lay down, much less sleep, when they were there for the watching. Jack couldn't sleep well, shifting this way and that to stay off his arm, and not being able to rest on his leg. I'd hear him cry out in his sleep, the only time he'd cry out. About to pop his buttons he was so proud of those broken bones. The sleepy whimpers sounded all the worse because he never made a peep all day long. And I noticed the difference in the sleep sounds more than I'd ever thought I would, although the whimpering wasn't as bad as when there were no Jack sounds at all.

The quiet made me think what if there weren't never more Jack sounds. Never again. Only a Jack as still and quiet as those bricks left on the side of the road. But we couldn't go after the brick company. Albert didn't want to. Not that I'd argue with the idea that we didn't need to be causing people trouble, but every time I raised my head, I saw the trouble that driver had caused my boy. Albert didn't want to hear it, but I sure wanted to say it. What I did instead was ask it, only once. When he said no, we didn't need to be thinking on that anymore, I only nodded. Not like Celia. She nagged at him, argued with him, sighed at him. I didn't see as that nagging moved him anymore than not nagging. He'd made up his mind and that was that.

I could keep at him, be quiet and cold and make him miserable, make us both miserable, or I could leave it be. I wanted to keep as much smoothness in our life as I could. Too much was already pulled and yanked out of place.

So I tried to smooth out my own thoughts at least, keep them pressed and folded. For a week, there'd been the shoes to do, which at least took my mind off why I couldn't bear to have my children out of my sight even to sleep.

It was only five cents for one of those stick-on shoe soles, and the holes in Tess's winter shoes was only getting bigger. But I hated to spend a single cent, at least not until Albert's hours had slacked off and we'd paid a good chunk of the hospital bill. Not that he'd have begrudged new soles. Just the opposite. If he'd seen me here cutting a piece of cardboard to fit inside her shoe, he'd have had a fit and gone to Bill's store himself. The cardboard only lasted a day, so I was back at the same spot every night, cutting a new piece. Tess didn't complain, even though she must've felt the damp on wet days.

More than saving money, it was something I could do. That nickel wouldn't make much of a dent in the seventy-five dollars we owed. But it about killed me to see Albert come in half dead at all hours of the night or morning, not even knowing what time it was, just knowing his shift was done and he needed to be back in however many hours. One night he'd walked in asking what was for breakfast when it wasn't even sunset yet. And we bought so little, it was hard to scrimp. I wasn't going to cut back on Albert's coffee. We couldn't do without the dry ice for the icebox. And nothing else was bought regular. I was used to working longer days than Albert, mending or cleaning supper dishes while he sat and smoked, and I didn't take to sitting while he sweated and strained. The empty space beside me made the bed seem harder, the clock ticking seem louder. It left me with a helpless feeling, all the worse for Jack tossing in his bed and me not able to help him.

So I cut that cardboard perfectly, not veering in the least from the lines I'd traced around the shoe. When it was done, I was tempted to patch some more shoes whether there was a hole in them or not. But I didn't. I didn't even put the sewing scissors down. I held them in my lap, Tess's shoes side by side in front of me. I didn't blow out the two candles next to me, but I didn't really need the light. I sat there cross-legged in the middle of the front room, no fire going, not tired, not really thinking of anything much. It was easy to not think those wide-awake nights. I could turn my mind off and be an empty body. I stayed there and felt the cold floor under me until Albert pushed the door open.

"What're you doin' home in the middle of the night?" I asked, almost forgetting to whisper.

He whispered back, head to the side, "It's five, Leta-ree. Rooster's about to crow any second."

I'd always known that rooster better than he knew hisself. I didn't know what to say. The night pure got away from me.

"What're you doin' sittin' in the middle of the floor?" Albert asked. "And still in your nightgown. Jack alright?"

"He's fine."

"You feelin' poorly?"

I pushed myself to my feet, blowing out one candle and holding the other one toward Albert. Deep circles under his eyes. Even after a night of staring at Jack's bruises, one look at Albert's eyes sapped out any bitterness I'd worked up over who ought to be paying for this.

"Just wandered out here," I said, knowing he wasn't in no shape to press me on it. "When you headed back?"

"Night shift tomorrow."

"So you can sleep in?"

He nodded, already headed toward the bedroom. I followed right behind him with the candle. He'd changed after showering at the mines, so he only stripped down to an undershirt and his long johns, then fell into bed.

"Jack sleepin' through the night?" he mumbled, head in the pillow.

"See for yourself," I answered, just barely poking his side. "Tosses a little, but he's sleepin' good."

Lifting his head and turning it toward the boy took a few seconds, but he managed. His eyelids stayed open long enough for him to look over Jack from head to toe, then he flopped back down. "He knows I want to be here, don't he?"

"'Course he does. He knows you got to work."

"I ain't seen him awake in three days. What's he supposed to make of that?"

"That you ain't got no choice."

He pulled at the hem of my nightgown, inching me closer to his face. He'd remembered he hadn't kissed me, and he pecked my cheek when I got low enough that he didn't have to raise his head.

"Shoulders sore?" I asked.

He grunted, eyes closed. The girls weren't moving, but I thought Virgie might be playing possum. She woke at the littlest sound. Tess slept like Jack—might as well have been carved out of wood once they hit the bed.

"Want me to rub 'em?"

He more hummed than grunted that time. I sat on the edge of the bed, rubbing my hands together to warm them. Between the cold air and showering after every shift, the skin at Albert's neck was dry like newsprint. The muscles underneath had turned to concrete, no give in them at all, and I knew his arms would be the same. But he started snoring before I even made it past his shoulders. Shoulders maybe harder, stronger than when I met him. Thought he could run into a rock wall and the wall'd give before he did.

I kept on rubbing even after he was asleep. He'd feel the difference when he woke.

Virgie IT FELT GOOD to have Jack back home, his old self, only quieter. He couldn't run into things nearly so well with the casts on his leg and arm. I knew he'd soon enough figure out how to leave his mark with a crutch, though and that Tess best stop poking at him and learn to keep her distance.

Mama didn't like to talk about Jack's accident. She'd talk about it fine if you brought it up—she wasn't one to shy away from anything—but I could tell she'd rather focus on talk about the chores and our schoolwork and what was going on with relatives. She never mentioned that truck driver or what became of him or how lucky Jack was or how scary it had been seeing him in the hospital for the first time. Jack's accident was a wild, unpredictable thing, and Mama liked things to be regular and orderly. I always thought I was exactly like her that way, and mainly I was. I wouldn't ever be like Tess and sling my shoes all over the place, one under the bed, the other propped against the nightstand. I liked them to be pointed in the same direction, their toes and heels touching. But a small part of me, only a small part, wanted to see what would happen if I put those shoes on opposite sides of the room and pointed them in opposite directions.

I'd finished changing my clothes and tying a rag around my hair before Mama had the varnish measured out. So I started sorting through the paintbrushes laid out next to her.

"You remember Robin from the hospital, Mama?" I asked her as she poured out the last bit of varnish into separate pails for each of us.

"That cute little nurse?"

"Yes'm. She was nice ... and real good at takin' care of the patients."

"I'm sure she was."

"You ever wish you'd stayed unmarried, Mama? Earned your own money? Moved somewhere far off?"

"Why're you askin' me about somethin' I don't know nothin' about?" She set the can down and handed me one of the buckets. She hadn't spilled a drop of the varnish.

"You never thought about it?"

"Lord, no. Who's got time for thinkin'? There's floors to paint."

We'd have painted the floors earlier if it weren't for the accident. As it was, the cold wind outside had turned the floors icy enough that I needed to tuck my dress under my knees to warm them. Mama took the kitchen, Tess took the bedroom, and I took the den. I had on my oldest dress, cream-colored belted cotton, with the hem frayed and a dark stain on one arm that wouldn't come out. I never could figure how I spilled anything on it. But I only used the dress for housework, and it was good for sprawling on the floor and making even, up-and-down strokes with a paintbrush full of varnish. Every fall the floors started looking dusty and dull, and Mama would want to shine them up with a new coat. It was hot work, messy, too, and even with Papa's old work gloves for each of us—he never wore gloves, so I didn't know how he managed to have old ones—I still got varnish sloshed on my arms, shellacking down the little hairs. I'd crawl a little too far and stick my knee in a wet spot, then dirt would stick to my knees. A few hairs worked their way out from under the kerchief tying them back, and they got shellacked from me trying to keep them out of my face.

We didn't keep a fire going with us all working so hard.

Jack sat out on the porch—even with the windows open, Mama worried about him breathing in the fumes. I heard him call my name as I was trying to unstick my knee from the floor without setting my gloves against anything.

"What is it?" I answered back, blowing at a loose hair.

"That boy and Lois are walking up the road."

"Orville?"

"That whistle boy."

One night before Jack got hit, a boy that called on Lois had brought his cousin Orville from Jasper on a visit. The two boys and Lois came over, and everybody agreed without saying anything about it that I would be the fourth. We just sat on the porch for a while and Papa decided as long as he met any boy involved and we weren't gone too long, it'd be alright if I went somewhere with a group of boys and girls occasionally. As long as it wasn't an actual date. The next time Lois's fellow was in town, they came over and Orville brought me a wooden whistle he'd carved for me to take to Jack in the hospital. He was a sweet boy.

But I didn't want him dropping by right then with me such a fright. I wished there was some way people could let you know when they were about to show up at your door.

I saw Lois and Orville wave at Jack as they turned up the walk, and I hid myself by the window, peeking out to see how close they were. As I heard them climbing the steps, I yanked off my gloves and did my best to smooth my hair back under my kerchief. I used the inside hem of my skirt to wipe my face real fast. I didn't have time to do anything about the dress.

"Virgie," called Lois at the same time she was knocking.

I counted to three, then opened the door. "Hi, y'all. We're all paintin' the floors, so I'm sorry for bein' a mess."

I could tell by the look on Lois's face that I really was a mess, but Orville looked calm enough. "Hi there, Virgie," he said. "Nice to see you."

He stepped back and held the door open for Lois to come in first. The nicest thing about Orville was he had wonderful manners. He was always tipping his head to me, almost bowing when he said hello. He never forgot to open a door or pull out a chair or walk on the roadside of the sidewalk.

"Sorry we caught you by surprise," Lois said, waving her hand in front of her nose at the fumes. "We were just goin' to walk to town to meet some folks and thought you might want to join us."

"Oh, no, I couldn't," I said. "Not like this. And it'd take me ages to clean myself up. I'd need to..." I stopped, not sure it would be right to mention bathing in front of a boy. "I'd need to redo myself from head to toe," I said instead.

"You look fine," Orville said, and I could tell that he really did think so. Which was nice enough, but sort of silly.

Lois was still frowning at the smell; I opened the door again and shooed her toward it.

"Let's go sit on the porch—I don't want you passin' out," I said. I didn't want them wandering over to where I'd already varnished, either. So Orville held the door again, and we all sat in the rockers on the opposite side of the porch from Jack, who was throwing rocks at a tin can a good twenty feet into the yard.

"I'm sorry, but I just can't," I said again. "I couldn't get ready to go—it'd take way too long."

"We can wait for you," Lois said.

"I'm really, really sorry," I said to Orville. "I'd love to go with y'all but I just can't this time. I hope I'll see you next time you come to visit."

We went round and round about it a little more, and I sat with them on the porch for a few minutes, but I didn't change my mind. So I brought out some iced tea and we all had a glass and then they left. I could tell Orville was hurt, but I really couldn't go. I was filthy, and it would have taken an hour or more for me to draw the water and clean up, plus I couldn't just leave without finishing my part of the floor.

Tess WE ALL FORGOT about the Well Woman after Jack's accident. Pretty much. My nightmares stopped altogether.

Neither Virgie nor I mentioned babies or mothers or solving anything. Everybody talked less anyway, so it wasn't like we'd made any effort to keep quiet about it in particular. Papa and Mama hardly slept, but they tried to act like they weren't about to fall over. I saw more lines in Mama's and Papa's faces, and I could tell Virgie was working harder than ever to help out Mama.

I felt the difference in the house, and I knew I should be all somber, too, but once I knew Jack would be okay, I couldn't seem to keep still. I'd come back from Birmingham twitching to do something, go somewhere. My head was full of the city. And if I couldn't go all the way to Birmingham—nobody seemed to be in any hurry to go back, and even if they did, they'd hardly let me explore any—I'd have to make do with something closer.
I thought about Lou Ellen Talbert and those dead babies buried in her backyard. I was curious. With her puckered side and pointy tongue and grown-up ways and buried babies, that girl lived in a world just as different as Birmingham. And it was close by. Lou Ellen wasn't at school all the time on account of helping around the house while her mama worked outside, but I kept an eye out for her. And as soon as I spotted her at recess one day, I asked if I could come see them babies. She was sitting by herself under a shade tree—I never saw her with other girls much— and she didn't act surprised that I asked. She didn't skip a beat before she told me she didn't think her parents would take to the idea of her parading a friend past the graves like it was show-and-tell, but if I could get out after her parents were asleep, she'd show me.

Sneaking out made the whole thing seem all the more exciting. I made plans to meet her the next night, after everybody else had gone to bed.

I didn't say anything to Virgie. I thought she'd scold me for thinking about those dead babies when we had plenty to think on right here at home, and she'd definitely scold me for thinking about sneaking out, which I'd have to do. Not that I'd ever asked about staying out late, but neither me nor Virgie had ever gone out past regular bedtime unless we were spending the night with a friend. Papa always talked about not understanding parents who let their daughters stay out 'til all hours of the night. I knew that meant we wouldn't be like those girls.

I tried to keep from feeling guilty about keeping a secret, telling myself I wasn't doing nothing wrong, only visiting a friend. It really wasn't lying if I just didn't mention it. Wasn't no reason to feel like I was disrespecting Mama and Papa.

When I came in from school the day I was supposed to meet Lou Ellen, Mama was drawing water from the well, her back to me. I wrapped my arms around her middle and made her "oof."

"You're gone squeeze me plumb in two," she said, not really complaining, reaching around with one hand to pat me as much as she could. "You have a good day, sugar?"

I didn't say "yes, ma'am" like I meant to. Instead I said, "I told Lou Ellen I'd come over to her house tonight," all the time wondering why those words were so determined to come out.

"After supper?" asked Mama, not seeming too concerned.

"A good bit after supper. Around bedtime."

"Why you goin' over there so late?"

I didn't like the idea of lying to Mama, but I wasn't stupid, neither. "We wanted to have an adventure," I said, thinking as fast as I could. "I never been out that late before, and we thought it'd be fun to be out by ourselves, have the whole backyard for a little while with the moon shining down and not another soul around. It'll be like we're the only ones in the whole world, and I bet it all looks so different late at night."

I thought about just what all that could involve, and I started seeing the nighttime as I described it. "Maybe the crickets get together and play in a big band after we're in bed. And I bet the owls are out and they have fun tippin' the birds off their branches while they're sleepin', to see if they'll wake up before they hit the ground."

"First time I heard you talk like that in ages, Tess." Mama usually told me to stop daydreamin' when I started imagining things, but this time she didn't seem upset about it at all. Instead she smiled, which made her eyes crinkle up like I hadn't seen in forever, and she ran her hand over my hair. "Never thought I'd miss it like I did. Not scared of possums or boogeymen bein' out there?"

I shook my head and didn't correct her that I was only nervous about the fairy-eating possums, not the normal kind. And I didn't think they'd be out that night.

"You waited late to tell me, didn't you?" she said, balancing the full bucket of water on the side of the well. "And don't think I didn't notice that you were tellin', not askin'."

"I'm sorry, ma'am. May I please go? Please? I just really wanted to get out for a little while and do somethin' different. And Papa always said he don't want us goin' out late at night. I figured you wouldn't let me."

Mama shook her head, half smiling. "He meant with boys. Don't know that he'd much care about you goin' to look at a yard." She looked up at the ceiling, the tip of her tongue sticking out from her teeth. "But then again, he's a might tense lately. Best not to mention it. You just go on and head over there when you need to…but he'll be asleep when you get in, so be quiet."

She didn't even tell me a time to be home, and I made up my mind that it wouldn't ever do no harm to tell Mama my business. She took it real well.

It did seem like a whole different yard by the time I got to Lou Ellen's a little after nine o'clock. Usually I watched the dark from the porch, but this time I was walking through it, smashing it down with every step. Not knowing what my feet were going to hit every time had me breathing quick by the time I got to Lou Ellen's, even though it was a short walk.

She was waiting for me on the porch, an itty-bitty shadow in a rocking chair. The shadow waved, then hurried down the porch steps, her slippers making soft tunk-tunk-tunk sounds instead of the usual thonk-thonk-thonk. Her nightgown came to her knees, and she hitched it up so she wouldn't get tangled in it.

She'd hardly said hello before she was pulling me by the arm past the house and toward the woods. (Even though most of the land was made up of fields, they did have one little patch of pines off to the side of the house.) I was glad for the feel of her hand around my wrist. Everything else seemed unfamiliar. The trees made one giant, dark wall, and with the shadows, the ground had a whole other set of black, flat trees. Patches of moonlight would break through when the branches swayed, and I wanted to play hopscotch on those bright spots. It was as quiet as it was dark—lightning bugs and even the crickets seemed like they were asleep. All I could hear was our feet tiptoeing and the wind blowing the pine trees.

Then my arm was let go, and I nearly ran into Lou Ellen where she'd stopped.

"Here they are," she said, pointing right in front of the woods.

I was only looking at ground. Dirt, a tuft of weed, and grass here and there. No markers—not even a stone, much less a name.

"Y'all didn't mark 'em?" I asked her.

"We know where they are," she whispered. "Papa measured out five steps from the three big pines. There's a baby in front of each."

She took a few steps and pointed straight down.

"So you just know?"

"Yeah," she said like it was obvious.

"And people go on and walk over them like they're not even there?"

"I don't know. I don't."

I wondered how long I needed to stand there. I wasn't quite as interested as I'd thought I'd be. But I knew it was only polite to stay a few minutes, so I started thinking about those babies tucked underground, wrapped in a sheet or blanket. I didn't think about what was under the blanket.

"Why do you suppose we put dead people in the ground?" I asked Lou Ellen.

"Where else you gone put 'em?"

Maybe that was it: no other choice. But I hated the thought of a baby in that cold, hard ground with worms and slugs and roaches rooting around.

"Are they in boxes?" I asked.

"Wrapped in cloth. Least the two I 'member are."

That made it worse. If it was my baby, I could see thinking our nice cool well with mermaids and sparkling fish was a better place. Maybe Virgie had been right and the Well Woman wasn't pure evil or out of her head. Maybe she had some good in her. Like Birmingham had some pretty street cars and also men tucked in coke ovens. It was still an odd thing to do, mind you, turning our well into a grave, but I'd never stared hard at the dirt before and thought what it would be like as a blanket. If I loved something dearly, I'd have a hard time wrapping it up and covering it with dirt like it was garbage you didn't want the dogs getting into.

I saw a shadow move across the only window that had a light, soft but bright enough for me to make out long hair, not electric, but like one of the oil lamps Mama kept around for when we had a thunderstorm.

"Your mama still up?"

"Nah, that's Aunt Lou."

"You think she's noticed you're not there?"

"Prob'bly, but she'd just think I came out to go down the hill." She nodded toward their outhouse. "She's just pacin' anyway. She don't sleep too good. Walks around and talks to herself. Don't know where she is sometimes."

"She alright?"

"Sometimes. Other times it's like she ain't even in the same room with you. Won't talk or nothin'."

"Oh." I started to turn away, thinking to say I needed to head on home, but she kept talking.

"I took her by your place one time, you know. Before she even moved down here. She wanted to get a look at the town when she was visitin', and Mama sent me out to show her y'all's house since your papa owns the farm."

"Why didn't you come in?"

"Didn't know you then."

A thought came to me. I knew why most people had been walking past our house. "Were you out showin' her where the baby got throwed in?"

"This was before that happened."

"Oh."

"She moved down here ... well, couldn't have been more than a couple of weeks later. She's sort of a gossip. Likes to know about people. Mama knew that, so I was just supposed to point y'all out and tell her about you."

"So what'd you tell her?"

She shrugged. "That your sister's real pretty. That your mama and papa give away to anybody that comes askin', that they're big on goin' to church, good people. Your papa don't never talk down to us or act like he's better than us."

"Nothin' about me?"

"Um, I dunno." She looked like she was thinking hard as she could. "I don't think so."

I wished I hadn't ever asked her to jump on cotton, even if she did have dead babies in her backyard. She must've read some of that on my face, because she was quick to add, "But I did tell her that Mama says if anybody's doin' God's work, it's the Moores."

I still thought I could have been mentioned by name. Some people thought I was real personable. Plenty she could have said. I started to say that, but the front door to their house opened, and we ducked down behind the porch. It wasn't Lou Ellen's mama coming to yell at her for being out so late—it was Aunt Lou who'd come out on the porch.

She was a big woman, broad across the shoulders. It was only a crescent moon, but it caught her face just right. She was the woman from the revival.

I got home without thinking, putting one foot in front of the other and winding up at our front door. I climbed in bed and barely got the covers over me before I fell asleep. No bad dreams at all. And I woke up clear-headed, even though it seemed like I'd just closed my eyes. I loved waking up to the smell of coffee and the sounds of the fire crackling. I only had my ears and nose to tell me things while my eyes stayed closed. I could hear Mama clanking pots in the kitchen and Papa making the floorboards creak while he finished getting the fire going and fetching water for our basin. I wished it was the thick smell of bacon that had drifted under the covers along with the coffee-flavored air, but biscuits were nice, too. I could stay buried under the quilts for at least a few minutes and do nothing but soak it all in. But this morning I wanted to do more.

"Virgie. Virgie. Virgie." I kept saying it even when I saw her frown. "Virgie."

"What?" She didn't even roll over, just stayed perfectly still, arms crossed over her chest.

"Virgie."

"I said 'what?'" She sounded annoyed and still half-asleep. She wasn't moving at all, and I wanted her to be a little more enthusiastic about this whole to-do. I was the one who'd gotten in late and had to tiptoe around and find the key Mama left for me on the porch and jump every time Papa shifted or snored and try to stay away from the squeaky board on my side of the bed. Virgie had been dead asleep. And I'd laid there bursting with the news for what must've been hours and hours and hours.

I leaned close to her and talked right in her ear. She hated that.

"I'm pretty sure it was Lou Ellen Talbert's aunt that put the baby in the well," I said.

That made her roll over, one eye peeping open, head shifting a little. She'd drooled on her pillow in her sleep. "Why you say that?"

I told her about the babies' graves and Aunt Lou.

"So she would've known who we were," Virgie said, head still on her pillow, but eyes getting wider by the second. "Would've had some connection to us even. And you really think she was that upset at the revival?"

"She was beside herself."

"We don't know that she had a baby."

"Well, we don't know that the sun'll come up in the morning, but it always does." I'd heard Papa say that before, and it always sounded smart when he said it.

"What are you talking about?" asked Virgie, rubbing at her eyes with one hand.

I tried to move along, not sure about the sunshine explanation. "We can't know for sure unless we talk to her."

"You didn't ask the Talbert girl?"

"Lou Ellen. No, I didn't ask her."

She raised herself up on her elbows, looking down at me. "Why not?"

I raised up on my elbows, too. "Now how do you think I should have worked that in? 'So do you know if your aunt had a baby she didn't tell nobody about and threw it in our well just for fun?'"

"Shhh," she said, looking toward the kitchen. "Don't get bent out of shape. I just thought it might be easier to ask her than to ask a grown woman we don't even know."

"Why do you think she'd tell her little niece about a baby? About havin' one or dumpin' one?"

Virgie flopped back on her pillow with a whoof, and I wondered that the pins in her curlers didn't stab her in the brain. She lay there and I sat up Indian-style, my knees jabbing into her left leg. But she didn't move her leg or even look at me at all.

"Can you keep a baby a secret?" she asked, face half in the pillow again.

I shrugged. "If it don't cry much." Then I remembered. "But she's from Brilliant. She could maybe keep the secret if the baby hadn't never been here. Never been to Lou Ellen's."

"You might be right, Tess," she said, drawing her knees up so they banged into mine. "It might really be her."

She laid and I sat, so quiet I heard an egg hit the frying pan. Then the oven door open. Maybe the biscuits were ready.

"So what do you want to do?" I asked. "Tell Papa? Maybe have him call Chief Taylor?"

She was all the way out of bed and pulling a dress out of the wardrobe before she answered. "No. Let's go talk to her ourselves."

I didn't think that was such a great idea, but I had to admit I was curious.

Leta   JACK HAD SHOT a squirrel from the front porch, and I added it to the stew for dinner. We'd had a lot of stew and cornbread—filling stuff that made the children miss meat less. But squirrel was perfect for stew; the meat was too overpowering to eat by itself.

Everybody sliced their cornbread into triangles and spooned stew on their plates, quick to take a bite and tell Jack how tasty it was. He smiled with every bite he took.

"Next time I'll get a rabbit," he said.

"Next time get a deer," said Tess.

"Might as well tell him to get a buffalo," said Albert, eyes not looking up from his plate. For the first time in a while he was getting to eat with the children, and I hoped he finished quick before he fell asleep in his stew.

"I could shoot a deer," Jack said. "I could."

Nobody argued with him. I thought the stew could have used a little more pepper. And a touch more onion.

"We were thinking about the baby in the well," said Virgie, her face down while she wiped at her mouth. "About how…"

Albert shook his head and interrupted her. "Not now. Not that. Just talk about school or your friends or what the neighbors are up to. I don't want to talk about anything but what'll make me smile. Nothin' to make me think."

We all watched him as he shoveled in more stew, hand propping up his head. Virgie only nodded, looking heartsore and guilty.

"Missy's little brother fit a whole frog in his mouth at recess," said Tess. "He won a piece of licorice off some other boy. But I bet it tasted like frog."

"I could fit two frogs," Jack said.

9 Coffee and Supper

Jack THAT NIGHT SHE WENT OVER TO LOU ELLEN TAL-
bert's was the first time Tess snuck in. By the time we were
teenagers, she was doing it at least once a week. She always
told Mama where she'd be, and if Mama ever happened to say no,
she wouldn't go. But most times Mama would nod at her, and
Pop would never notice she was out late because he went to bed
so early.

Once she was tiptoeing up the back steps and stepped in
the slop jar—which was really an old pot to pee in, not a jar—
that stayed on the porch at night so you didn't have to walk all the
way to the outhouse. Pop had his bed to himself by then; his
breathing had gotten bad enough that he tossed and turned all
night and didn't want to disturb Mama. Pop slept like the dead
even with his tossing, which was always puzzling because he
had an internal alarm clock that beat all I'd ever seen. You could
tell him you wanted to wake up at 4:33 in the morning, and you
could bet money—not that we ever would—that it wouldn't be
4:32 or 4:34 when you felt him shaking your shoulder.

But he didn't hear Tess walking up those porch steps the
night of the slop jar. The rest of us did because she tripped
and clomped loudly on the planks as she got near the door. Then
she hissed, "Shoot!" as loud as she'd clomped. After that, the
clatter and slosh of her stepping in the slop jar pushed us over the
edge. Mama's bed was squeaking from her laughing. And still
Pop didn't wake up. By the time Tess hopped in trying to keep one

foot—the one without a shoe and sock—off the ground, we'd quieted ourselves.

"At least nobody's gone number two," she whispered, and that made us all shove our heads in our pillows to keep from waking Pop.

Tess still lives in the family house, after outlasting two husbands and moving back to take care of Mama. She's there by herself now, with a schnauzer that tries to eat dirt out of the flowerpots.

Virgie started teaching after two years of college—she graduated the last year you could still get a teaching certificate after only two years. I sold papers with Tess helping me, and we all scrimped and saved for her college. Nobody got new shoes those two years. Then she started teaching about thirty miles from home and lived with another girl in a boarding house. She loved it, and she met the man she married when they were both at Troy State College for the summer upgrading their certifications. She kept teaching all during the war while he was overseas. Then when he came back, she quit and started on her family.

She lives in Birmingham and her sons take her up to see Tess for long weekends or weeks at a time. Sometimes I join them and we argue over which was Pop's favorite pie and who snored the worst at night and which of Virgie's boyfriends was the one who accidentally opened the door while Tess was peeping through the keyhole and gave her a black eye. We talk very little about politics or books or movies—we like to unroll the past and touch up the details. And between us all, we can fill in each other's gaps.

Albert I SLEPT FOR sixteen hours straight the first day in November. Then I ate a bowl of vegetable stew and went right back to sleep for another ten. By the time I finally got my head on straight again, I couldn't hardly remember why I'd wanted Jonah to come over. But I knew I'd decided it was a good idea and didn't much matter what anybody might say.

When I asked him, he said no.

I'd driven over to his house, knocked on the front door, and taken in the porch floor while I was waiting. The door and walls of the house looked solid enough, but whole sections of the porch were rotting—Jonah'd laid plywood across the bad spots on the floorboard. His wife opened the door before I could lean down to get a better look.

"Ma'am," I said. She was a strong-looking woman, maybe a head taller than Leta. I couldn't think of her name, though I was sure Jonah must've mentioned it sometime over the last few years. Surely.

"Mr. Moore," she said back. "You need Jonah?"

"I'd appreciate it. You doin' alright?"

"Yessir." She turned, then stopped before her hand left the door. "You like some tea? Fresh made."

I could tell she didn't expect me to take her up on the tea. "That'd be real nice."

When Jonah came out, I was leaning against the railing, not putting much weight on it, hands in my pockets. I was thinking how he could best patch the porch more permanent, without having to replace everything.

"'Afternoon, Albert," he said from the doorway. The screen closed behind him when he took a step. "Kids know better than to play out here," he said, seeing where I was looking.

"All the wood goin' bad?"

"'Fraid so. Ain't got around to trackin' down some new."

His wife came out with two glasses of tea, handing me mine first, which I thanked her for. He called her Renee when he thanked her, and I tucked that away.

"So what brings you by?" he asked after a sip. "Somethin' wrong?"

"Nothin' wrong. Just wanted to see about you comin' by for supper tomorrow if you're not workin'."

"Supper?"

"Nothin' special. You could bring Renee."

He ran his hand over his chin like he was feeling for stubble.
"Well, I thank you. I didn't think you knew what you was sayin'
when you asked me the other week. Not sure you do now. But I'm
gone say no just the same."

I hadn't thought about him turning me down. "Why not?"
I asked.

"You got to stand there and ask me why not?"

I wished he wasn't making this so difficult when it'd already
taken me long enough to ask. "Look, ain't no reason to say no.
I been thinkin' on it. Figured out I was actin' wrong."

He looked at me like I'd sprouted wings. "What're you
talkin' about? You ain't done nothin' wrong."

"That's what I thought," I said, glad he'd given me that little
bit of help. "I thought I treated everybody fair, so none of the
rest of it mattered." Nigger Town, laws about restaurants and such,
police takin' coloreds in whenever they felt like it. 'Cause it
wasn't me. But this was me. This visit. "What you said about the
woman and her baby, it surprised me. Shouldn't have, though,
long as I've known you. Wanna do better by you."

He took his time drinking his tea, kicking at the porch a
time or two. It was a clean porch, well swept, but no paint on it or
the rest of the house. Paint would've helped with the rotting.

"The rest of it still matters, Albert."

I shook my head. "I was wrong, and I know it, and I aim to
make it right."

"The rest of it still matters," he said again.

"Not to me. Not now."

"You askin' any more colored men over for supper? Writin'
any letters to the governor sayin' we ought to be able to eat in
y'all's restaurants?"

I only looked at him.

"You a good man, Albert, but it ain't ever not gone matter."

I'd watched Leta argue with the children before, and
I noticed she usually talked less than I did. I'd go back and forth
with them, trying to tell them why they was wrong, and she'd

only repeat herself until they gave in. In the back of my head, I knew it usually worked on me, too.

"Come for supper," I said.

"Ain't gone do that. But I thank you."

"Come for supper."

"Albert..."

"It'll be fine."

"Might be fine. Probably would be. But might not. Ain't worth riskin' the might-not."

"Come for supper."

"Mule-headed." He set his tea glass down, stared at the ceiling long enough to draw a few breaths. "You so set on it, I'll come for coffee tomorrow."

"Why not stay for supper? Ain't no difference."

"You know the difference." And I did—with coffee we could sit out on the porch, and it wouldn't be the same as having him inside the house, much less at the table.

Virgie I FINALLY GOT to meet Naomi's preacher and potential husband, Bradford. She invited me to go with her family on a night they were having a fellowship supper after church, and Naomi and Bradford and Tom and I stayed long after Aunt Merilyn and Uncle Bill headed home. At the beginning of his sermon, Bradford told a story about a preacher who told his congregation that they should throw all their whiskey and homebrew into the river. Then the song leader stood up and announced that the closing hymn would be "Shall We Gather at the River." I did laugh more than I usually did during a sermon, and I laughed a good bit on the walk home.

Naomi couldn't stop looking at him. I tried looking at Tom out of the corner of my eye to figure out if I could get captivated, too, but it only made my head hurt.

We were still a good ten or twelve houses away from home when the sky opened up. Busy talking, we hadn't noticed any clouds, so we froze when that first sheet of water hit us, then started yelling and running, with the boys asking if we wanted their jackets. We didn't want to stop long enough to take them. As we ran, I felt my dress twist around my legs, and I couldn't seem to keep it straight. After we'd made it a couple of blocks, I realized that it wasn't just that the material was wet: my crepe dress was shrinking.

"Naomi, we got to stop at your house!" I yelled over the sound of our feet hitting the dirt and puddles. "My dress'll be up to my hips by the time I get home!"

She clearly thought that was about the funniest thing she'd ever heard, and she stopped completely, throwing her head back laughing with the water pouring off her face, running into her mouth and down her chin. Her dress was plastered to her, and I knew mine looked the same, but neither of us had curves for it to look too shocking.

"Get home," Naomi said to Tom and Bradford when she'd gotten hold of herself. "God might strike you dead if you get a look at Virgie's legs."

"I didn't say that…" I started, knowing she was teasing me for being prudish but thinking it sounded like a comment about my legs, which were just fine.

"Quick," she shooed. "Her knees are about to peep out."

And they were, even though I was pulling at the skirt as hard as I could. Tom looked about to split in two, not wanting to look like he was after a peek at my legs, but not wanting to leave me.

"You ought to head on," I said to him. "Naomi and me'll be fine." All this had gone on with rain so hard you had to squint your eyes, and I think the weather made the boys agree quicker than they normally would have. They wished us goodbye and took off.

By the time we got to Naomi's house my dress was several inches above my knees, and it was short instead of long-sleeved. We banged on the door, not wanting to drip inside, and Aunt Merilyn didn't open the door all the way before she turned and ran back for towels. By then Naomi and I were both talking at once about my dress, and soon enough I had a towel around my head and Aunt Merilyn and Naomi both squatting on the balls of their feet yanking at my dress. I pulled at my sleeves, wondering how I'd get home without my dress shrinking back up. Tess and I were going to see Lou Ellen Talbert's aunt the next day, and I felt a little frivolous thinking more about crepe than about that dead little boy. But the truth was that I'd thought about him—and his mother—less and less. Somewhere between the basketball game and sitting with Jack in the hospital, the dark, awful life I'd pictured for the mystery mother got harder to imagine. Then she got less dark and awful. More normal. And a little more boring.

Watching Naomi and Bradford hadn't been boring. It was like she was under some sort of spell.

"If you marry your preacher boy, you won't be runnin' around and havin' fun like this," I said to her, water dripping from my chin to the top of her head. I ran the tip of the towel over my face for the third time. "You'll be stuck at home."

Naomi had both hands on my dress, not moving at all so it would hold the stretched shape. She'd opened her mouth when Aunt Merilyn said, "Sure she can have fun."

"How many married women you know who laugh on their front porches soaking wet at night?" I asked.

Aunt Merilyn let go of my dress and stood up, then took three big hops down the steps until she was in the yard. Arms raised, spinning in circles, she got as soaked as we were in about ten seconds flat. Then she grinned and calmly walked back up the steps and knelt down at my feet again, licking the rain off her lips.

"One at least," she said.

Naomi and I hadn't said a word during her whole rain dance, but we both lost it then, laughing even harder as Aunt Merilyn tried to wring out her dress.

"Shoot, it ain't all misery," she said, giving up on her dress and going back to tugging at my sleeves. "And there's other kinds of married besides being married in a coal town. You don't want to do it, that's fine. But don't make up your mind just because this is all you've seen."

"I saw Birmingham," I said, but she acted like I hadn't said anything.

"You pick the man you marry, Virgie. You pick whether you make your beds or go gossip at the post office. You're a smart girl. Sweet. Pretty. I seen you with Jack and Tess—you got as much motherin' in you as any woman twice your age. You got more choices than most. Have some fun with 'em."

"I don't want to get stuck," I said. "I want to be able to support myself like those nurses so I don't have to take some man just so I can eat."

"Lord, you could be a doctor. Be a senator," Aunt Merilyn said.

She was joking, of course. But the thing was, I didn't want to be a doctor. I didn't want to live in some far-off place or do some remarkable thing. And I didn't want this. I didn't want to give every last speck of energy to my husband and houseful of kids and have no time at all for any pleasure of my own. I wanted something left for myself. All that was left was to figure out what was in the middle between remarkable and Carbon Hill.

Tess ME BEING FRIENDS with Lou Ellen made it easier to meet Aunt Lou. The Well Woman to my thinking. I couldn't tell Lou Ellen why we wanted to meet with her aunt, of course—I said we thought it would be the neighborly thing to do. So we got there and said hello and sat around all uncomfortable for a good while chatting with Lou Ellen while Aunt Lou sat in her rocking chair hardly saying a word. Finally, after it seemed like days must've passed, Lou Ellen said, "I got to get to work on some chores now. You wanna come with me?"

We'd been waiting for that. Lou Ellen never got to sit still for long.

"Nah," I said. "We'll sit here for a little bit and then come on out later."

She sat there a moment, head cocked, purely confused but not knowing how to ask us about it in front of her aunt. "You sure?" she said.

"We're sure," answered Virgie.

Lou Ellen sort of backed out of the room slowly, like she was giving us time to change our minds. I couldn't blame her—I wouldn't know what to make of one of our friends coming over and visiting with Aunt Celia instead of us. Well, maybe I could, but Aunt Celia was a whole lot more fun than Aunt Lou seemed to be.

Finally Lou Ellen had thump-thumped down the front steps, and Virgie and me and Aunt Lou sat facing one another in the middle of the Talberts' dark sitting room. Aunt Lou'd made coffee, but she didn't think to offer us anything to drink. We didn't mind.

We'd had a little while with only the clinking of Aunt Lou's spoon against her cup when Virgie said, "So do you like Carbon Hill so far, Miss Lou?"

"'S'alright."

"We're glad you moved. I'm sure Lou Ellen's glad to have you around."

When Aunt Lou didn't say anything, Virgie glared at me like I wasn't pulling my weight. So I said, "Bet you're a help to everybody. I sure would like to have my Aunt Celia or Aunt Merilyn around more."

She didn't answer that, neither. Matter of fact, she didn't even look at us, hadn't hardly looked at us since we came in. Hadn't smiled, hadn't yawned or sneezed or licked her lips. She had a plain, pale face, but it was worth looking at just because it seemed frozen. She glanced out the window toward the fields every now and then, but mainly she stared down at her lap, her shoulders slumped a little and her knees not quite together so that her pink-flowered dress stretched tight across her legs. Mama told us we should always sit with our ankles crossed, but since that was so uncomfortable, I didn't blame Aunt Lou for being more relaxed.

"I guess you heard about the baby that was put in our well," Virgie said.

I was glad she quit dawdling. We'd decided before we got there that she'd bring up the subject and just see what Aunt Lou had to say about it. We thought we'd be able to tell if she knew anything about it.

Aunt Lou kept on stirring her coffee. There wasn't even any steam coming off it.

"Of course, Chief Taylor knows that the baby was ... that he wasn't alive by the time he was put in there," Virgie added.

"So it wasn't a crime. What the woman did. There wasn't anything illegal about it."

Nothing. Her stony face didn't budge.

"But we sure wish we knew who it was," Virgie kept on. "Tess's had awful nightmares about it, and we've all been thinking on it for months now. We'd like for the baby to have a name, to make our peace with it, you know."

Still nothing. I didn't think she would ever take a sip.

"Did you put that baby in our well?" I asked.

Virgie kicked my foot, but Aunt Lou finally looked at us, really looked at us. She didn't seem offended at all.

"Hmm?" she said, forehead all crinkled up. She had a little voice for such a big woman. More like a girl's voice, high and thin.

"The baby," I said real slow. "Did you put him in our well?" When Virgie rolled her eyes at me, I added, "Ma'am."

"You came down front at the revival," she said to me. "With the nice woman."

"Yes'm, I did see you at that Baptist revival. You were real upset. Like you had somethin' big on your mind."

She started stirring that stupid coffee again, like it was more interesting than being accused of putting a baby in the well.

"So you were upset at the revival, Miss Lou?" asked Virgie, sweet as pie.

The coffee spoon stopped moving, and that childish voice piped up again. "I wanted to ask for forgiveness. Same as everybody else who felt the call."

"It's okay if you put the baby in." I kept my voice soft and low, like when we tried to get a colt to come eat a carrot. "We're not mad. We just want to know."

"Wouldn't put my little George in a well," she said.

"Who's George?" I asked.

"I ain't told nobody."

"We won't tell," said me and Virgie at the same time.

Aunt Lou looked toward the door, then toward the kitchen. Then she covered her belly with the hand that wasn't holding the coffee. I'd seen women carrying babies do that same thing.

"Don't matter now. It's eatin' me alive—might be good to get it out of me," she said, hand still on her belly. Patting and circling.

We sat forward on our seats just as she heaved herself out of hers. She grunted a little as she pushed off the rocking chair, then she walked behind the chair and stood with her hands resting on the back. She fiddled with a little tear in the cane, flicking it back and forth with her finger until I wanted to scream. My mouth got dry with the waiting.

"My George was a secret," she finally said.

Then nothing. More flicking of the cane.

"A secret?" Virgie asked.

"Really?" I asked, encouraging and friendly and not-shocked-at-all-sounding.

"Didn't know I was carryin' him for the longest," she started again. "But I was livin' alone then, so it didn't much matter when I started gettin' big. Nobody noticed. Delivered him myself—I'd watched women cut the cord before."

She stopped and cocked her head at me and Virgie, making a little "huh" like she hadn't noticed us before. "Feels good to have the words out of my head," she said. "Nobody never asked me about it. Anyhow, I took care of him that first month or two, nobody ever seein' hide nor hair of him. I aimed to say I found him on my doorstep whenever he got big enough that he couldn't be a secret no more. And then one morning he was dead in his crib. House was lonely then, full of him, so I came here."

She wasn't married, so she shouldn't have had a baby at all, but I didn't bring that up. She'd left out the end of her story, which was more important.

"But you didn't put him in our well?" asked Virgie, sounding almost disappointed. "It really is alright if you did it."

"Why would I want to put him in a well?" she asked, and she did look puzzled, finally setting her cup down on the floor and smoothing her hands over her dress. She took a deep breath and stood up, walking to the window. "What I did was baptize him."

Virgie and me looked at each other. Her mouth wasn't quite closed. When Aunt Lou didn't explain, I waved at Virgie to say something, and she waved at me.

Finally Virgie said, "Did you baptize him while he was alive?"

I thought that was a nice way of putting it.

Aunt Lou shook her head. All we could see of her was her back and the knot of her hair. "Some people do that, you know. Baptize babies. He wasn't old enough to accept Christ: that's what a baptism should be. But then he died, and I got to thinking that bein' baptized as a baby would be better than not being born again in Christ at all. I had him all ready to bury when I thought of that. Didn't have no church to take him to. But God touched me, showed me the way. For what is a church but godly people?"

She used a preacher's voice to ask the question. We didn't answer, and she went on. "I knew where godly people lived—my niece showed me. And godly people have a baptismal font where we are reborn clean and pure. With everlasting life." She turned and held out one hand palm-up, her chin high. "The ground is for death—water is for life."

She took two steps toward us and leaned down, looking over her shoulder real quick. "A baptism, that's what he needed."

As happy as we were on the one hand to have her admit to

everything—or at least admit to it in her own cloudy way—we were getting nervous, too. I was glad when she backed away from us and sat back in her chair, her face as empty and calm as when we'd first started talking to her. She didn't seem to have much else to say.

"Thank you for telling us," Virgie said.

When she didn't respond in any fashion, we weren't sure what to add. We thanked her again, told her we hoped she'd be alright and to let us know if we could do anything for her, but with her still as a stump, pretty soon we wished her goodbye. We walked as fast as we could and still be polite, only slowing down when we were on the main road. I didn't even find Lou Ellen to say goodbye.

"What're we gone do?" I asked Virgie.

"Nothin'."

I couldn't believe that. "We got to do somethin'!"

"You want to tell on her?" asked Virgie.

"We can't just not say anything."

"She's not quite right, Tess. Maybe it's just missing the baby. But whatever it is, she didn't do any real harm. And everybody'd talk about her and look at her and treat her like dirt if they knew. And what good would it do? Leave it be."

Leta "I ASKED JONAH if he wanted to come for supper."

I couldn't believe those words had come out of Albert's mouth. I was already hot from standing over the boiling turnips, and I felt almost dizzy when I turned my back to the stove and faced him instead. I looked at him until he started talking again.

"He said it wouldn't be right."

"Well, thank goodness one of you had some sense."

"I thought you liked Jonah."

"I do, of course."

And I did. Jonah was a hard worker, helpful to Albert. Polite. He always offered to carry things for me if he happened by while I was hauling laundry or feed. But there was a reason Negroes lived in one part of town and we lived in another. They were different, inside and out. And we were all better off as long as we remembered that.

"It just isn't done," I told him.

"Why isn't it done?"

I wanted to grab him by his shoulders and shake him once, hard, like I could Jack when he got too difficult and words didn't come close to sayin' how wrong he was. After all we'd been through with Jack, with all those extra hours Albert had spent below ground, things were finally falling back into place. Jack's casts would come off soon. The circles under Albert's eyes weren't as dark as they had been. Even the talk about that dead baby had died down. We didn't need any more uproar.

"Oh, for heaven's sake, Albert, it just isn't. You know that as well as I do. Yes, Jonah is a nice man, and that wife of his seems perfectly nice herself. But there ain't no reason to go stirrin' up everybody, makin' people talk and carry on, just 'cause you get it into your head to go invite a Negro for supper."

"I just don't think we ought to treat him different."

"So now you're for mixin' races?"

"No, I'm for havin' Jonah for supper."

I heard the water boil over and hiss against the metal, so I turned back and took the pot off the open eye. I looked in on the cornbread, which was beginning to brown. Albert was between me and the jar of beets. I wanted to put them in a bowl—it looked nicer on the table.

"Pass me that, please," I said, pointing to the jar.

He did, never taking his eyes off me. "How do you know anything about him, Leta-ree? Or any Negroes. You ever talked to them? I'm the one standin' next to 'em all day."

Sometimes when I didn't answer back, Albert would burn out like a fire starved of air. I stirred the turnips even though they didn't need it, feeling sweat on my throat. I didn't mind the heat of the stove, really. It was familiar, regular as breakfast, dinner, and supper. I scooted closer. With my face burning, my breath harder to come by, I could almost block out Albert.

"I just want to have the man for supper, Leta. Does it have to be more than that?"

"Yes, Albert. It does and you know it."

"Doesn't matter. Like I said, he won't come anyways."

I felt my shoulders relax some.

"He said he'd come for a cup of coffee instead."

I didn't turn around, only waited until I heard him walk out. He was my husband, and I wasn't going to tell him who could or couldn't come to his house. But for the first time since I met him, I didn't know what to say to him. And it wasn't that I didn't understand him liking Jonah. I wasn't like some who thought Negroes were something less than human. I knew they were people. But there was a pattern to how things were done, rules we followed. Not following meant not knowing what might happen.

I'd kept quiet about the truck that hit Jack, made my peace with Albert's way of thinking on it. Left it in his hands. Let the anger run out of me while I stared awake at the ceiling, listening to Jack breathe. Put it all out of my head and focused on putting things back together like they was. But Albert wasn't back like he used to be, even though everything was still in his hands. All of us were in his hands, and my own hands didn't feel like they could do anything but set the table and cut up the turnips.

Tess "MAMA, I KNOW who put the baby in the well."

"You do?" She asked it sort of singsong like I'd said a bird started talking English to me on the way to school.

"I really do. It was Mrs. Talbert's sister, the one that came to live with them from Brilliant."

She set her dish cloth down and pulled out a chair. The table was shining, still damp. The dishes were all put away. One little bowl of turnips was still setting out, and she'd been reaching for it before she decided to sit down. "What would make you say such a thing?" she asked me.

"She said she did."

"She said she put her dead baby in our well?"

She hadn't used those exact words. "She said she'd baptized him but he ..."

"You can't go around accusin' a woman of such things."

Her chair scraped on the floor when she pushed it out, dishrag back in hand.

"But Mama ..."

She was tucking a cloth around the turnips, and I couldn't tell for sure if she was talking to me. "Everybody tryin' to turn things upside down around here. Goin' against common sense."

"I'm not imaginin' this, Mama."

"I don't want to hear it." Mama never yelled, but she closed in on herself when she was madder than she could stand. It didn't happen much, but I knew what it meant when her voice got small and tight. "Talk like that has no place in this house, Tess. No place at all. When I say you don't talk about somethin', you don't. And that's the last thing I'll say about that."

And that's the last thing I ever said about it to her. Or anybody. I took it as a sign that Virgie was right and we should leave Aunt Lou to work out her problems and her sadness on her own. I didn't mind. Funny how once I had a face to put to the Well Woman she wasn't scary at all. And the baby wasn't sad to me. They fit together in a snug sort of way, not exactly happy, but tolerable.

Virgie PAPA WAS UNDER the house, checking potatoes.

They kept longer under there, weren't as likely to rot, but Mama also liked to keep a sackful in the kitchen. A sackful of potatoes could weigh a good bit, and Papa'd said he'd carry it up for her. I hated to interrupt him, but I wanted to talk to him while I had my nerve worked up.

"Papa, I want to talk to you about what I'm doin' after school."

His head and shoulders were under the house, and his answer echoed a little under the porch. "You wantin' to go over to somebody's house? Ask your mama about that."

"No. I mean after high school."

"Um-hm?" I could tell he was still thinking more about potatoes than about me.

"Well, I've got to do somethin'. I know that. Somethin' to bring in money." He'd backed out from under the porch, two potatoes in each hand. He probably could have held three. "What're you thinkin', girl?"

He asked me like he was truly curious, and like whatever answer I gave would be a smart one and a right one. Like he'd asked Mama something, not me. "Hours aren't so good with nursin'," I said. "They work long shifts, days and nights. And I don't care too much for sick people."

He nodded, still holding the potatoes.

"I was thinkin' maybe teachin'. Miss Etheridge says I would be good at it."

He leaned against the house, hands in his pockets. "Teacher's college costs money."

I'd thought of that. "Two years of school. And I know I'd have to look to you for help. I s'pose that's what I'm askin' you, Papa. If you'd help me to go."

Papa smiled a slow, lopsided smile and took a step toward me. He reached out and tucked my hair behind my ear, which I couldn't ever think of him doing before. "I figured you'd be headed somewhere, Virgie. Knew you'd be up for makin' somethin' of yourself. Been plannin' on sendin' you to school. I didn't know what kind you'd want, or even if you'd want it really. But it sounds like you been puttin' some real thought into it."

"I have."

"You know I'd do anything in the world for you, girl. I can't tell you how, but we'll find a way to make school happen for you. I promise."

I knew if Papa promised, it would happen.

Albert HAVING JONAH ROCKING next to me on the porch
wasn't much different than having Oscar or Ban. Didn't say
too much. We'd mention a cardinal or a blue jay that lit nearby.
Point out a woodpecker or a chipmunk. Mostly we rocked. Leta
brought us a refill for our coffee, smiling at Jonah and waiting
on him like she would any friend of mine. Whatever thoughts she
might have, she'd never be rude. Didn't have it in her.

"So you think I'm bein' foolish," I said to Jonah finally,
second cup of coffee half gone. "You sayin' you ain't bothered by
bein' treated different, treated like a Negro not a man?"

"Oh, I'm bothered by it. More than you'd ever get a handle
on. But I know who I am, where I am."

"What's that supposed to mean?"

"Who's gone change things, Albert? You? Me? Shoot, when's
the last time you slept more than six hours straight? When you
didn't work longer than the sun does? Ain't no time for shakin' up
things, Albert. Ain't no energy left for it."

"Don't mean we can't try."

"You tell me where you're gone carve that time outta your
day, when you gone fit in changin' the world?"

I liked to think the white fellows I worked with didn't much
care who I had to dinner. I knew for a fact most of 'em wouldn't.
But if a few took offense, the wrong few? Might mean a tough time
at work, might mean Jack not getting a job when he got ready
for one or the girls' friends bein' told not to come visit. I needed
every penny, every scrap of goodwill to get Virgie to college. But
even if it weren't for her, I couldn't stomach the thought of all that
ugliness. Men in this town had put their backs to the wall for us,
saved us when it came to payin' that hospital bill. I needed that,
my family needed that safety net if anything happened to me.
I knew it, and Jonah knew it. Knew it before I did. I just didn't
want supper to mean so much.

"So you ain't gone do supper," I said.

He shook his head.

"But coffee's alright?"

He coughed out a laugh. "Reckon it is."

"You want another cup?" I asked.

"If you're offerin'."

Tess   JACK DID SHOOT a deer the next summer, like I'd asked him to. Papa skinned it and cleaned it, then gave away a good bit of it. We still had so much left that Mama came up with a week's worth of venison recipes. The first night we had great hunks of venison on our plates, spiced heavy from all Mama's little glass jars. She'd spooned the meat over a plateful of mashed potatoes.

The burn of the black pepper and the relief of the mashed potatoes made me think of the deer. Soft hide and sharp antlers.

"How did it feel to shoot that deer, Jack?" I asked. "Were you scared? Did it look dangerous? Or did you feel bad about it 'cause it was pretty?"

He answered with his mouth full. "Both, I guess."

He figured that out quicker than I did. That the right answer could be more than one thing at the same time.

Current Titles

At Hawthorne Books, we're serious about literature. We suspected that good writers were being ignored and cast aside as a result of consolidation in the publishing industry, and in 2001 we decided to find these writers and give them a voice. We publish American literary fiction and narrative non-fiction, although we won't turn down a good international title if we find one. All of our books are published as affordable original trade paperbacks, but feature details not typically found even in casebound titles from bigger houses: acid-free papers; sewn bindings which will not crack; heavy, laminated covers with French flaps and built-in bookmarks. You can probably buy Hawthorne Books wherever you buy books, or from our Web site (*hawthornebooks.com*) postpaid* and for a substantial discount. If you like to read, we think you'll enjoy our books. If you like to write—well, send us something. We're always looking.

* Free postage available only for orders shipped within the United States. Sorry about that.

Core: A Romance
Kassten Alonso

Fiction / 208pp / $12.95 / 0-9716915-7-6

This intense and compact novel crackles with obsession, betrayal, and madness. As the narrator becomes fixated on his best friend's girlfriend, his precarious hold on sanity deteriorates into delusion and violence in this twenty-first-century retelling of the classic myth of Hades and Persephone.

"Jump through this Gothic stained-glass window and you are in for some serious investigation of darkness and all of its deadly sins. But take heart, brave traveler, the adventure will prove thrilling."
Tom Spanbauer Author of *Now is the Hour*

501 Minutes to Christ
Poe Ballantine

Essays / 174pp / $13.95 / 0-9766311-9-9

This collection of personal essays ranges from Ballantine's diabolical plan to punch John Irving in the nose during a literary festival, to the tale of how after years of sacrifice and persistence, Ballantine finally secured a contract with a major publisher for a short story collection that never came to fruition.

"My soul yearns to know this most entangled enigma. I confess to Thee, O Lord, that I really have no idea what Poe Ballantine is talking about."
St. Augustine

Decline of the Lawrence Welk Empire
Poe Ballantine

Fiction / 376pp / $15.95 / 0-9766311-1-3

Edgar Donahoe is back for another misadventure, this time in the Caribbean. When he becomes involved with his best friend's girl and is stalked by murderous island native Chollie Legion, even Cinnamon Jim, the medicine man, is no help—it takes a hurricane to blow Edgar out of the mess.

"This second novel ... initially conjures images of *Lord of the Flies*, but then you would have to add about ten years to the protagonists' ages and make them sex-crazed, gold-seeking alcoholics."
Library Journal

God Clobbers Us All
Poe Ballantine

Fiction / 196pp / $15.95 / 0-9716915-4-1

Set against a decaying San Diego rest home in the 1970s, *God Clobbers Us All* is the shimmering, hysterical, melancholy account of eighteen-year-old surfer-boy/orderly Edgar Donahoe, who struggles with romance, death, friendship, and an ill-advised affair with the wife of a maladjusted war veteran.

"Calmer than Bukowski, less portentous than Kerouac, more hopeful than West, Poe Ballantine may not be sitting at the table of his mentors, but perhaps he deserves his own after all."
San Diego Union-Tribune

Things I Like About America
Poe Ballantine

Essays / 266pp / $12.95 / 0-9716915-1-7

These risky personal essays are populated with odd jobs, eccentric characters, boarding houses, buses, and beer. Written with piercing intimacy and self-effacing humor, they take us on a Greyhound journey through small-town America and explore what it means to be human.

"Part social commentary, part collective biography, this guided tour may not be comfortable, but one thing's for sure: You will be at home."
Willamette Week

WINNER, 2005 LANGUM PRIZE FOR HISTORICAL FICTION

Madison House
Peter Donahue

Fiction / 528pp / $16.95 / 0-9766311-0-5

This novel chronicles Victorian Seattle's explosive transformation from frontier outpost to metropolis. Maddie Ingram, owner of Madison House, and her quirky and endearing boarders find their lives linked when the city decides to regrade Denny Hill and the fate of their home hangs in the balance.

"Peter Donahue seems to have a map of old Seattle in his head ... And all future attempts in its historical vein will be made in light of this book."
David Guterson Author of *Snow Falling on Cedars*

www.hawthornebooks.com

Clown Girl Introduction by Chuck Palahniuk
Monica Drake
Fiction / 298pp / $15.95 / 0-9766311-5-6

Clown Girl lives in Baloneytown, a neighborhood
so run-down that drugs, balloon animals, and even
rubber chickens contribute to the local currency.
Using clown life to illuminate a struggle between
integrity and economic reality, this novel examines
issues of class, gender, economics, and prejudice.

"The pace of [this] narrative is methamphetamine-frantic, as Drake
drills down past the face paint and into Nita's core ... There is a lot
more going on here than just clowning around."
Publishers Weekly

So Late, So Soon
D'Arcy Fallon
Memoir / 224pp / $15.95 / 0-9716915-3-3

An irreverent, fly-on-the-wall view of the Lighthouse
Ranch, a Christian commune the eighteen-year-
old hitchhiker D'Arcy Fallon called home for three
years in the mid-1970s, when life's questions over-
whelmed her and reconciling her family past with
her future seemed impossible.

"What would draw an otherwise independent woman to a life of
menial labor and subservience? Fallon's answer is both an inside
look at '70s commune life and a funny, poignant coming of age."
Judy Blunt Author of *Breaking Clean*

The Tsar's Dwarf
Peter H. Fogtdal Translated by Tiina Nunnally
Fiction / $15.95 / 0-9790188-0-3

Due out September 2008 Soerine, a female dwarf
from Denmark, is given as a gift to the Russian Tsar,
Peter the Great, during his visit to Copenhagen.
Soerine travels to St. Petersburg where she becomes
a jester at the Tsar's functions. She enjoys her new
life and falls in love with the Tsar's favorite dwarf, but
disaster strikes in the shape of a priest who wants to
"save" her.

September 11: West Coast Writers Approach Ground Zero   Edited by Jeff Meyers

Essays / 266pp / $16.95 / 0-9716915-0-9

The events of September 11, 2001, their repercussions, and our varied responses to them inspired this collection. By history and geographic distance, the West Coast has developed a community different from the East; ultimately shared interests bridge the distinctions in provocative and heartening ways.

"September 11: West Coast Writers Approach Ground Zero deserves attention. This book has some highly thoughtful contributions that should be read with care on both coasts, and even in between."
San Francisco Chronicle

Dastgah: Diary of a Headtrip
Mark Mordue

Travel Memoir / 316pp / $15.95 / 0-9716915-6-8

A world trip that ranges from a Rolling Stones concert in Istanbul to meetings with mullahs and junkies in Teheran, from a cricket match in Calcutta to an S&M bar in New York, as Mark Mordue explores countries most Americans never see, as well as issues of world citizenship in the twenty-first century.

"Mordue has elevated *Dastgah* beyond the realms of the traditional travelogue by sharing not only what he learned about cultures he visited but also his brutally honest self-discoveries."
Elle

FINALIST, 2006 OREGON BOOK AWARD
WINNER, SAMUEL GOLDBERG & SONS
FICTION PRIZE FOR EMERGING JEWISH
WRITERS

The Cantor's Daughter
Scott Nadelson

Fiction / 280pp / $15.95 / 0-9766311-2-1

Sympathetic, heartbreaking, and funny, these stories – capturing people in critical moments of transition – reveal our fragile emotional bonds and the fears that often cause those bonds to falter or fail.

"These beautifully crafted stories are populated by Jewish suburbanites living in New Jersey, but ethnicity doesn't play too large a role here. Rather, it is the humanity of the characters and our empathy for them that bind us to their plights."
Austin Chronicle

www.hawthornebooks.com

WINNER: 2004 OREGON BOOK AWARD;
2005 GLCA NEW WRITERS AWARD

Saving Stanley: The Brickman Stories
Scott Nadelson
Ficion / 230pp / $15.95 / 0-9716915-2-5

These interrelated short stories are graceful, vivid narratives that bring into sudden focus the spirit and the stubborn resilience of the Brickmans, a Jewish family of four living in suburban New Jersey. This fierce collection provides an unblinking examination of family life and the human instinct for attachment.

"Focusing on small decisions and subtle shifts, *Saving Stanley* closely examines the frayed ties that bind. With a fly-on-the-wall sensibility and a keen sense for dramatic restraint, Nadelson is ... both a promising writer and an apt documentarian."
Willamette Week

WINNER: 1983 PEN/FAULKNER AWARD

Seaview Introduction by Robert Coover
Toby Olson
Fiction / 316pp / $15.95 / 0-9766311-6-4

This novel follows a golf hustler and his dying wife across an American wasteland. Trying to return the woman to her childhood home on Cape Cod, the pair are accompanied by a mysterious Pima Indian activist and shadowed by a vengeful drug dealer to the novel's apocalypse on the Seaview Links.

"Even a remarkable dreamer of nightmares like Nathanael West might have been hard-pressed to top the finale ... Unlike any other recent American novel in the freshness of its approach and vision."
The New York Times Book Review

The Well and the Mine Introduction by Fannie Flagg
Gin Phillips
Fiction / $15.95 / 0-9766311-7-2

In 1931 Carbon Hill, Alabama, a small coal-mining town, nine-year-old Tess Moore watches a woman shove the cover off the family well and toss in a baby without a word. The event forces the family to face the darker side of their community and seek to understand the motivations of their family and friends.

"Gin Phillips is the real thing. *The Well and the Mine* is a stunning triumph: haunting, lyrical, a portrait of the southern family, a story of the human predicament."
Vicki Covington Author of *Gathering Home* and *The Last Hotel for Women*

Leaving Brooklyn — Introduction by Ursula Hegi
Lynne Sharon Schwartz
Fiction / 168pp / $12.95 / 0-9766311-4-8

An injury at birth left fifteen-year-old Audrey with a wandering eye and her own way of seeing; her relationship with a Manhattan eye doctor exposes her to the sexual rites of adulthood in this startling and wonderfully rich novel, which raises the themes of innocence and escape to transcendent heights.

"Stunning. Coming of age is seldom registered as disarmingly as it is in *Leaving Brooklyn*."
New York Times Book Review

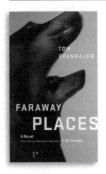

Faraway Places — Introduction by A.M. Homes
Tom Spanbauer
Fiction / $14.95 / 0-9766311-8-0

This novel marks the end of childhood for Jake Weber and the beginning of trouble for his family. An innocent swim ends with something far beyond anyone's expectations: Jake witnesses a brutal murder and is forced to keep quiet, even as the woman's lover is falsely accused.

"Forceful and moving ... Spanbauer tells his short, brutal story with delicacy and deep respect for place and character."
Publishers Weekly

FINALIST, 2005 OREGON BOOK AWARD

The Greening of Ben Brown
Michael Strelow
Fiction / 272pp / $15.95 / 0-9716915-8-4

Ben Brown becomes a citizen of East Leven, Oregon after he recovers from an electrocution that has turned him green. He befriends eighteen-year-old Andrew James and together they unearth a chemical-spill cover-up that forces the town to confront its demons and its citizens to choose sides.

"Strelow resonates as both poet and storyteller. [He] lovingly invokes ... a blend of fable, social realism, wry wisdom, and irreverence that brings to mind Ken Kesey, Tom Robbins, and the best elements of a low-key mystery."
The Oregonian

Soldiers in Hiding Introduced by Wole Soyinka
Richard Wiley
Fiction / 194pp / $14.95 / 0-9766311-3-X

Teddy Maki is a Japanese American jazz musician trapped in Tokyo with his friend, Jimmy Yakamoto, both of whom are drafted into the Japanese army after Pearl Harbor. Thirty years later, Maki is a big star on Japanese TV and wrestling with the guilt over Jimmy's death that he's been carrying since the war.

"Wonderful ... Original ... Terrific ... Haunting ... Reading *Soldiers in Hiding* is like watching a man on a high wire!"
The New York Times